D1563069

CRIPPLED JACK

ALSO BY BOSTON TERAN

God Is a Bullet
Never Count Out the Dead
The Prince of Deadly Weapons
Trois Femmes
Giv— The Story of a Dog and America
The Creed of Violence
Gardens of Grief
The World Eve Left Us
The Country I Lived In
The Cloud and the Fire
By Your Deeds
A Child Went Forth
How Beautiful They Were
Two Boys at Breakwater

CRIPPLED JACK

BOSTON TERAN

Copyright 2022 by Brutus Productions, Inc.

All right reserved under International and Pan American
Copyright Conventions.

ISBN: 978-1-56703-101-0

Published in the United States by High Top Publications LLC,
Los Angeles, CA, and simultaneously in Canada by High Top
Publications LLC.

Special Thanks to: Kenneth Koch—One Train May Hide Another

Interior Design by Alan Barnett

Printed in the United States of America

To those who make the fight, who understand all to well the shadows closing in from every corner of our darkest thoughts, words and deeds, and if they must, die with a dream on their faces.

ACKNOWLEDGMENTS

To Deirdre Stephanie and the late, great Brutarian…to G.G. and L.S and M.K…Miz El and Roxomania…the kids…Hotrod…Natasha Kern… Janice Hussein…Melissa Brandzel…The Drakes at Wildbound…Charlene Crandall, for her brains and loyalty…And finally, to my steadfast friend and ally, and a master at navigating the madness, Donald V. Allen.

PART ONE

PART ONE

CHAPTER 1

What tortures await the lives of men? What degree of exile from goodness makes up their souls?

The boy was near about eight, maybe nine years old. His hands and feet had been bound up with heavy rope. His mouth lashed tight with cotton strips so he could not cry out.

He was lying just off the Chihuahua Trail where it fed south from San Antonio toward Helena. He had been placed on the most degraded soil, by the remains of a rotted wagon and the sanded-down bones of an ox. A page from the Bible had been torn loose and pinned to his ragged and filthy shirt. And in a fine handwriting was written this:

— It's up to God now —

• • •

For days the boy survived on his muffled cries and desperation to stay alive as he caterpillared along, his arms tied behind his back, a thing to behold, crawling inch by inch over rock and gray brown and scrub brush that scored the flesh. Threading down through gullies, his skin blistered, courtesy of the hideous Texas sun. He used his jaw and shoulders and the bottom of his bare bound feet to edge toward a road that grew farther and farther out of reach, until there was no more of him to struggle with.

He lay there alone, awaiting death, in all that unmerciful emptiness with one thought—Why did God hate me so much?

CHAPTER 2

God's traps await…Let neither the just nor the unjust believe otherwise.

Ledru Drum was making his way south, following the Chihuahua Trail. Not on the trail itself, mind you, but keeping it within sight, staying to the narrow slopes and shadowed coulees that could afford one protection. A wary, steady, unremitting man, he would stop and watch through field glasses, scanning the country behind him for any sign of the four who were out to see his downfall.

He rode a sorrel mount with stocking feet he had taken from the wilds and led a mule who carted his foods and grip and an assortment of telling weapons. The dog, Corporal Billy, was always out front taking in the rooty stench of man or beast that clung to the earth or was carried upon the wind. The dog was the canary in the coal mine. A warning sign of ambush or assault that might be lying in wait.

Somewhere up ahead in an unseen wash came the unsheathed cry of that dog. Ledru Drum reined in his mount and took a ram horn that hung from the pommel of his saddle and sang out a pitched call, but the animal did not come. There was a raw edge to the dog's cries, and those were the only sounds upon that blighted land. Whatever it was up ahead ruled.

Drum reached back to the mule and from one of the half dozen scabbards roped there retrieved his Yellowboy. He then set the rifle across the saddle and came forth slowly.

Ascending a sandy rise and keeping the sun to his back, ready for whatever he might run afoul of, what does he see in a gravel strewn basin but the bound and gagged body of a child that Corporal Billy circled while snapping at the air. At first Drum thought the child dead, but then the body balled up as the dog closed in, crawling along on its haunches.

Drum scanned the terrain around him. Road agents used every vile trick to lure pitiful fools to their demise, but there was nothing in that purgatorial waste save the scuffing of his mount's hooves and him ordering the dog back.

He dismounted and kneeled over this pathetic vision with the dog there beside him. The boy was a burnt and beaten thing, and the eyes staring up at him above the endless wrappings of cloth spoke to almighty terrors.

He removed a slipjoint from his coat pocket and opened the blade, and the boy gave this muffled cry and recoiled.

"The knife is to rid you of those rag strips. Free you to drink down some water, is all."

The child closed his eyes while Drum went about the business of cutting away the rags and then the ropes that bound him. It was while doing this that Drum noticed a page from the Bible pinned to the youth's shirt.

Retrieving a canteen from the pack mule, Drum looked the page over. It was the damnedest thing…torn from a King James Bible…Chapter 22…Genesis. That ancient sorry faced story of Abraham offering his son up to God on a burning altar to prove his faith…and in this neat and educated handwriting, someone had inked, "*It's up to God now.*"

As Drum knelt and offered the boy a drink, he said, "What the hell is this?" shaking the Bible page in his fist. "What does it mean?"

"My fatha lef me here. Took my motha and sistas. Lef me." He pointed up there on the hill.

"Why?"

"Poor. No money. No food. Me a burtin'."

"A burden."

"A crip'el."

CHAPTER 3

Drum looked the boy over hard. He should have seen right away. The boy struggled to sit upright. He reached for the canteen with his left hand. His right was pressed against his chest, and when he moved it, Drum saw the wrist was carried at an odd angle and the fingers moved with a stiff and knotted clumsiness.

"How long you been bound up?"

The boy raised two fingers.

"Just left you like that, did they?"

"Tey did."

The boy was so weak. It was hard standing and when Drum went to help him the boy brushed the offer aside. He wanted Drum to see he could wrestle the weakness on his own. Two days in the wilderness, tied up, no water, no food, manhandled by the elements.

He was dizzy and listing and Ledru saw the boy's right leg was sort of bent in at the knee so his shoulders were pitched a bit at an angle. While the boy gathered himself and drank, Drum took note of the markings of a trail that snaked its way up through the ravine bottom where the boy had crawled and that led up the hill to the peak, which was a goddamn quarter mile away.

The boy had the palsy, that was a fact. Drum had seen children like this from his own days in the foundlings and the orphanages. The cast asides, the abandoned, the helpless. And always the poor.

"You crawl all the way down from that peak?"

"More dan dat, mista."

The boy even had that slur in his speech where the words sometimes are a struggle.

Drum took the page from the Bible and folded it up and slid it into his pocket.

"You got the palsy, yeah?"

The boy nodded.

"I'll say one thing for you…you're a gamebird."

• • •

Drum rerigged the mule, creating a space for where the boy would ride, and off they went. Corporal Billy in the lead, one behind the other. A strange looking crew to say the least, keeping parallel to the tired and dried out Texas roads.

"What's your name?" Drum called out to the kid behind him.

"Marion…Marion Eno."

"Marion…Don't like it," said Drum. "Not at all." He shook his head vehemently.

The boy did not know what to say.

"I'm not gonna call you that. You need something I like calling you."

Drum rolled a cigarette and then smoked, shouting out names here and there, to see how they sounded on the wind. He listened to their echo, then he shook his head, "No."

The boy thought a few were fine, even good. But he did not offer an opinion.

Finally Drum turned, grinning. He pointed his cigarette at the child there on the mule. "Matthew," he said. "Now there's a name you can wear under all circumstances…And every day of the week…It's biblical, which is good…I knew some hard assed bastards named Matthew…And when I was a boy I had a mule named Matthew…Did I love that mule. That's the name you'll answer to." He shouted it out. "See how good that sounds."

The boy was going to tell Drum you can't *see* how something sounds, but he thought better of it.

"I hope you like it. Cause if you don't, it's too damn bad."

The boy took a little time, silently saying the name, imagining himself the owner of it, and what kind of person he might be with that name.

"Mine is Ledru Drum. You can call me Mister Drum…until and unless I tell you otherwise."

From time to time, Drum would stop and survey the landscape behind him with field glasses. And he took his slow and precious time about it.

The boy thought Drum to be a cockish looking fellow. And one who was either coal or snow.

"How ole are ya?" said the boy.

"None of your goddamn business," said Drum. "But I'm twenty-eight. And am told I'm a fine lookin' twenty-eight. Don't you think so?"

The boy nodded.

"Can you read and write?" said Drum. "I'll bet you can."

The boy nodded.

They camped at dusk and Drum perched his hat back and panned the blue and softening distance with his field glasses. He hummed to himself quietly as he went about his task.

"Wha' ya lookin' for?"

"Wolves of the empire."

The boy did not understand and said, "Wha' kina wolves?"

"Matthew, there's four men out there somewhere on the road hunting me out. Mean to kill me…If they should be so fortunate." He put his field glasses aside. "Now what do you say to that?"

CHAPTER 4

Drum called to the dog and it came loping out of the dark. Drum sat by the fire and rolled a cigarette. The boy labored over and sat where he could study this man.

"Scared?"

"Shudin' I be?"

"You know what I was thinking when I first found you? No…of course, you don't. I was thinking…I'd cut you loose. Give you enough food and water. And leave you. The men following my tracks would eventually come upon you. What would they do? Would they take you with them, like civilized gents…knowing that taking you would slow them down? Like you're slowing me down. Or would they just leave you?"

The boy was swept up in what Drum was saying. He was frightened because he did not understand.

"How old are you?"

"Near nine."

"You ever shot a gun?"

"A pistol…few times. But in my lef' hand. A rifle and shagun…Twied. Righ sholda is too weak…clumsy."

"I didn't take you with me 'cause it was the right thing to do. I want you to know that."

Drum lit the cigarette. He put his head back and nonchalantly blew smoke up into the night. Corporal Billy lay at the feet of where Drum sat. His eyes were on the boy.

"I did it," said Drum, "because if I left you, I'd be a coward. It would mean I feared that trash catching me. But I'm not afraid. I am not a coward. And it's not important you know that. Or anyone knows it. It's only important I know it. Because…they will catch me. I'm going to see to it."

The boy saw something in the man he had not seen before in any man. Something he did not understand. Something in the look, beyond the lean mouth and hardened cheekbones, intent as he was on the smoky fire. As if the boy were not even of that place where they camped, but was watching from another world, one that was not quite born yet. What he was seeing was what other men would describe as the agate stare of a killer.

"Wolves?" said the boy.

Drum now turned to the boy. He smoked. He quietly rode a few seconds of time elsewhere until he was there again at the fire.

"Wolves of the empire is what I called them. They're Pinkertons. You know what a Pinkerton is?"

The boy did not.

"Well, young Mister Matthew…they carry badges, but they are not the law. Though they act like such. They are an army of paid trash. A posse, militia, a gang that works for the wealthy mine owner, the oil company lord, the industrial robber baron. Their job is to keep the poor and disenfranchised in place. Even though they themselves are of that class."

Drum flicked his cigarette ash at the fire. "We need a few dead kings on the altar to even up the score."

His face there near the flames was deeply shadowed as he turned to the youth. "You have no idea what I'm talking about, do you?"

"No, Mista Drum."

"You will. 'Cause you're living it. Those two days in the desert. You think about your folks? What they did? Why they did it?"

The question carried with it some terrible omen of what the boy was still too young to understand, but of the age to feel.

"I was mosly tinkin' why God haded me so."

"You don't actually believe God takes sides in matters like this?" said Drum.

The boy nodded that he did.

"Watch this," said Drum. He held up the cigarette. He flicked the ash. It was barely visible against the fire even for a moment. "We're the ash," he said. "You and me. The fire is the world. That's the fight."

The dog's head rose suddenly, and both Drum and the boy went on guard. Drum held the dog by the flesh on the back of his neck and listened for whatever might be out there moving with the night wind.

"Whatever it is," said Drum, "it isn't them."

The fire yawed and rose, and the boy watched and the boy listened to the sound of sand whispering over the rocks and he felt the world moving, and he managed to rouse the courage to wonder, "Why dey afta' you, Mista Drum?"

CHAPTER 5

The Great Depression of '73 stripped America of its rampant sense of invincibility. There had been a drive after the Civil War to connect the country by rail to achieve its gluttonous dreams of manifest destiny. So the government, in all its left-handed wisdom, offered huge land grants and subsidies to a burgeoning industry. The aspiring railroad president had become the Lord of the Manor.

Thanks to investors and speculators, the endless urge to rape the industrial battlefield for profit knew no ends. The banks lent beyond their means, overexpansion became the state of affairs, stock traders existed on promises they knew they could not keep. An industry was racing toward its downfall as there were no profits to be had, no exit strategy within sight. One future was a long way off, the other was closing in fast.

Since loans could not be repaid, it was left to the worker to bear the brunt of corporate avarice and instability. Across America the railroad companies lowered wages, increased work hours. Double headers—two locomotives pulling one long extended train—meant a single crew was forced to do the work of two.

Across the next few years among the workers, you would hear words like—protest, organize, unionize, strike. Then came the hints of violence, then the violence itself.

There was a growing revolt in the railyards from Virginia and Baltimore to Pittsburg, Chicago, St. Louis, Galveston, and onto San Francisco. Other trades began to feel the strains of a nation losing its corporate grip on the workingman. Miners, longshoremen, tradesmen of all colors and stripes, even cowboys in west Texas, to a fault talked about organizing to achieve more security and power.

In response to the threat to their power, the Lords of the Railways began to hire security of their own to protect what they owned. Skullcrackers with badges and writs is what they were, often under the aegis of the Pinkertons. Famous already for exacting their own brand of cruel and clever reality.

• • •

The San Antonio railyard was under virtual lockdown on orders of John James Vandel, the security and crisis chief for the railroad. There had been the killing of a former brakeman and union organizer. He had been shot to death on railroad property allegedly preparing to derail a train. There was doubt, in the newspapers and among state authorities, as to the veracity of the circumstances in the brakeman's death.

But his body still hung from a railroad signal track as a warning to other malcontents when a coal train slowly entered the yard around midnight. The train was stopped and searched. Security guards under Chief Vandel went from gondola to gondola with their lanterns and weapons at the ready.

Ledru Drum could hear it all. The crisp, clear order from Chief Vandel. From where Drum lay buried under the coal, he could see faint traces of light as the railroad police walked literally over his body.

CHAPTER 6

The train was switched to a siding where it would be rerouted in the morning. It was a track parallel to one where a locomotive and tender were hooked to a flatcar for horses and an extended caboose. This was the railroad security train when they traveled, and where they drank and played cards when they were in the yard.

Drum came slowly up out of the coal, all black and dusty, like some ancient primordial creature. A canvas messenger bag hung from his shoulder by a single strap. In the bag were a handful of dynamite sticks all bound and a length of fuse.

He was going to deliver a message, no doubt about it. Unless he were gunned down.

His head crept up over the lip of the gondola. He searched the darkness to be sure it was safe. A few men with lanterns moved here and there about the yard. Feeling the moment right, he slid over the side and crawled under the railcar. He snaked his way along the ties until he could see the caboose windows all burning with light, and hear the men going about their drunken chatter.

Drum lay on his back and readied the fuse. After that he checked his pistol, then slid it under his coat. It was now about the darkness when he heard John James Vandel.

He was striding toward the caboose as if there were blood in the air, and he went after that swaggy loose mouthed bunch. He was not a man for small talk or diplomacy. He ordered the men he thought a little too relaxed to get their asses up and back out into the night air.

The men double timed it, and Vandel let part of another crew that were walking behind him take a break.

Did Drum hope that Vandel would allow himself a cup of coffee or a drink, but he was too dedicated, too driven and was not one to join his men. He was of their class, but desperate to escape it. The ones he did chase out, one day they'd tell this story about how fuckin' lucky they were.

Drum had been that near Vandel. He could practically spit on his boots. Drum knew him by reputation. Vandel always wore a gentleman's hat, and a white shirt with a tie. He always wore a tie. He could be dying of thirst in the desert, but he'd be wearing a tie.

They were about the same age, he and Drum. And no matter how different the two men looked and acted and dressed, they had one thing in common, this Drum knew. They were the types that would get even, and they'd burn down their souls seeing to it.

Once Vandel had walked off with his crew and the world inside that caboose settled back into the usual rot, Drum cut a fuse that might stretch out to a minute. Enough time to let him clear the explosion anyway.

He noted a stack of lanterns on the tracks by the caboose platform, which gave him an idea. He got out a match and took a long breath. It was all passion and consequence now. He lit the fuse. It started that sparkly hissing.

He was out from below the gondola like nothing as he strode to the caboose with the dynamite held behind him. Beneath a car window he knelt and set the dynamite up in the wheel well.

He was up fast and as he strode away he grabbed a lantern and he lit it and looked back over his shoulder. He could see the faint spark of the fuse burning even faster than he'd guessed.

He crossed the tracks with the lantern swinging at his side, trying to pass himself off as just another yard rat on the midnight shift. A security officer came up through a lane of freight cars, running his lantern over the slatted doorways. The two men crossed paths. Something caught the officer's attention. He held out his lantern.

"Where's your badge?"

Drum kept on like he had not heard.

"Vandel," said Drum. "He's got a flame up his ass tonight. Wants me to do another turn of the roundhouse."

The man repeated himself in no uncertain terms.

Drum turned. "Here's my badge," he said. And flashing his pistol, fired.

The man dropped like a weight upon the lantern that he held and his clothes set to burning. The shot was heard far across the tracks. Men shouted, men came running from the deep shadows. As Drum knelt and tore the badge from the dead rail boss's shirt, there was a blinding explosion.

The caboose was torn asunder. Burning strips of wood and metal were catapulted over rows of freight cars and for a time it looked as if heaven were raining down a fiery rage. The few men that had survived the bombing staggered or crawled through the smoke.

Amidst a frenzy of guards and burning remnants of the railcar and men trying to quell flames that had spread to the freight cars, John James Vandel, on the next row of tracks, was organizing them, ordering a crew to hunt out the saboteur. And here came Drum, not fifty feet away, moving through a choking heat and smoking body parts with a dead man's badge pinned to his coat, only to slip into the darkness at first chance and just disappear.

CHAPTER 7

Drum awoke to crying that no one in the world heard, except him. It was a mortal sound he thought to be coming from somewhere within his own body. Turned out it was the boy, there by the campfire, being hunted through his rest by a nightmare.

Drum sat and stared at the child's pitiful and hitched sobbing. He reached out and touched the boy's shoulder and the act woke him with a frightened gasp.

It took a moment for the boy to realize who and where he was, and he sat up and wrapped the blanket around him, and by the fire wiped at his eyes and tried to rein in his sorrow.

"Dreamin'?" said Drum.

The child nodded. "Fa certin'."

The boy took to staring at the fire, then he put out a hand and let it get as close as he dared to the flames.

"My fatha'," he said, "was a teechur."

And just like that, in a voice tainted with shame, he began to spill out how he got left in the desert to die.

His family had lived in Silver Reef. It was a mining town in Utah. When the economy began to suffer, the company executives cut wages hard while they increased workers' hours, firing those who wouldn't comply. His father, being educated, was asked to write up a list of the workers' demands.

This cost him his job. Ostracized, the family was forced to the road. Day work or nothing, traveling by wagon from town to town with their meager possessions. The boy had two older sisters and the three children were sent out to beg.

"It was dat beggin'," said the boy. He was ashamed by it, humiliated. And his being crippled made it all the more awful. He would see the look on the people's faces when he asked for a pittance of change or a scrap of food, a piece of fruit, a raw potato.

Drum understood. The boy saw himself as a deformed thing, a flaw in the universe, a failure of the energy of creation. And the boy told Drum how other boys who were begging would beat him mercilessly because they knew he would be given preference over them. That he would reap a reward for his imperfection and defect, a reward that they would feel in their pocket.

He told his parents that he would not beg. That they should send him to a foundling home, or give him up to anyone who needed a laborer. Anything but begging. That he would be one less mouth to feed.

But it was his palsy that paid best. And when he refused to beg, he was no longer fed. His family had grown to hate him, his sisters warred with him. And so it came to pass that he refused once too often. And his father took action.

He fought against his father and sisters. He saw his mother's silence for what it was. Before the leaving, his father knelt down over his bound up son. As he wiped the sweat and dirt from the boy's face, he said, "Whatever happens, you'll be better off. God will see to it."

There by the fire, the boy started back where he'd left off, crying.

"God mus' hate me sumpin' tearable."

Drum had gotten up and retrieved a pocket bottle of whiskey from his mule pack. It wasn't fair, Drum thought. The boy was too young to feel so worthless. But fair is not the state of things. And at its best, pure guesswork. He sat beside the boy.

"Ever had whiskey?"

"Once."

"It's pretty raw and cheap. It'll burn the wood on a bar." He offered the bottle to the boy. "One drink may help to calm you down."

The boy wiped at his tears and took the bottle. He studied it and sniffed it, then he took a sip and damn near spit up.

"Poverty," said Drum. "That may be the original sin. The worst sin of all. You know about original sin?"

"Some."

They sat by the fire like two longtime pards. The wind kicked up burning ash from the fire and the night around them lit up with a thousand tiny starbursts.

"Well, young Mister Matthew…I got a question for you."

"Yes, sir?"

"How's your talent for lying?"

CHAPTER 8

When the sun began to bleed light, Drum took out his field glasses and scanned the countryside behind them. There was nothing to see, no telling signs for concern. At least that is what he said.

But it was different for the boy.

"Ova dare," he said, pointing.

Drum stared skeptically at first. But the boy took to jabbing a finger where he wanted Drum to look.

And sure enough. The faintest shadows were coming up through a causeway where the ground dipped and rose. It took Drum a few moments, but there they were, swimmy outlines coming on with haste. There, then gone, and then there again.

"You can see that?" said Drum.

The boy nodded. "I see…'xtra good."

• • •

The boy could see the dusty approach of riders in the warm Texas sun. He sat on a rock like a lizard by the side of the road with a half empty canteen hung from his shoulder by a long leather strap.

Four men soon drew down upon him, and he was frightened as hell. They were a tired, dirty looking crew, and all wearing iron. Not a gent among them, to be sure. They slowed when they came upon the boy and reined in when he said, "You ta' men followin' him?"

"How come you said that?" said the one who seemed to be in charge.

"He took me from da deser' days ago. Tole me…was gonna use me as ransom…but his hoss got sick and he lef' me."

One of the men began to circle the road, looking out upon the countryside. Another used his field glasses to scan the road ahead. The one who had spoken said, "What he look like?"

The boy gave the perfect description of his father, who certainly did not look like Drum.

Then he was asked the man's name, and the boy gave his father's name, not Drum's.

"He left the kid to try and weasel us," said the man who had been circling. "Get us to take him…slow us down."

The boy rose from the rocks. "You won' leave me?"

They saw he had the palsy.

Before the one in charge could speak out his decision, there was a shot and the fella with the field glasses was hit square in the face. The damn glasses shattered, and he pitched back in his saddle.

The men scattered, but to no avail.

The boy threw himself on the ground.

The one who had been circling, his horse was shot out from under him. As it tottered over, he couldn't get loose of the stirrups and was pinned. The third man was shot in the side and as he reeled his mount around was shot in the back. The one who had questioned the boy was sprinting up the road, his mount too was shot, and its legs accordionned, and the horse went down and the rider went with it.

From out of a still bastion of rocks came Mister Drum. The boy watched him from where he lay. Drum was chambering more rounds into his Yellowboy. He stood over the rider pinned under his mount. The youth watched Drum raise the rifle and fire. The man's body jerked, then stilled.

Drum strode past where the youth lay. "Matthew…you earned your name today."

Drum proceeded up the road with the rifle slung up on his shoulder to where the first rider lay motionless and pinned by his dead mount. Drum knelt over him. He was unconscious.

"Bring me rope, boy. And snag one of their horses."

With the youth's help, Drum managed to get that unconscious man up into the saddle. He strapped his legs together under the horse's chest. Then he roped the man's arm around the withers and under the animal's neck. The final touch was tying a sack over his head. By the time he came around his struggles would be useless.

From the papers he carried Drum found out his name was McSorley, and he had a railroad security card and a badge, all of which Drum kept.

Drum shook that sacked head. "Listen to me, you cracker whore. I'm sending your poverty row ass back down the line so you can tell them what happened here.

"You and the rest are traitors to your own class. You think good will come from what you're doing. You'll always be day wages until the railroad Czar or the mine owner or some other landlord has had enough of your sorry ass. Then you know what's left? Your unbathed reek."

With that, he whipped the horse with his hat and off they went back to where he'd have to explain himself.

CHAPTER 9

Drum left the bodies in the road where they lay. A statement for scavenger and stranger alike. He and the boy's shadows lengthened as they rode and when they stopped to rest and water the mounts, Drum said, "You haven't spoken a word all day."

The boy looked at anything but Mister Drum.

"Never seen men killed?" said Drum. "The real way of it?"

"No, sir."

"It isn't fair, really," said Drum, washing his face with a wet handkerchief.

"What?"

"Being thrown into the world like you have. I'm sure there's no comfort knowing you're not the first, and you won't be the last. But there it is."

The boy looked at the man with uncertainty.

"You a killah, aren' you, Mista Drum?"

"I am that," said Drum. "Among other things."

As they went to mount up, the boy said, "Mista Drum…what gonna happen ta me…Whahe da I go?"

• • •

It began to rain that day. A slashing downpour that quickly flooded the roads. Lightning in the gray black sky flashed before them, and Drum saw the remains of an abandoned farm on the crest of a hill.

"There," he said to the boy. "Follow me."

The roof of the house had long since caved in from a fire. But the huge barn itself was serviceable, and it is there they camped to wait out the storm.

Drum stood at the open barn door smoking and watched the rain fall upon the darkness. The dog lay at his boots, the eternal watchman. The boy was poking at the fire with a stick. Strangers they were, at the raw edge of the world.

"Mista Drum…what you gonna do wit' me? Gonna drop me on some street corner somewhere? If ya' mean to, at lease' tell me."

21

He turned to the boy, who'd told Drum how he'd witnessed an auction at the depot in San Antonio. Children from an orphan train. And there was a kid there with the palsy like him, and no one bid on him even for chore labor. And the boy went on reminding Drum that he could read and write real well. That he'd even kept a ledger, and the job had lasted a whole week. And that he didn't want to end up like the kids he met while he was begging, who were his own age and already drunks or drug addicts.

Drum listened to this plea of desperation, for that is what it was. And before he could rightly give an answer, Corporal Billy rose and the hair on his back stiffened. Drum could soon make out the outline of a wagon trundling its way up the hill.

"We got company," said Drum.

Drum got hold of the dog and leashed him with a rope to a tall gate with a highwayman's hitch. From his saddlepack, he retrieved a pistol. A baby Paterson, which he handed to the boy. "Slip this in your coat. And be quiet as the dead."

The wagon pulled up to the barn doors, and in moments, a man entered with rain dripping off his slouch hat which he removed. Stepping into the light you could see this was a hard scrabble character, maybe fifty, who introduced himself as Ezra Skinner. Soon after, behind him, were his two adult sons. One stood supporting his wife. She had two children with her, a boy and a girl about Matthew's age. The woman was mighty pregnant and didn't look too well.

"My daughter-in-law is under it," Skinner said. "The wagon, the road. You know how it is. Mind if we set up camp here for the night?

"We got our own grips and food. We'll set our own fire. We're all house broke," he said, grinning.

Drum pointed to the half of the barn they were not using.

They set the woman down in a stall on a blanket. Skinner was talking away while his sons unhitched the horses.

"How are you gents called?"

Drum gave the boy's father's name as his own. Then made up one for the kid. Skinner used his hat pointing out his family, naming them.

"Where are you all heading?" said Skinner.

"San Antonio," said Drum.

"Coming up from the south?"

"Yeah."

"Then you didn't see the killing?"

Matthew looked up at Drum, who put on at being utterly confounded.

"What are you talking about?" Drum said.

"Men and horses shot dead in the road. A sinful portrait. Sinful indeed. Had to shield the children's eyes from a sight straight out of Revelations."

CHAPTER 10

Drum did not like the way Skinner had suddenly taken to staring at the boy. Not at all. If they had come upon the dead, then they may have come upon the rider. And if they had come upon the rider and freed him, he might have spoken of Drum and a boy with palsy.

Skinner pointed at Corporal Billy, who was not at all friendly.

"That animal looks to have quite the mean streak."

"That depends on which side you're on."

Skinner laughed out. It was a phony laugh. He was spinning his hat with a finger inside the crown. And still watching.

"I think I'll help my boys with our grips."

As he walked out, Drum took up a pan from by the fire with strips of bacon that he offered to the two children. But he was watching the barn doors.

He set the pan back down and Matthew whispered, "He knows, don' he?"

"I believe you're correct."

Drum then proceeded to place himself between the dog and the boy, so they were both within arms' reach.

The barn had a small back door on leather straps that came smashing open and in plunged one of the sons with a big bore rifle. From out of the rain Skinner and his other son rushed into the light and they were loaded down with iron.

Skinner ordered Drum, "Don't you move now. And keep that beast where it is."

"You mean to rob us…?"

"I mean to sniff out if you're the one the newspapers are calling the 'Coffin Maker' who bombed the railroad and kilt them men on the road."

The pregnant woman did not understand. She was frightened at the sight of all those weapons and called out to her husband, who told her, "Be silent."

"Open your coat," Skinner told Drum. "So I can see if you're bearing a weapon."

"This isn't right," said the woman.

Her husband told her to shut her mouth.

"We came upon a fella on the road," Skinner said. "Lashed to his saddle…He was one of the Pinkertons hunting the man who bombed the railroad. Said the man had a boy with him stricken by the palsy.

"Now," Skinner said to the boy. "Get up so I can see if you're crippled."

The boy looked to Drum.

Skinner stepped forward and cracked the boy across the face. "You don't need to look at that fool. Get up."

"Don't hurt him," said the woman.

Her husband shouted for her to keep damn quiet.

The boy stood. As he did, he glanced down to where the gun was hidden inside his coat. As he stood, Skinner saw the twisted arm, the tremor, and he knew. And when the boy took a hitched step toward Drum, that sealed it. Skinner howled with joy. "There's a reward on that one that'll carry us to eternity."

"Do you think it best we bring them in dead?" said one of the sons.

Near tears, the woman called out, "You can't do such a thing."

"Listen to the woman," said Drum.

Drum was ordered to be silent, but wasn't. "You're living at the edge of a terrible mistake."

"We're not gonna kill him," said Skinner, trying to calm the moment.

But it was too late. The dog was near rabid and could barely be kept, the children were crying 'cause their mother was frantic and pleading, holding her swollen out belly. The men were sweating and nervous and in over their heads, and the rain was coming down on that tired old roof getting louder and harder, and then came the lightning and then came the thunder, and one of the sons said, "What do we do?" And the boy, in desperation, took a chance. He made a clumsy step toward Drum, turning, and lost his footing. Skinner told him to sit. But didn't see him pass Drum the gun he had under his coat.

Drum pulled loose the hitch on the leash and the animal lunged forward. Skinner got off a shot but missed and the dog buried its teeth in his leg. A flurry of gunfire and smoke and screaming ensued, and when all was said and done, one of the sons had been shot through the ribs and lay all balled up on the barn floor. A mount of theirs was dead in a stall, shot through the brain. The other son had dropped his weapon and raised up his arms as he pleaded for his life. His children and wife wailing for him not to be hurt. Drum pulled the dog off of Skinner, and waving his pistol over this human catastrophe, said to the old man, "Look what you got for your greed."

CHAPTER 11

The pregnant woman called out, "You're not gonna kill us?"

"If I was the man that you said I am, what else should I do?"

Drum kept them at gunpoint while they lay the wounded brother down in the stall on the blanket and while he writhed in pain they went about exorcising the bullet.

Theirs was the same old tale of woe that was plaguing the country— the unmerciful conflict between labor and management.

The family had been workers in the meat packing industry. Eleven hours a day, seven days a week, rock bottom wages, benefits be damned, no protections against accident, fires, disease. And when they tried to make a stand to better their lives were run out and replaced by the poorer and more desperate. And so they became the next generation that's left to feed on its own, and in doing so, to lose every trace of their soul.

• • •

The gray storm light cleared the next day. Drum and the boy left that abandoned farm and battered family to live out their fates.

Drum was silent for hours, and the boy wondered about this but felt it wrong to just ask.

The man was thinking how much his life had been altered since finding the boy. How it was being tested in ways he could not have imagined.

In time there would be more Pinkertons on the road if they weren't already. They would wire ahead if they hadn't already. They would collect descriptions and put out rewards, and the child would now be as hunted as the man.

The road was still muddy and spotted with pools of brown filthy water where Drum could see their reflection framed by the sky, there for a moment then trampled away by the hooves of their mounts and the paws of the beast. And he was marked by this indecipherable feeling he would never return to the person he'd been.

"We'll pull off the road, up there by that outcrop…and get down to business" was the first thing he said.

The road where they stopped was edged in by hills strewn with rocks broken down by centuries of runoff from rains. Drum took from the mule the canvas messenger bag with the strap that he used to carry dynamite.

"You're a smart boy for your age. And you're composed. Just look at last night. How'd you come to be that way? Not from your folks, that's for sure."

The boy shrugged as he opened a canteen.

"Hate them, I bet," Drum said.

The boy wanted to show how he felt. For sure they didn't love him. And that hurt more than peril itself. He squatted down and cupped a hand and filled it with water to let the dog drink.

"You're a survivor," said Drum. "Any fool could see it that day in the desert. Did you go mad being left there like that? Don't know if I'd a stood up as well."

The boy was overwhelmed hearing such, but tried to act like it was nothing.

Drum smiled to himself at the brace of this kid. "Maybe someday you'll get even…in ways you never imagined."

The boy squatted there with the dog lapping up water, as great heavy drops dripped from his fingers. They looked like old pards at the gate to whatever came next.

Drum had taken the satchel and slung its strap over his shoulder and began to fill the damn thing with rocks. It was a strange sight the youth was watching.

"Wha' ya" doin?"

"Got your curiosity up? That's good. Didn't know I was an eccentric bastard? No…how could you?"

He kept dropping rocks into the sack.

"A boy with your eyes…if he could learn to shoot could enrich himself in any number of ways. But, of course, you'd have to be able to shoulder a rifle."

"When I'm ola…mehbee."

"We're gonna get to repairing that right now."

The boy did not understand.

When the satchel was partway full, Drum took to juggling how heavy it was, and when it seemed to him, for whatever reason, right, he called the boy over.

Matthew stood and capped the canteen.

Drum loosened the strap and said to the boy, "Hold on now!" and draped the strap over the boy's ruined right shoulder.

The weight of it almost sunk the poor kid.

Drum held him up, listing from his left to his right, and dumped out rocks until the boy was weighed down but not so he couldn't keep upright.

"Walk," said Drum, and he pointed to where they were going. Matthew looked up a road that seemed to go on forever.

CHAPTER 12

The boy labored along and wove like a drunk with Drum walking behind him, leading their mounts, the dog loping in slow time beside the struggling youth. He could barely lift his leg with the weight of the rocks slapping against him.

"You'll always be lame, but you will get stronger," Drum shouted. "Today you go as far as you can…tomorrow a little bit farther. And so on and so forth, till hell freezes over."

The boy walked till he dropped from exhaustion. Drum dumped out the rocks except for two that you could clump in each fist.

He lifted the kid, gave him a drink, wiped the sweat from his face, cooled his neck and dropped one stone in each of his hands.

"Hold them and walk," he said to the kid.

And he started off all over again.

"Your hands will get stronger and harder and so will your arms and so will your shoulders. And like I said…you'll always be lame but soon you'll be able to brace up a gun."

They tramped through a misery of dust and the few strangers on the road that they passed—lone riders, families in wagons, freight pullers all—stared in disbelief at what seemed to them a cruel punishment of sorts.

"They may think me vicious or mad," Drum said, following along behind the kid. "But I learned this trick from a nasty old woman, tough as a boot, and twice as ugly, who ran a home for kids like you. And who, by the way, beat me through and through because I was a belligerent and disobedient bastard, and she loved me dearly."

The boy found a private elation in the quiet sympathy of these strangers and not because he was lame or suffering but because the suffering meant something. He was learning to carry himself.

He wanted badly to warrant praise for who he was, for what he could do. That he might lift himself beyond his limitations. And rid himself of the shame that he bore inside him as if he were a bottle.

He fought the thought that haunted him—Why did God hate me?

He looked through the heat that turned the road into an endless mirage and wondered where his parents and sisters might be. Were they thinking of him, that he might be dead? Did such a thought cause them grief, pain, sorrow, or shame? He hoped that it did, but he didn't believe it.

And this made him stronger. This made the suffering in his hands and his arms, from his neck down to his legs, all the more worth it.

I may be lame, he told himself, but from now on I will never be weak.

For a moment it happened, it came in a flash—he felt liberated. It was there, then gone like a ghost, but he knew it existed.

They kept on through the heat of terrible days. Hardening the body and testing one's soul. Listening to strangers at watering holes—freighters and cowboys handling stock, wayfaring families at crossroads and hamlets—talking about the endless transgressions of avarice and deceit, that fueled an American dream leaving its people powerless and broke, and that the Lords of the Manor better beware, because there was a comeuppance being prepared.

Drum was wary and silent and forever watchful for men on the road that were hunting. He called out to the boy while he was carrying rocks, "This is livelier than the labors of Hercules, don't you think?"

The kid had no idea what he was talking about.

The boy woke one morning looking up into the sun and who should be framed there in shadows.

"Well, young Mister Matthew, you know what this is?" said Drum, and he made a little flick with his jaw.

On his shoulder rested a gun.

"A rifle...sir."

"It's a Remington Rolling Block...Vintage '70...A damn fine piece of craftsmanship. And simple as sin. It's also a powerful voice when you're past trading in reason."

CHAPTER 13

And so began his instruction, and not in values, morals or beliefs, but in the art of the weapon. He was tutored on this gun's perfect simplicity. No brass, no frills. Just a creation for killing.

Drum went about teaching the boy what was a breech lock and a separate hammer. How to use its rear sight and set trigger. He was made to take it apart and clean it, even when blindfolded, before he ever shouldered the thing.

It was about the best damn single shot there was, used by armies all over the world.

"It's good for three hundred meters or more."

The boy wondered what a meter was, as he did not know.

"It's past where my eyes can see," said Drum, "but not near as far as yours."

The boy carried the rifle now slung by a strap from his good shoulder, even as the other was weighed down with rocks. They crossed the San Gabriel River upstream from the town because Drum had learned Pinkertons were putting down a strike at a gristmill.

With his field glasses, Drum saw mounted riders chasing down workers, driving them into the water. The road was strewn with the wounded and dead who were trying to improve their lives.

The boy could see small puffs of smoke rising up over the rooftops.

"Mista Drum…What is it ya' seein'?"

"I'm watching the meek inherit the earth."

Up in the hilltop set back in the trees were the remains of a mission where whites and Indians had fought to the death. It was a hollow of stone and a downfallen steeple. A forsaken place overgrown with thicket and wholly forgotten. A reminder now of what might have been.

"This is as good a place as any," said Drum. He held up a brass cartridge, and the boy understood. He suddenly reeled with excitement.

In the open church doorway with weeds up to Drum's waist, he pointed out a huge cross carved into the stone where the altar had been.

"See what you can do with that," he said, handing the boy the heavy caliber cartridge.

The boy's hands trembled as he cocked back the hammer, then rotated the block and inserted the shell and shut the curved breech block back down. He hoisted the weapon against his bad shoulder and aimed. Frightened to death, he was breathing in flashes.

"You'll find out it gets easier," Drum said, "once your target starts shooting back."

Dumbfounded the boy looked up at the man and there he was grinning.

"Shoot the fucking thing," Drum said, "before he rises from the dead."

And that is just what the boy did.

To his amazement, his shoulder, legs, and back, strengthened as they had been, held up. The shot was errant, missing the cross. Drum had a lineup of cartridges held between each finger and offered the boy another.

"You'll get him eventually," Drum said.

• • •

From the woods by the church they watched a cadre of riders chase those poor mill workers on up into the hills. Drum set his field glasses aside and told the boy, before they were stumbled upon, they better get out. Looking back into long riffs of dark, the boy saw men were being hunted by lantern.

When they crossed the train tracks just east of San Gabriel, the boy saw Drum lean from his saddle and spit on the rails. He cursed out a couple of names, and the boy asked him why.

"A Lord of the Lords of the Manor," said Drum. "Parasites with bankrolls. Like Gould. Remember the name. The bastard owns one mile in ten of every bit of track that crosses the country. All that and Western Union. The money he cheats from his workers he uses to pay his private police to make sure he's not killed."

Drum wiped the angry sweat from his face. "If only injustice worked both ways."

CHAPTER 14

America had reached a flashpoint. It was social justice, equality, and fairness for all, or there would be nowhere safe, nowhere free of insurrection and violence. The poor will not lie down and just die peacefully in the road while they are forever run over.

In the morning they came upon a slat bridge that crossed a nameless creek. Roped upright to the rotting boards was a naked man. He had been shot dead. A strip of slat had been nailed to his chest with one word painted on it—ANARCHIST.

The body swarmed with flies. Corporal Billy was lapping at the blood that pooled around the dead man's feet. They passed around him silently. He had been a huge man in life. The boy looked up into the lifeless stare of this once formidable creature. The force of death in the morning quiet had the boy look away.

"Mista Drum…Wha' does…"

"Anarchist," said Drum. "A person who wants to destroy the government."

"You an…Anakiss?"

"No," said Drum. "I'm worse. I don't want to destroy the government…just the bastards that own it. It'll probably get me killed one day… but there it is."

They were walking down a country road with its wild thicket and high grass. The boy grabbed Drum by his coat.

"You can' say such."

Drum was caught off guard. Then saw what he'd said had hit the boy hard.

The dead man roped up at the bridge. They could still see him. His skin all white and shiny in the perfect sunlight.

"You hea' me," the boy shouted. "You def'…or stoopit?"

"Mostly neither, Matthew…But sometimes both."

• • •

Houston spread out beyond the marshland before them. They followed the road along Buffalo Bayou. They were among the living now and lights from the first buildings began to make their silky appearance out of the dark.

Drum led them into town and at Moody Street they dismounted. Drum left the boy with the horses and dog. "Wait here," he said, "no matter what. It may well be hours."

Drum crossed the street looking about him and went around to the side of a two-story building. The first floor looked to be a mercantile shipping office. Drum climbed an outdoor stairway and knocked on the door. He waited and watched and seemed to be anxious. A man finally answered. A short looking rough with a flashy moustache and derby hat. A man the boy would eventually learn was known as "The Cook."

When he saw Drum, he threw his arms around him and hustled him in, scanning the street as he swung shut the door.

The boy could see in a triptych of windows a small group of men rally around Drum as he entered the room. And just like that they began to draw down the shades and the last the boy saw, someone handed Drum a newspaper.

The boy was in a vacant lot between buildings. From there he could look out over the waterway where steamboats and barges were being loaded for shipment. And on the flats flanking the wharves was the railyard and a huge roundhouse stacked with locomotives. All of it ringed by men with torches, guards, hired thugs, Pinkertons, there to make sure nothing like San Antonio would happen again. A freight was pulling out on into the night in that slow march of iron couplings and wheels. It had to cross a trestle that spanned Buffalo Bayou as the tracks made their way through Texas. Bonfires had been set up on both sides of the shore where the shadowy figures weighted down with weapons kept watch.

A gang of drunk youths came coursing up through the vacant lot. They couldn't have been a half dozen years older than Matthew. They were chugging beer and chasing it down with whiskey, and they took to screaming insults and hatred across the river. Giving the guards every known notion of shit. They were part of the crowd that was watching the railyard. Everyone there alive to the terrible that might happen, and some probably praying to the Good Lord for the terrible *to* happen.

One of that drunken rabble took notice of the boy standing back from the crowd in the black of the building with a roped dog and a Remington strapped over his shoulder. He had the hitched walk of the lame.

"Hey," said a youth to his friends. "Look at this here."

That gang of kids laughed and wheezed and made lurid remarks.

"How old are you?" one of them said.

"Almost nine."

"Nine? That rifle a Remington?"

The boy nodded.

"Loaded?"

"No good 'ith it weren'."

"Fucking right," said one of their number.

They tried to coerce him, bribe him first with beer, and then with whiskey, to take a shot at that rail trash down by the trestle.

"You don't have to kill no one...just give them a little testimonial."

And like that they were on their way, and the boy heard one of them repeat what he'd said, "No good if it weren't." And over the laughter, another said, "Tough little cracker."

Then it settled in, what they'd said, as they strode through the crowd, being drunken shits and nasty. The way he'd been looked at and talked to. He was not some lame thing to be mocked or made sport of, shunned, cast off, stared at. He was...a tough little cracker, bearing a rifle.

CHAPTER 15

An explosion shook the ground beneath him. Smoke the color of pure sand marbled the night sky. The best of the men knew it was where the tracks arced down toward Galveston that had been dynamited.

Then the fierce report of gunfire rolled up out of the darkness. The blue teeth of powder all along the train line and across the railyard. The guards hired by the company were firing wildly into the night. The guilty and innocent alike were sprinting from the shore, from the docks and warehouses, from the streets facing the railway, scattering to hell and its neighborhoods to escape the wrath. You could hear men shouting though, calling down the company, calling down Gould by name.

Men came scattering up through the dark. Petrified, cursing, spottings of gunfire all about them. The boy looked to the building where Drum had gone. The windows were now black as night and everything still.

He heard men shouting. "He went up that way…" "See…" "There…."

The boy squatted down against the building wall and held the dog close to him. He saw a man come laboring up through the trees. A tall ungraceful man, narrow from ankle to shoulder. He was holding his side where he'd been shot.

The boy had not dared to move from the shadows. The sweeping shape of the man stumbled toward him. He fell and then crawled along as he tried to stand. He clawed his way to his feet. He saw the boy and the alley between buildings that was filled with refuse and debris and the stench of human waste.

He got down on his hands and knees and caterpillared into that filthy miasma until he disappeared. He looked back and saw the boy at the edge of the dark staring right at him.

The boy remained as he was, where he was. The boy buried his face into the animal's chest, as if somehow this would help him hide. Moments later men with weapons drawn came out of the trees, breathing hard, enraged. They asked had the boy seen a man they described to a fault. And when the boy hesitated a man bore down and violently hit him. The boy's shoulders and neck shook and he buried his face into the animal's side even farther and then pointed.

He had pointed to the street.

He waited until it felt like forever and the empty lot got quiet and the gunfire distant, then he eased himself up and peeked into the alley, pitch black as it was, and he whispered, "Mista'...ta' men are gone."

Nothing moved, nothing at all. The boy's matchless vision could not pick out a sign in that graveyard of garbage.

Even the dog was silent.

And then the faintest scraping and the dog leaned toward the outline of a man rising up from the garbage and feces.

He leaned against the wall holding a pistol, breathing out pain from the wound.

"Thanks," he said, and then he slipped off into the night.

CHAPTER 16

Drum arrived with the light. He was filthy and worn out and his forearm was bandaged with strips of bloodstained cloth.

"We got to move," he said to the boy. "And I mean now."

He hurried to the mule and tried to tell Drum about the man in the alley when Drum cut him off with, "We know."

They left on the same road they'd come in, pushing for time. The road was already trafficked, and travelers were talking up how the tracks just east of town had been blown.

They hadn't gone but a mile when a man signaled Drum from a long sweep of trees. The boy saw it was the one he'd come to know as "The Cook."

There was a freight wagon hidden up from the road and in the back, amidst all the crates, a bespeckled gent with his sleeves rolled and arms slathered with blood, digging a bullet out from the man in the alley. The wounded man's teeth bore down on a strap of leather to keep from screaming in agony. He caught sight of the youth and nodded his head, the strap and his lips all drenched with saliva.

The boy watched the blood pool and stream where the surgeon's tool kept digging until the man passed out. The doctor pressed on, probing down into the flesh, cursing all the while, and when he was done, when he held the bullet up to the sun and stitched the wound shut, he ordered the boy up into the wagon. He stuffed a rag clump into his hand, "Hold this against the wound. Keep it there," he said, "until the bleeding stops or the bastard is dead."

Drum covered the boy and the wounded man with a tarp and he drove the wagon with his weapons on the seat at the ready, because there were Pinkertons on the road hunting for radicals behind the bombing.

The boy could hear it all as they trundled along. The wounded man was named Koons. He'd been a rail yard manager, well thought of, respected, until he started talking an eight hour day and an increase in wages. Then he was given the walk. The doctor was called Momont. He attended to a number of railroad and mining officials. He never talked politics, but he always listened. The one they called "The Cook" was a German named Ammerman. He owned a drug store and was known as The Cook because he organized and plotted acts of sabotage and was a link to other small cells committed to fight.

The boy had not noticed Koons' eyes were open, not until the wisp of a voice said, "Where are we?"

The boy was caught off guard, like the dead had risen. He leaned over just to be sure. "On ta' road," he said.

"The bullet?"

The boy made his jerky motion with a thumb to show it was out.

The wagon suddenly veered. The wheels rose and fell, then the wagon began to shudder as they crossed the rickety slats of a bridge.

"I think we're home," said Koons. "See, will ya?"

The boy peeked out from under the tarp. It was an encampment of the kind the boy had seen along the roads of this country. Some scrapboard shacks lined the edge of a marsh. But people mostly lived in their wagons, or tents, even makeshift huts of tree branches and fronds. The smoke from their fires tinted the air.

It was home to families untethered from livelihood, who could no longer pay rent or buy food. There were men on the move, hobos and tramps. And everywhere, children. A legion of the bathless and underfed, thin from suffering want.

The boy described what he saw, and Koons closed his eyes and breathed with relief. "At least if I die now," he said, "I'll have my loved ones around me."

Koons lived in one of the shacks that backed up to the marsh with a wife and two ragged little sons.

The boy had lived in a hovel like this, shit boards and tarpaper. Right down to the smells, it reminded him of a world that had been lost and for no other reason than being born lame. Standing by himself and watching this family gather around the stricken man, a trail of memories were having at him, and the boy had no idea what they promised or what they meant, only that they possessed him.

Drum and the boy took to the road alone on their mounts with Corporal Billy leading the way. The dog seemed to know where they were going because it was just a few miles farther ahead he veered off the main highway and toward a ramshackle hacienda graced with crumbling walls and a dried out creaking gate.

"We're home," said Drum. "At least…I think."

In the compound were chickens and pigs and a slat sided burro rooting around in dirt, when the front door opened and out onto the porch stepped a woman.

Drum told the boy to dismount. The dog ran to the woman and swirled all about her, and she called him by name. She was leathered and lean and wore men's filthy trousers held up by rope she passed for a belt.

She looked from Drum to the boy and approached them with arms crossed over her heart.

"Grandmother," said Drum. "It's so good to—"

Without a word, she slapped his face as hard as she could, so hard, in fact, that she knocked the hat right off his head and got his nose and mouth to bleeding.

"Now that we've got that out of the way." She threw her arms around her grandson and grasped him tightly and with long held affection. "Two years…not a word. I should beat you like it was religion. But I see we have a guest. Do you have a name, child?"

"I call him Matthew," said Drum.

She put a hand out. "Well, Matthew. Do you always tote a rifle slung over your shoulder?"

"As of recenlee," he said.

"I also see you got blood on your hands," she said, "and on your shirt."

"Yes, ma'am. Ya' right."

CHAPTER 17

Missus Drum set a place on the portico for the boy to eat. She left the dog with him. Then she and her grandson went inside so they could get down to the hard matters at hand.

The old woman brought out a bottle of rye and glasses and she and her grandson sat at the dining room table under the veneer of a kerosene lamp. He with his drink and rolling a cigarette, and she with her two worked down, arthritic hands, folded together, watching over her boy like the judge of ages himself.

"Did you read about the bombing in San Antonio?" she said.

"I heard about it."

She had also brought a newspaper which she slid across the table so he might see for himself what had been written.

"The newspaper is calling…someone…the Coffin Maker," she said.

Drum did not seem overly moved or impressed.

"They've taken a little privilege on the facts," he said.

"There is now a five thousand dollar reward out for information leading to the—"

"We kill one of theirs and we are murderers and assassins," he said. "They kill one of ours and they're exterminating vermin…anarchists… filthy radicals…America haters."

He slipped the cigarette between his lips and lit the match on the table and a ribbon of smoke shot up out of nowhere. "You didn't know you'd raised an assassin, did you?"

"I can't take all the credit," she said. "Or all the blame."

A look passed between them, a look that took in the history of their years.

"Whose idea was it to blow the tracks west of town?"

Drum sipped at his glass of rye.

"Ammerman, right?"

He set the glass down.

"They should have targeted the trestle bridge on Buffalo Bayou," said the old woman.

"The years haven't slowed you down, have they?"

"They have operatives working the camps now," said the woman. "Infiltrators. The camp where Koons lives…it's a hotbed. If you know what I mean."

"Yeah."

"And this reward—?"

"I know it'll turn angels into rats. I'm gonna stay just long enough… Mary Jones is set to speak here. I want in on that."

"There'll be a show of force," said the old woman. "The railroads will have thugs in there making it look like the protestors were instigating all the violence. And there will be violence."

Her eyebrows rose, and she carried this expression of someone who had charted years of insurrection.

"What about the boy?" she said. "What is his story?"

"He needs a home."

"And you thought to leave him here with me?"

From his coat pocket Drum took out a page stolen from a Bible. She looked it over. Read… *It's in God's hands now….* She said, "What does it mean?"

He told her the story of a lame child bound up and left in the desert and she listened with case hardened compassion.

"You think you've heard it all," she said. "No one's heard it all. Not even God has heard it all. And who's got a better ear?"

She looked out the window at this solemn faced youth swabbing his plate with a scrap of bread and minding his own damn business.

"He's got the palsy," said Drum.

"I'm not blind. Is this your attempt at redemption?"

"I don't think I'll live long enough to be redeemed," he said.

She reached out and slapped his face. "I can say that…but not you."

He grinned as one who has taken most everything. "I can't keep the boy with me," he said. "He's too young. I would if I could, but—"

"You've got too much killing to do."

"I've got too much killing to do."

"You're getting to feel the loneliness, aren't you?"

"I'm getting to feel the loneliness."

"Good," his grandmother said. "It will give you a little insight into my life."

He smoked. He emptied the glass of rye. He poured another. He was a hard traveled young man in need of a miracle and there were no miracles running 'round loose...that he knew of.

"I failed you," he said. "I know that."

For a moment of surprising tenderness the old woman reached out and took her grandson's hand.

"The truth is, I knew how much blood it would take to change America...And it is terrible when the gap between what you know and what you choose to believe is insurmountable. My boy...it may well be I failed you by setting you on this course."

"That was no failure, Missus Drum...that was just the call of providence."

CHAPTER 18

Missus Drum walked out onto the portico followed by her grandson. The boy had finished his food and sat quietly in the shade studying the pigs and chickens that roamed the yard around him.

"Had enough to eat?" said the woman.

He was a quiet boy, thoughtful, she sensed, and observant. And when he looked at you, he looked at you. But he also looked lost.

She swept an arm across the unkempt courtyard. "This used to be a home for children," she said. "Orphans, the infirmed that parents could no longer afford to keep, or didn't want. But the city fathers shut us down. Courtesy of the railroad and freighters' management. Complaints filed against us. Said we were poisoning children's minds with ideas like a shorter workday and better wages, benefits for the sick or those hurt on the job. All the children are now in the Houston City orphanage."

The woman went and sat, and the Corporal came over and rested his head in her lap.

"The only thing they didn't get was Corporal Billy here. Ledru found him down the road five years ago. He was a pup. Been bit by a rattler. Leg was all swelled up, fevered. We were sure he'd die. But as you can see—"

She held the dog by its jowls, and she leaned down and kissed his filthy, scraggled face.

"We named him after my late husband. Everyone called him Corporal Billy. He was shot dead one night on the Bayou Road. He and Ledru's father, both. No one was ever brought to pay, but we know who was behind it."

The boy noted the bitterness that both grandmother and grandson bore.

"It was the same people that shut this place down," she said. "And that drove people like your parents out onto the road and made them do desperate and terrible things. That created camps like the one you went to. That birthed a nation of homeless tramps and hobos and—

"Do you have any idea what I'm talking about?" she said to the boy.

"Some, ma'am!"

"We preached revolution here and how if this world isn't changed there'll be just these islands of the rich in an endless sea of the poor. I have friends in Houston…a few. And I have enemies…a few too many."

She stood now. Straightened. Put a hand on the boy's shoulder. "You have a home here, Matthew…Free to come, free to go. And you don't have to wear that rifle all the time, but you are welcome to."

• • •

The Union Pacific called their new surge of Pinkertons Fact Gathering Committees. They should have been defined as Death Squads.

In the Gould mission statement for the press, they described these new committees as search and surveillance groups who were to hunt out radicals that were intent on disrupting and destroying railroad property under Gould ownership, including that of Western Union.

Gould had had the acute foresight to take over first the Atlantic and Pacific Telegraph Company, and then Western Union itself. This gave him control of the national media. And so Western Union became the propaganda arm of the railroad, allowing it to defame and destroy labor organizations and strikers by constantly describing them as virulent radicals who meant to undermine the American way of life and turn the country into a socialist dictatorship.

Published reports in the newspapers began to surface that Mary Jones, the infamous labor organizer who was coming to speak to a rally at the Houston Fairgrounds, was, in fact, part of a veiled plot to incite a riot. And that she and her anti-American "minions" should be denied access to the fairgrounds.

Of course, Mary Jones, known to the rank and file worker across the nation as "Mother," refused to be intimidated by such harassment and said she would go on with the rally as planned.

"Permit or not," she told reporters as she boarded the train, "I will speak wherever the people will gather. In a cow pasture, on the road, or in a cemetery, if that's what it takes to stem the tide of manifest greed and so give the workingman and woman their due."

As the date of the rally approached, a "Committee" of six men was making its way from San Antonio. This particular "Committee" was the special purview of Natale Prince, who was one of Gould's private security officers. Prince had served in the Russian Imperial Army during the Crimean War, and when he emigrated to the United States changed his name to seem more "Americanized."

The leader of the six was John James Vandel, recently fired for his failure to stop the bombing at the San Antonio railyard. Under him was McSorley, who had also been fired for his failure in pursuit of the bomber, and for being captured and humiliated. Both of the men were being given a chance to redeem themselves or face what would be described by Prince as "a professional execution at the hands of their employer."

The Committee did not ride to Houston bereft of possibilities. A family named Skinner had answered one of the railroad reward ads in the newspaper. At a private meeting with Prince in an office across from Alamo Square that he used as his headquarters, the Skinners described their confrontation in an abandoned barn with a man they believed to be the bomber. And that he was traveling with a boy about eight years of age, who had the palsy. The Skinners described both the man and the boy, and the description of the boy matched that of the youth McSorley had come upon just moments before the attack on the road.

Prince paid the family for their information, even exceeding the amount offered in the press, while at the same time warning them in no uncertain terms of the wrath that would be exercised against them and their children should they fail in one matter—that matter being absolute silence.

CHAPTER 19

Matthew fed the chickens and tended to the pigs and made sure that slat ribbed donkey had grain or hay. As he went about these chores, he wore the canvas satchel weighted down with stones.

"My grandson taught you that," said the woman upon first seeing this. The boy told her it was true. She pulled his shirt loose and saw his shoulder was already heavily calloused and the flesh a raised and discolored epaulet.

In the afternoons, the boy would take the dog and the donkey and go to the remains of a stone corral behind the compound and there he would practice firing the Remington.

He had a room to sleep in and a world to live in and the word —"home"— had some truth to it. And he thought, as a boy thought, that his life would be like a boy's again. But he was no longer a boy, though still in a boy's body. And his life since that day in the desert would never be a boy's again.

He would have moments, flashes of feeling, that sparked his child's spirit, but he was something else, something different. Within that lame body of a child existed a shadow, a shadow that had been hovering over his cradle since the dawn of his birth. It was the shadow of a crippled country.

The boy knew, even young as he was, that life at its most honest was temporary. And more than temporary—it was filled with dangerous secrets.

Even here. How many times did some rider arrive with a letter that Drum and his grandmother would go off alone to read and then answer and pass their letter to the rider who waited silently in the quiet of the portico? How, after dark, Drum would stand at the compound gate, checking his watch until he saw a yawing light on a hilltop close by, and he would then disappear into the night, often until dawn.

• • •

There would be violence at the rally—wherever Mary Jones spoke, hatred and hostility followed. "If you mean to change the world," said the woman they called Mother, "then you must expect the world to have something to say about it."

Drum left for Houston the night before. His grandmother and the boy watched him ride out of the compound and into the pitched darkness. They followed the next day on mules. The boy had the rifle slung over his shoulder. Missus Drum thought the youth looked like a threadbare little soldier, but said not a word.

There were people on the road in wagons, people on horseback and mule, people walking. They kicked up long swaths of dust on their march to the city. And they all had one thing in common. They were poor.

There were men posted at every crossroad, every juncture, every street that led to the marsh beyond the fairgrounds where Mary Jones was to speak. These men were hired by the railroad to pass out fliers, and they were adamant that anyone going to the rally accept one. The fliers were unadulterated warnings that Mary Jones was a mercenary radical and her labor movement bred socialism and anarchy. And that those who stood with her would be committing themselves and their families to a life of hardship and suffering.

The railroad also had people at the depot passing out fliers to an army of unemployed and homeless awaiting Mary Jones' arrival. Among them was Drum and his small coterie of saboteurs, as there were expectations of violence, even a possible assassination attempt against the woman.

When the train pulled in you could hear the cheers for blocks. The crowd pressed the edge of the station and almost swept Drum under the wheels. And in a rolling wave of steam as the wheel brakes tightened down onto the far platform stepped a woman. A tiny, birdlike creature all dressed in black, with white hair and wire rim glasses. A woman so small Drum could hardly see her above a sea of upturned arms, not ten feet away, and when she finally got the people, her people, to settle down, to still, so she might be heard, she said in a voice filled with pepper, "My name is Mary Jones…and I've come here to raise hell."

CHAPTER 20

Flanked she was by factory hands and dockworkers, shop clerks and day laborers, women who worked the sewing shops and food kitchens and as maids. That legion whose clothes were shabby beyond humiliation and who were chronically ill but bore it in weary silence, and block by block their numbers grew.

And a part of this moving protest, the Committee was hard at work. Vandel and McSorley, each with two men, searched the crowd, hunting for a boy that was lame, crippled, had the palsy and was about eight. Everyone they came upon they demanded a name, where they lived, who they were with. For McSorley, he'd know that filthy little nothing on sight.

Mary Jones was led to the edge of the marsh just beyond the fairgrounds where the city could not legally keep her from speaking. A small stage had been erected from where she could address the crowd.

"Well," she said, looking out upon the people there, "this should not surprise you. They get the well kept fairgrounds...and we get the muddy and bug ridden marshland. Now where have you seen that before?"

There was applause and bitter laughter...and there were condemnations.

"I look at you all and you know what I see...I see myself. And that is what I hope you will see when you look at me. That you see yourselves. In this we should be rock solid. Our survival demands we are one."

In this the crowd spoke violently in her favor. She held up the flier.

"I had a chance to read this as I walked up from the station. And I'm sure one of the railroad's hired henchmen was kind enough to offer each of you one."

This earned a rousing jeer, and it was suddenly raining down crumpled up fliers of propaganda and threats.

"The Lords of the Manor," said Mary Jones, "want to convince you that the worse life is...the better off you are. And that everyone and everything is evil...except them. This flier is an unveiled attempt to force your obedience. It is, in fact, a dog leash...it is a harness...a yoke...a set of chains...and a rope to lynch your future with. The leash, the harness, the yoke, chains, and rope are made of fear."

She then crumpled up the flier she held in her tiny white hand and threw it in the mud.

"I want to tell you a little of my story…because it is also your story. As a little girl in Ireland," said Mary Jones, "I saw men hung for no other reason than they were poor, they were hungry, and they were desperate. But such as this, is not new to your suffering. I was married once and had children. My husband died from Yellow Fever in the Epidemic of '67. But such as this, is not new to your suffering. And my children. They died one by one in the Epidemic. This too is nothing new to your suffering. I had no money for doctors or food. The basic needs were beyond me. Except by begging. This is nothing new to your suffering."

Most of the people there didn't bother much with books or newspapers. There was the Bible, the ordained word. Except, of course, for fliers such as the ones handed out. Or eviction notices, pink slips, foreclosures, death certificates.

"We are not the leavings of creation," Mary Jones said. "We are creation. Though the rich and powerful would not have it so."

Her words would not stand in for feelings and ideas. They were feelings and ideas as they came from her mouth because people were moved. And what the people heard and felt is what the boy heard and felt, without really understanding. The words seemed true because he saw other lame children around him. Lame, infirm, missing limbs, emaciated to the point of death with sickness, and to them the words seemed true.

He wondered if his own parents were there in the crowd, and if so, his sisters. Would they be ashamed now by what they were hearing and feeling? He looked up at Missus Drum. She was crying. He asked why she was crying, but before she could tender an answer there came a scream—

CHAPTER 21

The boy saw two men standing over a child. They had the child in their grasp. The boy could see the child was about his own age and lame, and standing by him was what had to be an older brother. He was the one who'd screamed for the men to "Let the hell go of my brother."

The two men wanted the boys' names and where they lived and who were their parents. The older youth kept shouting, "It's none of your goddamn business."

And then things got violent. The older youth hit one of the men square in the face and rocked him. The man slipped and lost his grip on the younger child. The man was up fast, got a lick in, and the youth, hit and bloody and flat on his back, began to yell out for help. A couple of ragged protestors stepped in and things only got worse. It was fists and boots and men slogging about in the mud.

About then, McSorley pressed through the crowd, his weapon unholstered, and Matthew got a glimpse of him. His instinct was to run. He moved with a hitched panic as best he could and like some feral creature fled back into the crowd leaving Missus Drum there, shocked, yelling to him, "Matthew…where are you going…Matthew?"

He didn't answer her. He just disappeared into a world of protestors intent on Mary Jones, all the while looking back over his shoulder in desperate flight. Had McSorley recognized him?

For a moment, their glances had passed over each other. A moment that stole every ounce of hope and freedom within him.

• • •

There was an explosion on the wharf at the end of Labranche Street by the gas works. A barge containing naphtha and bales of cotton had been set off during Mary Jones' speech. Wood particles were hurled almost as far as the stage where Mary Jones stood addressing the crowd. Those at the rally could not scatter fast enough to keep from being burned by paraselenes of cotton and hull fragments that fell from the sky or escape that toxic fear of what might come next.

Drum was part of a group of men who ringed the stage. A blue collar private guard on the chance this was the first move in an assassination attempt.

Mary Jones wouldn't have it. "I'm not afraid of dying, gents!" she shouted. "Especially when there's work to be done." And with that she marched from the makeshift stage and went tromping through the mud, making for the wharf to see if there were wounded who needed tending.

And Mary Jones was not lost on the value of the press. Being the lone woman's voice in a man's war had taught her much. It bought her notoriety, as much as her courage and dedication did. As the reporters crammed in around her she took up a dramatic place on a bluff with the burning barge at her back as the flames twisted violently.

From the shoreline, a hellish vision of smoking wharves, and she had a question for the reporters, "How long will it take for the railroads and the ship owners to blame the working man for this? How long will it take for Western Union to tell America what they need to know…or should I say…what Western Union wants it to know?"

CHAPTER 22

Drum thought he heard his grandmother calling out to him. Her voice ghostlike from where he stood on the bluff above the barge now listing in flames. The water hissing steam and everywhere people scattering like mad creatures.

The smoke hugged the bluff, and it was hell to see flesh and blood detail with his eyes burning so and watering down his cheeks like someone swept in tears. But it was her all right and Drum cupped his hands over his mouth and choked out some smoke, then called to her.

Her voice came back again and like ships in a fog they closed in on each other until he finally saw her, frail and spent, at the edge of a light that had speared through the smoke.

She could barely keep upright. He got hold of her and took his bandana and covered her mouth so she might breathe a little easier and she managed to force out a few words.

"The boy," she said.

Drum looked around as if he should be somewhere close by.

"What? Where is he?"

"Before the explosion…something spooked him and he took off running."

When he asked what it could possibly have been, she told him about the incident with the lame boy and two men roughing him up, forcing him to give them his name, and then a fight broke out…and Drum could take a better guess at what it all meant.

He led the old woman to where they had shed their mounts up on Moody Street. It was behind the office where Drum and his fellow conspirators met. The boy's mule was gone.

Missus Drum was shaken, to say the least. "Could violence have befallen the boy?"

"This is the country for it," said Drum.

• • •

When they returned home the compound was nested in shadow. Drum took out his revolver and told his grandmother to wait. They had locked the dog in the house, and he was at a window barking and clawing at the glass. Drum dismounted and paced about. It was all still but for that ungodly beast of a dog. Drum waved his grandmother in.

"They didn't get him," said Drum.

"They? How do you know?"

He opened the door and Corporal Billy sprinted out circling Drum and then he was up on his hind legs against Drum's chest.

"Go get him," said Drum. "The boy…you son of a bitch. Get him."

The dog took off out of the compound gate leaving small puffs of dust in his wake for Drum to chase.

Drum tracked behind the dog up past the stone corral and on into the hills along a switchback where the slope narrowed, and the way grew more treacherous and dark. It was slow and careful going now. His mount had to be prodded and it tried to turn back, but Drum booted the horse forward and there at the edge of a black coulee was a small plat of rock where the dog had come upon the boy, who now stood.

"You picked a good spot," said Drum. "You can see it all from up here."

"Was waitin' on til I wa' sure it wa' safe."

"I guessed that much. The man on the road. It was him at the rally. The one I sent back."

"Yeah."

"Did he see you?"

"I ting so."

"Did he recognize you?"

"Don' know. He din' caj me. And I don' run sa fas'."

Drum reached out. "Climb aboard, son. Let's go home."

Somewhere among the black shapes of rock where the broken trail led back to the compound, the boy leaned forward and said to Drum, "I did awright?"

Drum reached around and patted the boy on the shoulder to let him know how well.

CHAPTER 23

Missus Drum stood in the doorway of her grandson's room watching him pack a handful of essentials into his grip, and she knew. The half choked cries would come later.

"You'll watch out for the boy?" he said.

"You haven't told him yet?"

The boy was at the kitchen table having soup and bread when Drum walked in and set his grip down by the door. He walked over to the table with the boy watching all this solemnly.

"I can't take you with me," said Drum.

"I knew dat," said the boy.

"It's too dangerous…too hard…you're too young."

The boy nodded. He set the spoon down.

"I'm leaving Corporal Billy with you."

The boy stared at the bowl. "T'ank you," he said. "I tae' goot care a him."

Drum did not know what to say now. He did not know what human action to take. Shake the boy's hand, grip him by the shoulders like an old pard?

His grandmother had no such problems. "Kiss him goodbye, you dumb bastard. And get on with it."

Drum pushed out a smile, but it was bittersweet. "Yes, ma'am."

The woman and the boy, with the dog on a rope, walked Drum out into the compound where his mount and mule stood at the ready.

"Do you know where you're going?" said the woman.

"Where they've written for my handiwork, of course."

He climbed up into the saddle and in the light of the veranda lanterns looked over those he was leaving.

"Keep the Corporal with you," Drum told the boy. "It'll give you someone to thunder around with."

The boy wanted to beg Drum to take him along. That he would not be a burden, that he had proved himself worthwhile. But he knew begging would only make him seem like a boy and more of a burden and so less worthwhile. He hated this feeling, as much as he'd hated himself for so long for being lame.

His only chance to go with Drum, he thought, what little chance he had, now rested in his silence. Would be graced to him because of silence. And the silence born of being able to bear what seems unbearable. That somehow his silence would be a sign of his respect, admiration, affection that the man would recognize and so change his mind.

The boy did not walk to the gate, to follow after Drum even for a little longer. He had to hold the dog back with both hands on the rope. The grandmother came and placed a hand on the boy's shoulder. They were, for a moment, a family portrait looking out through the gate and into the darkness.

What they did not know, would never know, was that when he reached the road, he reined in his mount and remained there looking back at the faint light for what was and had been his only home. He was leaving everything from childhood to manhood behind and without self regard.

You take all the feelings and ideas, he could cast them aside and go back. He could escape the empire of troubles and just live. It was there and hungry within him to do and be just that.

But the country was on fire, and he was born of that fire and until it was put out, put to death, condemned to a perdition of decency, or he himself was put to death, there would be no home.

CHAPTER 24

For the next few months Missus Drum and the boy lived a careful life, keeping the boy out of Houston and away from stray eyes. On one of her supply trips to town, the woman stopped at the apothecary and "The Cook" talked to her secretly as he filled out her order, warning her the Pinkertons had people there trying to run down their suspicions. And that they would pay well to have their suspicions answered.

On one of her trips, the last one, in fact, Koons was at a druggist getting medicine for his sick daughter. Missus Drum acted as if she did not know him.

He had survived his wound the night of the bombing, but one of the people at the homeless camp who had seen him brought home in a wagon that night, sold this information to the Pinkertons.

• • •

Koons would often tramp out into the marsh behind his shack with his Detroit Muzzleloader seeking a path through the high grass, hunting for swamp chickens to quell his children's constant belly hunger.

He would go far out to where the shadows block the clouds and the sunsets made the trees burn with color. He stood in the silence marked by the faint chittering of birds, waiting and watching, and then the fringed rustling of the brush forecast that he was not alone.

Two men appeared from a world of black tupelo and striding into the smoky daylight Koons saw they were bearing arms and...they were not alone.

Other men stepped from the high grass along the shore, the mud slopping up around their boots, and others slipped out of the shadow of downy branches that hung from on high to the earth, moving slightly in a tender breeze.

They were closing in and they all bore arms and one of them, Vandel, called out, "You can put the weapon down, or make a fight of it. Yours to choose."

Koons thought to run, but he set the rifle down instead.

Dusk was softly settling in as six men surrounded Koons. They reeked of whiskey and stale beer and tobacco. They weren't there to extort money, that was for sure. This was pure power and politics. Koons was already sweating so bad his damp shirt was skinned to his back.

"You know why we're here?" said Vandel.

"No, sir…I don't."

"Anarchists," said McSorley, "make the worst liars."

"This is where you're going to die," said Vandel. "Look around. Then we'll toss you off into the bowers and there you'll rot forever and be forgotten. And tonight your tired out wife will stand at the back door of that shack you live in with your kids there like a couple of dogs sniffing at her feet waiting…waiting…waiting…until every dream they had grows dim and dies."

"Now what do you think of that, anarchist?" said McSorley.

"What is it you want from me," said Koons, "or think you want?"

"You're one of the anarchists," said Vandel, "that dynamited the tracks. The night of the bombing you were shot. You were brought to that miserable camp of yours by a man in a wagon—"

"And there was a boy," said McSorley. "We want the names of the man…and the boy."

One of the men squatted down and unsheathed a huge Bowie knife and drove it into the ground at the top of Koons' boots.

"I was in Houston that night like everyone else," said Koons. "To watch the goings. I was shot accidentally when everything went wild."

"You've been ratted out by one of your own in that camp," said McSorley.

Vandel reached into his vest pocket. He had a small packet of paper money already prepared for this moment that he tossed on the ground right by the knife.

"Those are your two paths," said Vandel.

"The man's name…and that damn boy's," said McSorley.

Koons looked the men over. Saw the calendar of his life had expired, but he tried anyway. "Do you ever think what will happen to you after you crush us? You think the railroad or the mining company or the steel foundry will take care of you?

"You'll make some money while you're killing us, but then you know what will be…you'll be us. Yeah…living in a camp like I'm living now. Poor and miserable and hungry. Or you'll be a tramp on the road living on dust. And what about your families?"

"That's the anarchist in him talking…the socialist," said one of the men.

"I say we hang him a bit. Give him a taste," said McSorley. "And while his legs are jerking, we light matches on the bottom of his boots and enjoy a smoke."

CHAPTER 25

The compound was lightless among the night fields. There was only the thinnest bit of moon where phantom shadows with a sense of purpose kept low to the ground. Once they had control of the gate and had climbed the walls and took aim on the windows to make any chance of escape impossible, Vandel called from the darkness, "We've come for you, Coffin Maker. Do you hear…Ledru Drum…We've run you down, boy."

Missus Drum was the first to awaken, the dog rising from beside the boy's bed a moment later. The woman walked down the hall bearing a poor candle and set it down on a table by the entry.

The boy was just stepping out of his room and the woman said, "Matthew, get back in there. Keep the dog with you and close the door."

Vandel ordered Drum out. One of his men pistoled a window, then another. You could hear the shattered glass hitting on the tile floor, but it was Missus Drum who answered. "My grandson's not here…but I'm coming out."

As the front door opened and the woman stepped into a slanting light from the entry wearing a sleeping gown, she was barefooted, her arms held tight across her chest. She stood at the edge of the portico while men from the "Committee" closed in around her as they had Koons.

Vandel and McSorley she recognized from her grandson's description. Vandel wanted to know who else was in the house.

"A boy," she said, "I am caring for. And a dog."

They could hear the animal.

"The boy a cripple?" said McSorley. "Lame…got the palsy?"

"Yes," said the woman.

"Tell him to come out here."

She called to Matthew.

"Where is Drum?" said Vandel.

"He left months ago to try and earn a living. Said he might try California."

"You're one of them," said McSorley.

"One of what?" said the woman.

"Murderers…saboteurs…anarchists…"

"I'm an old woman."

The boy stood in the doorway with the dog on a rope.

"That's the little bastard," said McSorley.

Vandel said, "Are you the boy on the road?"

"Yes, sir."

"And he admits it right to our face," said McSorley. "The filthy little—"

"Where is he?" said Vandel.

"Don' know, sir. And at's ta' truth. Missus Drum…she doesn' ether."

Vandel ordered two of his men to comb through the house, and one to search the stables. Then he looked from the woman to the boy, from the boy to the woman. He was making a private calculation.

"You know they're lying," said McSorley.

"I don't know that," said Vandel. "But I will come to find out."

He looked from the woman to the boy again. His features now stony. Then his stare shifted to the dog.

The man raised the shotgun, and the boy threw himself in front of the animal spreading his arms and using his body as a shield. The man would have to shoot the boy in the back to get at the dog.

The woman pleaded her cause. "Shoot me instead if that's what it's come to. But we don't know where he—"

McSorley grabbed the boy by the hair and kicked him in the back and dragged him from the dog and took his weapon and the dog rose up to defend the boy, teeth bared, mouth frothed with saliva, all muscle, from flew to withers, and in the rising up was shotgunned.

You could hear the poor animal's agony across the compound. You could hear it far out into the night and all the way to where only God was listening. A cry of utter and absolute agony. It lay in its own blood dying. It lay there in its own blood fighting, as we all do, for a last breath. It lay in its own blood trying to raise its head toward the boy who cradled him, held him, this dog that had discovered him in the desert, that was the reason the boy was still alive. The animal tremored violently until it was no more.

With the shooting the other men had rushed from the house and the stable and now stood in the night where a shattered boy knelt over the dead animal. The boy's hands dripped with blood, a courtesy of the darker heart of man.

Vandel looked from the boy to the woman and spoke over his sobs. "Which one of you is next?" he said.

The boy was rocking back and forth, his face smeared with tears.

"Where is the fuckin' Coffin Maker?"

"Here," said the woman.

Vandel turned. What had the woman meant? She had taken a step toward him. She had been holding her hands to her chest and no one had seen the derringer she possessed. She could almost reach out and touch Vandel and before he realized she shot him in the face.

He was on the ground writhing in pain and spitting out pieces of tooth and jawbone when McSorley put his shotgun against the woman's stomach and fired. The power of the weapon blew her off the portico and into the yard where she lay on her back, arms spread out, like some stark and shabby excuse for a cloth doll.

They put Vandel in a wagon, and three of his men made hard time for Houston and a doctor. McSorley and one of the men got the boy up on a mule and tied him to it.

The old woman and the dog were left to rot among the chickens and the hogs and whatever else sainted creation might have come along.

CHAPTER 26

The boy sat atop the mule, staring numbly at the devastation. His head swam with the horror of it all, the truth of it all.

"Whea' you takin' me?" said the boy.

McSorley leaned out of the saddle and slapped the boy hard across his face. "That's for helping make a fool of me on the road."

The boy kept his head bowed and watched the blood drop from his nose onto the pommel of his saddle where his hands were tied.

He closed his eyes. He did not realize he had fallen asleep until he near slipped out of the saddle.

In the morning he was not taken to one of the city orphanages, but rather to an administrative judge who had no affinity for the ongoing labor protests, or those who sympathized with such. And who would be willing to sign a detention order because of the child's orphan status, age, and his connection to certain hunted criminals and their subversive acts.

The place he was to be detained, until the legal age of sixteen, was known as Sugarland.

• • •

Southwest of Houston it was sugar country. Big plantations that demanded hard labor. And sugarcane production demanded labor that was not just hard, but heartless. Harvest the cane, press out the juice, boil it, get it prepped, packed, shipped—you had to contend with mosquitoes, blistering heat, disease, brutal work conditions, and endless workshifts. They say in Sugarland that hell was God's warm-up to getting sugarcane production just right.

Labor was the issue, always. The plantation owners did not want to pay commensurate wages for the work, so they were always scrapping for field hands. Then they came up with an idea to maximize their profits— they made a deal with the state of Texas to lease the prison population. You could work the convict till he collapsed. Let them die in their tracks, then replace them. Most of the prison workforce was black anyway. It was the modern twist on slavery.

The boy was brought to the plantation in a wagon with convicted felons. He got his first look at this horrid misery of a place. There were boys among them about his own age. He was the only white.

McSorley had followed on horseback and at the main gate the convicts disembarked from the wagon one by one in chains. McSorley dismounted and approached the boy. He had told Matthew in Houston, "'Fess up about Drum, name his confederates and fellow murderers, and you can walk out of Sugarland any time you want."

At the gate McSorley said to Matthew, "Now that you got a look at your new home, anything to tell me?"

The boy was stranded between fear and rage. He stared at the ground as he spoke. "Yea," he said. "For wha' ya done...I'm gon' kill ya."

McSorley glanced at the convicts who saw and heard it all. He climbed back onto his horse silently. Then said to the boy, "I await that day with enthusiasm."

Matthew was put to work in the kitchen scrubbing pots in a boiling vat of water. He was put to work digging latrines and privies. He was put to work loading freight wagons and tending the mules. He lived a twelve hour shift, seven days a week. An hour off for church. In the first six months he survived dengue fever. He grew so thin he needed to rope up his pants.

He had spent little time with blacks growing up, but he came to learn how most of the incarcerated in Sugarland were there for crimes of poverty—such as loitering, vagrancy. Crimes that were nothing more than an excuse for the state to fashion a free workforce. It was everything the boy had heard Drum and those close to him rail against.

And the blacks there knew about the boy. That his detainment was illegitimate. That he was being kept there to rat out social renegades who meant to change the system.

And this bought him alliance among the convicts. The boy had no idea that out of the mistreatment and cruelty he was being recreated.

• • •

He had been incarcerated for over two years when he was brought by a guard to the warden's headquarters. He was led into a small room. There the light from a single window pithed over a plain wood table with two chairs that faced each other. In one of those chairs sat Vandel.

"I see that you have survived," he said to the boy.

A look of complete shock came over the boy that this man could still be alive. He was reticent to sit, but he obeyed. He sat stiffly but straight. He wanted Vandel to see him as strong. He kept staring at Vandel. The left side of the man's face was a ruination of missing teeth and jaw partly caved and deeply scarred. The wound had healed, in a manner of speaking, but the flesh was inflamed and butchered.

"I'm here to tell you," said Vandel, "that Ledru Drum…is dead."

The boy who had been sitting there, determined to keep square and up, to overshadow his infirmity, began to sag. He did not mean to, he did not want to show weakness, but he did not have the power over such news to stop his body from reacting in such a way.

CHAPTER 27

Drum had been killed in St. Louis in what was to be the first major industry wide strike in the United States. The labor unions were confronting the railroad, demanding an eight hour day and the end to child labor.

Strikers had taken over the Central Depot. They had control of the river. Strikers marched in the street by the thousands, singing in protest—the Marseillaise, the anthem of the French Revolution, and a decided call to arms. The strikers were joined by factory and cannery employees, foundry workers, steamboat deck hands, and roustabouts. Soon no industry was untouched by solidarity with the strikers. Even newsboys quit selling their newspapers.

The governor, in fear, asked for federal troops, and a massive private police force was put together.

Drum and a small group of saboteurs had taken control of a freight train just outside the hub. Some say the engineer and brakeman were in sympathy with the strikers and let them commandeer the train. They uncoupled the locomotive and tender and were in the process of destroying track when they were confronted by a force of almost fifty security guards. The half dozen strikers took up a defensive position in a shack beside the Farm Association Grain elevator.

What ensued was a ferocious gunfight. That ramshackle building they were holed up in was being shot all to hell. Within minutes everyone in the shack had been wounded.

It was Drum who led their attempted escape. With a kerosene lamp he set the building on fire. In a wave of smoke they busted out a few wall slats and ran to the grain elevator.

That's where they made their final stand. Drum had a stick of dynamite which he used to blow the wall of the grain elevator. Besides being torched, grain began to spill out the seven story high elevator, creating a wall between the security forces and the strikers.

They couldn't last long. Ammunition was running low. Men were hit, bloody, choked from the smoke and exhausted. They faced a withering fire that was only getting worse.

It was bust out or die. Drum and the strikers tried to disappear into a maze of rolling stock that was bottled up in the yard. Drum might well have engineered his own escape, he'd done it before, but during their retreat into that dark sea of freight cars he went back to save one of his gunmates. His body was later discovered on the tracks, under of all things, a caboose.

Western Union sent out word of the killing. And they called the fact he was discovered under a caboose a kind of "righteous justice" for what had happened in San Antonio.

· · ·

When finished, Vandel's eyes honed in on the boy across the table. The child had aged commensurate with the brutality of Sugarland. The visage that peered back at the boy was like something carved from a nightmare. It was a nightmare because it was a world that had power over him.

The boy did not know what to say or do. Should he say or do anything? He had learned from his time with the black convicts of Sugarland…the benefit of silence. What little benefit there was.

"I'll not come here again," said Vandel. "No one will. You will remain here until it is your time…or you die. Now is your last opportunity to free yourself from this…pestilence."

The boy could see from Vandel's movement the wound was causing him pain.

"Drum had contacts in Houston…criminals, fellow saboteurs, anarchists, haters. If you know any of these, you can attain freedom."

The boy looked about as if he were trying to escape. The sun from the lone window was harsh upon his face. Vandel saw something in the boy's expression that challenged him.

"The strike was defeated," said Vandel. "They shut down half the railroads of America and were still defeated. They will always be defeated."

The boy stared at the window…all that light. All that freedom beyond it. His throat suddenly closed shut. All he could think of was the old woman and Corporal Billy lying there in the compound, their blood blackening the dirt. And now Drum.

The boy said nothing. He rose up and walked out, just leaving the Pinkerton there.

CHAPTER 28

The boy wept as he beat his fists against the gate slats to the mule stables. He had gone to this spot because he thought he'd be alone, but a crew of convicts came upon him suddenly to harness up extra cane carts.

In charge was a felon known as Little Red. He was hardly bigger than the boy, and once upon a time, he had been the minister of a black church down Galveston way. That was until the clapboard structure had been burned to the ground by "person or persons unknown." Little Red was later convicted for vagrancy and resisting arrest, and sentenced to five years hard labor. But it wasn't a mystery why he had been incarcerated.

Little Red was a different kind of minister now, as he kept the chance for revenge close to his heart. He hustled his crew along, then went to speak privately with the boy, who was trying to compose himself, hide his shame at seeming weak.

Little Red dampened a rag in a trough and went about wiping the blood away from the back of the youth's hands. "It's never smart, boy, to make yourself do the suffering," he said. "Leave that for the other fella."

Little Red looked around to make sure what he was about to say did not fall upon dangerous ears. "Get yourself some trousers, boy. A shirt, coat. Something to replace this striped suit we're wearing. Find a piece of tarp, burlap, bury the clothes somewhere safe in the stable."

The boy understood without explanation. Convicts had escaped before, but most had been brought home on their backs and then hoisted above the latrines like flags.

"The people you know are of the same persuasion as the people I know," said Little Red. "When the time comes...you can decide or not. 'Cause you ain't ever getting out of here, even when your time is up. You know what you are, Matthew?"

"No, sir...?"

"You're one of us."

• • •

He lay in his filthy bed, in a filthy caged barracks with row upon row of other filthy beds, where he was now unable to sleep even when exhausted. He endured heart racing and sweats and a stomach at the edge of some precarious fall, but after many, many nights he realized he was suffering from hope.

Weeks passed, months, then a year. Little Red never spoke again about his intention. So the boy just waited. He tried to understand. He grew more and more distraught and would sometimes dig up the burlap sack in the mule's shed that the clothes were buried in just to fight the feelings.

His family came back to him in his dreams. Feverish episodes that left him shivering. He was always a cripple in those dreams. Even worse than in life. And the shame…the hatred. They are the same, he lay in the dark knowing this once and forever.

As one year drifted into two, in a desperate moment, alone with Little Red while they harnessed mules to the cane carts, he whispered to the former Reverend, "Wha' ya' tole me…it been almose—"

The Reverend could read the boy. "Maybe it was just something I made up so your time would pass easier. Cause I saw you couldn't make it."

Matthew looked at the Reverend with such hatred.

He lay in that filthy bed with his hands behind his head, much like how he wore his hands behind his head when the guards gave such orders.

They say hatred lies to us. If so, can the truth be trusted as master?

"It's a common grave you're heading to, fucker…"

How many times had the guards said this, and how many times had it been born out.

He was staring up at the pitch dark roof. A roof he had stared up at for years, a roof out of reach, that blotted out the sky, the night, the stars, the moon, but not the dreams.

He had been asleep, for how long he had no idea, when he was awoken by a hand across his mouth, suffocating him. He fought the hand until he saw it was Little Red with that muted stare and a knotty black finger pressed to his lips.

He whispered, "Tomorrow is the day, child. It's the common grave… or freedom."

And then that little man was gone, slipping back into the darkness silently.

CHAPTER 29

The boy could feel it in the mess hall the next morning. Like the air before a desert storm, the hall was charged with a shared secret. This was not going to be a few men daring an escape. This was to be a camp wide assault on the system. An insurrection against the rule that pretended law.

The boy saw it in the faces of the men, men who had been beaten by backbreaking years, who had toiled in the endless desperation, men who were turned to stone thanks to a stolen existence. And boys his own age, younger now, yes, younger, reared and exploited like mules, cheated of everything…except death.

It would be a common grave…or freedom.

• • •

This was to be the first day of the harvest, when the sugarcane was set on fire. The fields were burned to trim down the stalks, rid them of their grassy tops, excessive leaves and straw, and so maximize their value. A mile of acreage had been pathed into blocks to be torched section by section. It was a controlled fire, not only because of the heat, but the smoke and ash the fire produced could blind and choke you to death.

But today the fire would not be controlled by the guards, section by section. On the contrary, it would be an apocalypse brought about by the convicts.

They set to torching the first section. The leaves and grassy tips began to heat, the water contained within them boiled, then came the crackling as they dried up, and once they dried, they exploded into flame. The smoke and the ash were sucked up into the air as if God himself had breathed it in.

And that was the signal.

The convicts had been hiding empty bottles for months, and filling them with stolen kerosene or naphtha, then they plugged them up with cloth to make firebombs.

The Reverend and his crew had opened the corrals and stall gates to let the mules escape. The boy had dug up the burlap sack. He was naked in an abandoned stall slipping on the threadbare trousers and shirt and could see a collection of guards racing to the corral to gather up that chaos of mules.

Whatever they thought or suspected was answered. The mess hall had been set on fire, the worksheds set on fire, the stables set on fire. And as far as the eye could see, one section of sugarcane after another had been put to the flame. Then the guards realized this was an organized break and that's when the shooting started. The boy was slipping on the ratty coat he'd buried and was trying to run as best he could to join the Reverend when a convict a dozen yards ahead of him was shot to death.

They were still trapped within the prison grounds. The gates were made of wood and wire. The one gate they attacked opened to the road that flanked the cane fields. The gate had been set on fire, the guards defending it had run from an onslaught of prisoners. By the time the boy reached the gate the Reverend and his fellow convicts had grabbed a cane cart and used it to ram the gate. The boy shouldered in among the men with gunfire all around them. Covered now in dust they drove the cart through the gate that collapsed in flames over it.

The prisoners made a rush for the cane fields. Better to face the fire and the smoke and ash than an army of well armed guards on horseback coming right for them up the road.

And the mules—hundreds—came stampeding out of the gate being driven by convicts on foot, waving blankets and sheets of tarp. The animals, all frantic and braying, were being herded toward the oncoming guards.

The prisoners were ducking down and scattering into the fields, trying to find their way through the burning waves of cane to keep from being gunned. The boy could not move as fast as the others, but he kept the Reverend in his sights.

The guards were all along the main road now and moving down the paths between sections and firing at anything crossing that open ground.

It was a hot bright daylight but in those fields there was no daylight. Just an endlessness of smoke the color of a filthy shroud hanging over the cane and a storm of black ash blowing violently from the sweeping heat of the fires.

The gunfire ahead grew closer and more fierce. And a road to cross to the next field was where the Reverend held up at the edge of the flames.

He stripped off his shirt to use it as a bandana. The boy caught up to Little Red and was going to cross when the Reverend grabbed him by the arm and pointed to where he should look.

There was a turned over cart in the path and a convict was racing toward it for cover as he was being chased by a guard on horseback. The prisoner was shot in the leg. There was a stinging look of pain as he dropped. He struggled to his feet and was shot again. He fell to his knees and the guard trampled right over him. He wheeled about as the man was still alive and he fired into the body and a convict who had been hiding behind the huge two-wheeled wagon charged out into the path and leapt on the back of the horse. He was after the guard's pistol and the two men fought together on the back of the mount. The horse reared then spun about in a panic, lost its footing, and toppled over and men and mount tumbled into a swash of flames and no amount of screaming could save either of them.

CHAPTER 30

A convict came bursting through the cane like some scavenger from hell. "Can we get across?" he shouted.

Little Red told the boy to cover his face. The boy took from his pocket the burlap sack he'd buried his clothes in and made a bandana with it.

The smoke was death hovering above them, the dirt road blackening from ash.

"Does either of you know the way?" said the convict. "There's guards all up and down these roads and they're killing every bastard in their sights."

The Reverend wiped at his eyes, peeked up and down the road. He closed his eyes again. He turned to the boy. "My eyes ain't good enough. How's yours?"

The boy leaned over Little Red's shoulder and peered into what was a corridor of flames that sawed and leapt.

The convict was down on one knee, gasping for air, exhausted. He wasn't young, and he looked like he wouldn't hold up.

"Can we keep together?" he said. "I'm wore out. Don't know which way. Can't we keep together? I don't want to die out here."

Little Red looked at the boy. Neither knew how. While they held there trying to decide the boy saw something on that cart. It was stringed with strips of wire tacked to posts and the frame so they could fill the wagon to overflowing with cane. The boy motioned for the Reverend to stay there and then made straight for the cart. He started ripping loose the wire. When he got back to the two men, he tied the end of one strip to the end of the next until he had a rope of that flexible metal a good thirty feet long.

The boy took one end of the wire and pressed it into the Reverend's hand. He took the other end and wrapped it around his own palm.

"Yeah," said Little Red. "I got it." And he mimicked the boy. Then together, they helped the convict to his feet, and the boy gripped the man's hand and made him take hold of the wire.

"Don' let go," said the boy.

And with that, the boy set out into the road, leading way, the wire lengthening, the men following, while this man child tried to navigate the flames, to see through this whirl of fire and smoke.

There was a sudden rush of gunfire close at hand and men shooting and they weren't damn convicts that was sure, and the boy changed course cutting through a smoldering field where the heat coming off the remains of the cane could melt the leather off their boots.

The boy came upon a bloody corpse, the trousers in patches smoldering. A convict came scrambling out of the brush. "Thank God," he said. "I thought maybe you were with this bastard." He pointed the rifle that he carried at the dead man and then he wiped the blood from a slashing wound to his forehead. "Do you know a way outta here? There's fuckin' guards everywhere."

Little Red held up the hand with the wire. "Take hold, boy."

They pressed on, this chain of men clinging to a wire and led by a youth who God gave eyes to see with. A pack of mules speared out of the haze wildly, their features strained with torment, their eyes stormlit.

The boy followed the way from where they'd come and searched, his eyes like burning bits of coal, the skin around them being singed with black ash, until he saw through a thin cascade of flames—a road.

He tugged on the wire and again they labored forward. Reaching that path, they came upon what had been a pitched battle. Combatants lay dead, prisoner and guard alike. A number of them had been hacked to death.

While the Reverend relieved the dead of their weapons and canteens that he handed to the other convicts, the boy saw, or thought he saw, this vaporous fiction of a man emerge from the merciless heat.

It was one of the prisoners that the boy recognized. A huge black youth prone to silence and not much older than he was. The youth had a blanket wrapped around his bare chest and he was carrying a long scythe over his shoulder.

Little Red called out to him by name, but the youth did not answer and as he got closer, they all saw that he was streaked and smeared with blood—his arms, chest, blanket, his face...and the scythe blade.

"Do you know a way outta here?" Little Red shouted, and then he shook the youth and shouted again. "Do you?"

The youth gazed at the Reverend with a feral stoniness as if that was all there was to answer.

CHAPTER 31

Matthew knew, or felt he knew. He took the youth by his muscular arm and made him grip the wire. The youth only stared, but he kept hold as the boy squeezed his hand over the others, then with all in tow the boy started off down the only way left to them. It was the way from which the black youth with the scythe had come.

And so this strange caterpillar of lost men tethered to a wire made its way through a blinding creation. Trying to shield their eyes they leaned into a blizzard of burning refuse. They struggled and they stumbled with the Reverend calling out to God over the terrorizing sounds of the fire as the flames sparked and broke then shot out from the cane as if driven by menace.

The fire had blotted out the sun and the sky, and the place where the boy stopped to get his bearings was pitched gray and the heat such it could melt your throat. He was shaken suddenly and afraid. Panic set in. He wanted to let go of the wire, abandon the others and escape, run—but to where? He was no longer an innocent, but not completely hardened. And somewhere in that bereft moment a feeling revealed itself, having been left to die, and having been saved.

The men had crowded in around him. They stood there like beasts about to be slaughtered. While they called to him and shouted over each other, while the Reverend shook him about which way to go, the boy searched the smoke and then he saw, or thought he saw, was so desperate he believed he saw, what had to be a bit of sky over the lip of smoke just before him. And he used that bit of sky, real or not, as a kind of north star.

He followed its line straight down to where it touched ground because if that bit of sky was real, the ground below it was not burning.

He watched and he waited, and the Reverend shook him again, cursing the soul of the world, but the boy kept his vision fixed.

The boy was suddenly witness to something down the long pocket of all that fire. He rubbed his eyes to see better, to be sure. He blinked and lifted the bandana and spit into his palm, what little spittle there was, and wet each eye and then he cupped the hand over his brows to try and quell the ash as best he could.

Was it a moment of clarity amidst all those layers of smoke swirling in every which way?

He blinked again and then he shouted, "Look." He pointed. "Pas' ta smoke."

The men followed the line of his arm, and goddamn there it was, and it was no fuckin' mirage either.

They could see just beyond the bands of flame a strip of road, and across it, a cane field that had not been torched. They scurried forward until they cleared the fire and hovered at the edge of that causeway. It was quiet as hell. The skirmishes were well behind them. Not a rider or guard anywhere in the diminishing smoke.

"I worked that field," said one of the convicts. "It's marsh and woods beyond it. We free, man."

The Reverend unbound the wire around his hand. "It's time to go rabbit, boys."

He took off. They all scattered after that. Disappearing into the stalks. The boy did his best to keep up with Little Red but could not. And when Little Red realized, he stopped. When the boy caught up, the Reverend said, "What he doin'?"

He meant the youth with the scythe. The boy turned to see he was standing in the middle of the road like a piece of statuary. Little Red shouted to him, as did the boy. But he did not move. He just remained as he was, with the smoke all around him. Then he slipped the blanket from his shoulders and began to clean the scythe of blood.

They pushed on with hands balled up and beating back the cane. The smoke thinning, the heat dying off, they could breathe now and removed their bandanas. They came out of the cane into a trace of summer grass, then on to a grove of cottonwoods that coursed the shoreline of the river where they crouched.

"Can you swim?" said the Reverend.

Matthew nodded that he could, then admitted it was kind of a clumsy swimming, and the Reverend slapped him on his back it would be all right.

They eased out into the water, floating with the current. The water now black and filmy with ash and bitter to the taste and the Reverend kept pulling the boy's head up every time he bobbed, and they crawled up onto the muddy bank dripping wet and slipped into the heavy brush where they hid.

"You ain't a boy no more," said the Reverend, as if this were some kind of benediction. "Know what you are?"

"No…sir."

"You're wanted."

It was a thought that did not need pursuing, as it was pure truth. They remained hidden where they were, like wolves waiting on the night, and looked back across the river to an earth seared and blackening, the smoke clinging to the stripped stalks of cane or rising in still spires as far as the eye could see, as if some army had laid complete carnage to the countryside.

With the dusk, riders appeared across the river and began searching the unburnt fields. They dismounted and fired into the cane, demanding prisoners surrender or be hung when caught.

With nightfall, they fled. They kept to the road going west that followed the railroad tracks. Little Red's destination was Alleytown and the United Brotherhood of Friendship, who he knew would help and hide them.

As the raw edges of light came on they strayed from the road, but kept it within sight, as the Reverend knew Sugarland would have hired agents scouring the countryside for escaped prisoners.

Even though dressed like common tramps there was no lying about the chain marks on their ankles and wrists that marked them for what they were.

Matthew had lived this walk before, with Drum, following the way of a road, keeping the well traveled path in his sights but not being at one with the road. Moving in secret, living with secrets, ever worried, ever hunted. Heretics to the economic and social powers that be. Outlaws who do the dirty work of change then serve out their sentence in prisons or graves because the world as they knew it, counted them and those they were close to, as an enemy.

And the Reverend—whatever dream he harbored in his soul would never come to pass. He would not live long enough to reach some promised land he imagined in his thoughts. He was born too soon, and so too late. Somewhere along that street of dreams he was cut down, to become just another shadowy profile forgotten, with barely enough time to pass on a little revolution.

PART TWO

CHAPTER 32

Matthew sat in the unrelenting heat gazing out the railroad car window, the spare wildness of the country in his reflection. He was twenty-two and alone with thoughts of those lost to him when a young woman leaned down and addressed him, "May I sit there?"

She was pointing to the seat that faced his, and he nodded that would be all right. She was neatly dressed and comely.

Upon sitting she said to him, "I heard some of the men in the back talking," she said. "You're the marksman who travels to all those shooting contests, the one the newspaper calls Crippled Jack."

"Tat da' name I go by."

She watched how he tried to get physically comfortable.

"It can't be your birth name."

"Ma-hew," he said.

"Matthew...the tender apostle. How befitting."

There had been a tone in her voice he could not quite gather in.

"Last name?"

"No las' name."

"I thought it would be Drum," she said.

He saw now in her hands she possessed a pocket notepad and pencil. A quiet look passed from one to the other.

"I'm being questioned with that look, aren't I?" she said.

He nodded that she was.

"I'm a reporter for the *San Francisco Star.* I am to cover the labor wars. And anything else that is newsworthy...or arouses public interest."

"Min' if I smoke?"

"I mind nothing...within reason."

He took out tobacco and rolling paper and she watched as he went about the task. Having the palsy in one hand did not quite work well enough and a simple process became more dramatic and drawn out.

"Do you ever get used to being stared at as you go about such things?" she said.

"I fa'get from time ta' time. But da worl' see fit ta remin' me."

Then he spoke of how he'd been mocked once and told that the least animal on this earth had more grace then he would ever have. He struck the match on the car wall and it left a trail of smoke. He lit the cigarette, inhaled, and went to watching the brutal New Mexico landscape pass in a blinding sun.

"They say you're one of the best marksmen in the West. That's some form of grace, isn't it?"

"Dey say I'm ta best cripple marksman in the country…and no grace in dat."

She watched as his expression turned from that thought to another.

"A course…it's all in ta target anyway."

He smiled. The woman felt there was something to the smile that almost dared her to remark.

"You mean…some targets are better than others?"

He smoked, looked out the window a bit while the train rattled on. He took his time, then said, "Some brin' out ta bes' in you…I say dat much."

CHAPTER 33

"It's been five...six years," she said, "since you escaped Sugarland during the riot."

"Six."

"You were with that murderer—"

He was adamant the Reverend was not a murderer.

"The Rangers tell a very different story as those two dead in Alleytown attested to."

"You mean ta Pinkertons?"

"It was the United Brotherhood of Friendship who saw to your legal case and release."

"An' all black, to a man."

"Some say that's why you're so aligned to them and often speak of them at labor rallies."

"Maybe it's God's way?"

"Maybe you'd care to tell me your version of what happened that day in Alleytown?"

Matthew said he had told his version.

"I mean the truth," she said.

He smiled then flicked away the ash, as if the question were nothing.

"Drum was the man known as the 'Coffin Maker,' wasn't he?"

She was so assured in her manner and speech. It unsettled him, but he did not allow himself to be revealed.

"You lived with his grandmother for a while."

"Until ta Pinkertons and gunneys came one nigh' and gunt her down."

He rose up, using the back of the seat for balance, and then he walked out to the railroad car platform.

The country was flat and harsh and remorselessly the same and the scraggy hills seemed forever away. Matthew stood with his back against the railroad car wall for support, the air sweltering up from the tracks, dense with the smell of iron and dried out timbers, and it reminded him of the burning cane fields and the sorrows that went before it all the way back to the original sorrow.

He stole a glance into the railcar window. That girl had to be near his age, maybe a year or two older, but was double smart. She had put hammer to nail that he was lying about what had happened in Alleytown.

He wondered how other men remembered the first time they had committed a killing. Did they suffer the language of the Bible, or did they feel something much more uncharted?

He would always see the dust coming off the wagon wheels and three black men in their neat suits sitting tailorwise, their legs dangling down over the open rear gate. On the canvas tarp was written—UNITED BROTHERHOOD OF FRIENDSHIP, which the Reverend pointed out and winked as he led the boy from the trees to stride up alongside the wagon itself with a plaintive, "Hello, brothers."

There must have been a dozen men packed in that wagon, and all black. Alleytown had been a central rail depot for the Confederacy, but since then black migration put them at about a third of the population and central to its success. They were businessmen, they ran civic organizations, they were in politics and government—the mayor was black. Word had come down the pike about the riot and the private police hired by the Sugarland Farmers Association to exact any form of capture necessary.

The wagon pulled off into the margins of shade along a creek, while the Reverend made his dire plea for safe harbor for himself and the boy, at least until they reached town where they could jump a freight train west.

The members of the Brotherhood talked among themselves and prayed for guidance, and armed with nothing more than civility and courage they set forth with the Reverend and the youth huddled up in the middle of the covered wagon. They trundled along passing townspeople and travelers being questioned by heavily armed strangers and they crossed a bridge at the same time as an approaching posse, the hooves of their animals clopping on the wood timbers like the slow and troubling toll of a drum, the predatory stares of the hired gunneys just a short spit from the blacks.

You ask God to make you an instrument of good, even for some minimal purpose, but a prayer takes in a lot of road with turns to address and for redress. When they could see the first rooftops of Alleytown and the Church of Christ steeple, they were confronted by two men on horseback, with shotguns at the ready. One stationed himself at the front of the wagon and the other at the rear. The wagon reined in.

Then the man out front said, "Roll the canvas up so we can see who you all got in there."

"You need to show us you're authorized by the city," said the black in the box seat.

The two riders exchanged dark looks.

"If that answer don't reek of guilt," said the rider at the rear of the wagon. Then loud enough the rider up front called out, "We're gonna start firing into your fuckin' wagon."

CHAPTER 34

It got good and quiet all right. The Reverend called out, "I'm coming, brothers." He labored his way out of the back, his hands raised. "No need for trouble," he said. "These good Christians were kind enough to give me a ride, is all. They knew nothing."

The rider at the back of the wagon looked over Little Red. From the pommel of his saddle he took a set of hand chains and flung them to the earth. "Get 'em on," he said.

The Reverend had given it up so no one would be needlessly hurt. He had whispered to Matthew as he set his rifle down beside the youth. "Slip under the tarp on the backside. When I get out there, I'll make a run for it. You go for the trees."

The youth was desperate that he not consider it.

He took Matthew by his loose blouse and shook him. "Goin' back is too far from heaven for me."

Matthew reached for the rifle without ever thinking. Fear—the purity of the animal man to survive at all costs. He lifted the canvas on the far side of the wagon and slipped over the side as quiet as the clouds that passed overhead and shaded the sky.

The Reverend picked up the hand chains and looked them over like the would be grave that they were and with one single motion flung them right at the rider then charged the man and his mount.

The rider was bleeding down his face from where the chains had scored him. The Reverend had hold of his leg and the lip of the gun barrel but was not quick enough and a blast from that Damascus gun tore apart the right side of his body.

Then came a shot from the far side of the wagon and the gunney up front was hit in the chest and killed in that moment so cleanly he just slumped in his saddle.

Matthew came trudging around the back of the wagon. The clouds clearing, the sun going white, the shadows retreating in on themselves. The Reverend was lying there in the road on his back and gasping when the rider with the bloody face fired a second shot from the saddle and the

Reverend's body lifted into the air for a moment, as if lightning had struck him.

That rider did not realize his own fate had been determined when Matthew stepped into the rutted causeway with the rifle wedged against his crippled shoulder and fired. A long string of blood and dirt shot from the man's trousers high up on the leg. The bullet broke bone then passed through and skimmed the saddle before lodging in the horse, who reared and stumbled.

The second chambered shot killed the horse who collapsed as if pole-axed. The rider was now afoot with a broken leg, his shotgun lost to him in the fall. Trying for his pistol he was shot again. Crying out he went flat to the ground, crawling until he could hide behind the body of Little Red.

The blacks stood about the wagon, good Christian men all. They stared at Matthew and that battered walk, as he closed in on his quarry, now begging for life. One of the members of the Brotherhood muttered the word, "Mercy."

Was it a plea—or an expression of shock?

Matthew understood the killing had to be, for him and those all around him, otherwise their flesh and blood days would be over. Because this petty thug would have privilege over them with the powers that be. But that was not the only reason.

Matthew stood over that bloody castoff, now covering his face as if that could change anything. And there was Little Red, with his eyes open in the gaze of death.

Matthew heard that word again somewhere behind him. "Mercy."

He looked down the tunnel of that rifle barrel and fired. He could hear that shot echo across his lifetime. He killed the man not just because it was a necessity, but because of something hidden somewhere behind the necessity that Matthew did not as yet understand. Just as the utterance of the word "Mercy," where the meaning of the word at one moment may hide another meaning, as one mountain may hide another mountain, one building may hide another building, one shadow hide another shadow, one truth hide another truth, one lie hide another lie—Matthew killed the man because he had the heart for it.

CHAPTER 35

"You didn't even ask me my name."

Matthew turned. There on the platform was the young woman, one hand folded over the other.

"Didn' see reason for it," said Matthew.

She went and stood beside him. There was a strange intensity to his expression that was not lost on her.

"You were thinking very hard," she said.

"Is der any otha' way?"

She caught the slightest ripple of a smile that she would come to describe as fraught with trouble. "We have much in common," she said.

He offered no response.

"You have the palsy," she said.

He nodded.

"You're treated in places by people as an outcast, an oddity. Yes?"

He smoked, he listened.

"A woman going out into a man's world is treated much the same way. We don't belong, we're misfits."

"Yur after somethin'?"

"Yes," she said. "You."

He did not address this, but rather just stepped around her and went back inside, saying only, "'Scuse me."

He was in his seat when she returned. He had his hat pulled low over his eyes to shield them from the sun so he might doze. The train swayed as it carried up a slight grade into the hills.

"When we get into the station you ought to buy yourself a newspaper. There's an article that went out through Western Union about the 'Coffin Maker.'"

He did little more than cross his arms.

"You think you're gonna get away with it, don't you?"

She bent her head down a bit to see if she could catch his expression.

He scratched the side of his cheek with the tip of his fingers in a perfect gesture of disinterest.

"I give you credit…you're about as quiet as a child in a closet."

• • •

He did not need to read about what he already knew. The killings on the Alleytown road all those years ago had shown what he was capable of, so he'd gone about the business of steeling himself for the journey to come.

He'd begun with turkey shoots and rifle frolics, a crippled boy entering competitions for money against grown men, with nothing but an old Remington rolling block. But traveling from town to town, shooting match after shooting match, one ejected cartridge after another, with each shell left in the dust he was perfecting the talent that would make him an assassin.

Between Sugarland and those shooting contests he'd learned the art of weapons. As he scratched together a little savings, he bought himself a used Swiss Vetterli he'd had his eye on. The rifle had the same tubular magazine as a Winchester, and a unique bolt with self-cocking action. It had range, being a military gun. The magazine held thirteen cartridges, and a sharpshooter, a good and quick sharpshooter, could get off twenty one rounds per minute, with deadly precision.

One year bore two, became three, and in what was a comic descriptive coined by a reporter, he began to be known as the marksman called Crippled Jack.

He was listed as such in brochures and window posters for upcoming competitions around the country. It was not only a breath of entertainment and humor, it was a way of exploiting the fact he was lame and beating more seasoned marksmen who were sound of body.

But Matthew knew there was something else hidden behind the name, lurking there in all its worldly matter, just as one mountain may hide another, one building may hide another, one shadow may hide another. This was a way of reminding him he was lame. Of diminishing his achievement and rubbing his face in his physical infirmity. Though he could win a shooting competition, he would still go home as a cripple and be what he sees in a mirror. That even if you are dripping with insight, you can never walk taller, no matter how tall you walk.

But the sureness of movement in that lame body when it came to shooting, scored points of admiration with a hungry, back broken, ill treated, cast aside, and hope stolen public. One day a boy came up and asked Matthew to sign a scrap of paper with his name—Crippled Jack. The boy was missing all the fingers on one hand from an accident suffered while working in the mills. It started that inconsequentially, then spread, as if by the power of some anonymous hand.

A veteran missing both legs and an arm, a girl in a wheelchair, a woman with a Bible and a simpleton child. Others with no outward infirmity at all, except those that exist within us, that tear at us, that terrorize and torture us. They wanted something of him, because they were of him, and he was of them, and they knew the human mountain of disadvantage he had to climb, because it was theirs to climb.

Something came to him during those days traveling. A trenchant thought had been hiding behind all those shooting matches and signatures signed, and drawn from the wretched mistreatments and violence he had witnessed.

He made up a flier supporting the eight hour workday and child labor laws. He asked those attending to donate to Mary Jones and the Western Federation of Labor for the rights of the working man. That he himself was gifting part of his winnings to the cause. He passed these fliers out at competitions and frolics, to those he gave an autograph, to anyone who would take a moment and listen to his hobbly voice.

CHAPTER 36

He peeked out from under the brim of his hat to find this as yet unnamed young woman writing on that notepad of hers. She had not been honest with him. She knew who he was before she had asked, as if she had seen him just days before at the annual Red River Rifle Club Shooting Match.

It was a statewide affair with lots of pomp and Matthew had won some real money, and for a few minutes, he got to pass out fliers and speak before being politely pushed aside by Pinkertons. She had one of the fliers in her purse.

She also knew from the little clues she picked up Matthew had come to Houston for a very different reason. This was the home of Ledru Drum. Matthew had rented a horse and ridden out to the compound where he had lived with Missus Drum and Corporal Billy. It was now a roofless hovel where tramps and transients had set up little shacks and grew food on the patches of scrubland. He stood on the crumbling veranda where the old woman and the dog had been shot. He walked to the stone corral where Drum had taught him to shoot. A bristly wind brought with it all the old memories. He breathed in the bone dry past everywhere. This was blood country. Home to some of the worst scars he carried.

Rage went through him with the drive of a fuckin' locomotive and he could not remain in that place any longer. The dead still had business with the living and he was both message and messenger.

• • •

That night in Houston, he went to the building on Moody Street where Drum had met with his fellow radicals to plot out their violence. The address now was nothing more than a scorched shell at the end of a patchy dark block. As for the apothecary, the subversive known as "The Cook" owned, Matthew knew the man on sight. He was behind the counter when Matthew entered.

The years had dealt with him harshly. He needed glasses to see at all. And when he looked up and saw this youth with the clipped walk and rifle slung over one shoulder—

"I ba'leve," Matthew said quietly, "we know ich other."

"The Cook" glanced at the shop windows. In the evening street the lights had gone on. He searched for strangers. "I'm being watched now, act like you need something."

The druggist moved down the counter looking at his shelves while Matthew told him he wanted the names of the men on the Committee who had been gathered together to go after Drum. He knew Vandel and McSorley on sight, but not their whereabouts.

"Be at the plaza tomorrow...midday," said the druggist. He filled a packet with baking soda and gave it to Matthew.

"This will keep your teeth clean and healthy...so you can sharpen them for a fight, that will fall to you."

The next day Matthew did as was expected. The plaza was, as usual, filled with Mexican food stalls. It smelled of charred beef, boiled pig, and chili. There were stands with candies, liquor, and soda pop. It was a tourists' paradise and a place of kickbacks and payoffs for licenses—the hidden racism against migrant food as a public health hazard.

He'd seen the labor boys try to convince them to organize, but their immigrant status left them too afraid.

He wandered for hours. He ate and did his walkabout until an old woman called to him, asked him to help her get to a table where she might sit. And while he went about this polite task she slipped a letter into his pocket and quietly said, "Son...put all the wars inside you aside."

CHAPTER 37

The letter contained a list of names. One of those was Lee Steffens.

Lee Steffens had trained as a barber and lived that career for over ten years, but the labor movement changed all that. He believed it was the spawn of socialists and flag haters, that it was everyone's responsibility to achieve in life without the corrupting influence of unions, which were after power, money, and control. This led him to seek work from the railroads in security, and then with the Pinkertons.

Steffens had a huge round forehead and dense, puffy lips. His intention was to one day run for the legislature and believed his time hunting down radicals important to that end. Whenever he spoke at civic meetings in that loud, coarse voice, he made sure to detail his efforts in bringing about the death of the radical and murderer believed to be the "Coffin Maker."

He lived in a small cottage on the property of a rooming house owned by his uncle. No sooner had Steffens come home and was crossing the darkened parlor, he was wailed across the skull with a truncheon.

He took a severe beating after that and when he finally came to, his mouth tasted like iron from all of the blood. He used a chair to hoist himself and fumbled about for a kerosene lamp that he lit. He stood before a mirror, wobbling and disoriented, and saw his face in the gleamy light swollen as the corpse of a drowned man and veined with blood, one eye shut and the other staring at a note pinned to his chest.

• • •

Matthew, naturally, did not need to read the newspapers to know the news. The note he had pinned to Steffens' chest said only this:

The Coffin Maker

And the note he'd clandestinely left at a Western Union office read:

The Coffin Maker went visiting last night.
Ask the braggart, murderer, Lee Steffens.

On the train, the woman reporter sitting across from Matthew watched as he studied the letter that looked like the one she had seen the old woman pass to him at the plaza, when she said, "My name is Nola Dye…"

He looked up and politely doffed his hat. "Miss Dye."

She pushed her chin out toward the letter. "Good news or bad?"

He looked at her a long while, it was a cagey look, but one touched with cynicism. "Both," he said.

The way he'd slipped her probing didn't surprise her. He had, after all, in his few years escaped Sugarland and killed two hired thugs, though he and the Christian Friendship denied it.

"How ya' come to be a reporta'?"

"Believe it or not, I'm a product of the orphan trains."

His look questioned her further.

"My father was a peddler," she said, "who sold his wares from the back of a wagon in town after town. My mother died before I ever knew her. My father passed from swamp fever. And I ended up on the trains.

"I could read and write and was good at what my father called 'speech-ifying'…talking to the customers.

"I was taken in by a couple too old to have children. He is part owner of a newspaper, and she, a teacher. They didn't love me, but they treated me well. They made me study and learn, even attend college. I was to be a tribute to their hard work and kindness. And they were decent and kind and they are still and I care for them completely. But I'd rather be in that wagon with my father going from town to town and 'speechifying.'

"And that, Matthew, is the very short answer to the long question of how I got here today."

CHAPTER 38

Of course, her family name and position opened doors for her she'd gladly exploited but talked little about. People of position offered her courtesies they would not have otherwise. It was a swap meet of selfish motives she was clearly willing to take part in. She was ambitious to a fault but hid that behind a quiet, thoughtful manner. She would ambush the honest with the same dispatch she would the dishonest, because her destination in life was herself.

At Albuquerque they needed to switch locomotives as three more cars were being added. One was a private car. The passengers had to wait in the station. Nola watched Matthew from a distance where he leaned against the wall and read the newspaper. There was a taut musculature she noted in him that somewhat leveled the physical battlefield that was his body.

"As a reporter," she said, "I wonder why this Steffens was singled out?"

He looked up from the article. She had come upon him silently.

"His comment," she said, "it was because of his anti-labor sentiment in his run for the legislature seemed somewhat…self-serving and insufficient. Why do you think he was singled out?"

"Ta keep tem from sleepin' at nigh'."

"'Them,'" said Nola. "Who is 'them'?"

He folded up the paper. Tossed it in a trash box.

"Ya' know damn well who tem is."

He started away.

"Like you know who the Coffin Maker is."

Where the conversation would have gone was to be left unanswered, because within the station, on that day, a collision of worlds was about to take place. A moment was to be aborted where another would emerge to be written and rewritten about, detailing a trail of deaths that left their mark on all concerned and could not withstand.

• • •

There was a commotion at the far end of the station where the entry doors opened to the street. An armed entourage of Pinkertons formed a phalanx around a well tailored gentleman who could not have been but around thirty. There were men and women pressed in the doorways and windows, everyday laborers and tradespeople shouting obscenities and threats that echoed down the length of the depot.

A tramp tried to breech that wall of security guards and accost this seemingly implacable young man but was grabbed and beaten down. One of the men who took part in the kicks and pistol whipping was well over six feet and lean as a stick, and who Matthew recognized right off. He'd been at the gate of the compound holding onto the horses the night those vile members of the committee took time from their rancid lives to kill Corporal Billy and gun down that old woman.

He was on the list of names "The Cook" had written down and the woman had passed to him at the plaza:

*Charlie Bathlott – last known to be
in Colorado with Pinkertons*

Matthew watched as a pathway of awaiting passengers parted like the Red Sea before this violent grouping of well-paid, dapper dressed thugs and their stolid employer.

He studied Bathlott. The weapons he carried, how he comported himself, what quotient of guts he might be sitting on. Matthew made sure he stood where he could be seen by that fuckin' mercenary. They had an eye-to-eye moment, but nothing came of it.

Then that well tailored gentleman, handsome beyond anyone's right to be handsome, black haired, straight nosed, crisp eyed, smooth shaven, smiled and pointed right at Matthew, or at least that is what Matthew thought, until he said, "Nola…is that you?"

He put his arms out in some starved for affection pose and started toward her and the phalanx of men moved with him. He clasped her hands, and Nola tilted her head so he could kiss her on the cheek. It was all so civilized and fashionable and to Matthew utterly phony, set against, as it was, a litany of obscenities hurled in their direction.

"Are you taking the train?" he said.

"I am," she answered.

"I have a private car," he said. "Come and visit."

"Can I bring my notepad?"

"Why not?" he said. "You can even bring your friend."

She noted the way he glanced at Matthew, sizing him up. She made the introductions. "Matthew, this is Nathan Neihart. Nathan…This is Matthew. He's a champion marksman known on the shooting contest circuit as Crippled Jack."

"Crippled Jack." Neihart put out his hand. Matthew had to use his left as that was the good one.

"I'm a champion marksman myself," said Neihart, "when it comes to business."

Neihart and his security team moved on, unfazed. Matthew got one last look at Bathlott. He had a long dull stare in a long dull face with skin that was plaster like, almost bloodless. But he moved like a real soldier ant.

"You know who Neihart is?" said Nola.

Matthew did not.

"He's the major stockholder and president of the Americanus."

"The mine?"

"*The* mine."

Neihart and his men swept through the door to his private car that was being hooked up to the rear of the train.

"He knows how ta' mix charm wit' poysin."

As soon as Nola heard it, she knew she would steal it. On the train, the first thing she did was write the phrase down in her notepad. Because she knew what most did, you could feel it there in the depot, there was blood on the horizon.

CHAPTER 39

"We're heading into the heart of the labor wars," said Nola, as she watched the train make its slow and heavy exit from the yards. She also saw Matthew was still immersed in that letter.

Bathlott…Vandel and McSorley—the letter Matthew had been given from "The Cook" placed them as somewhere in Colorado.

It made sense if you thought of those coveted mines around Leadville— The Little Pittsburg, The Matchless, Cripple Creek, The Chrysolite, The Americanus. And all the smaller mines that consumed the hills—pit mines, tunnel mines, shaft mines. This was all about silver, gold, and coal. The true coins of the realm, that the coin of the realm is built on. In the state of Colorado, the nation was coming to its next violent crossroads where an untrammeled capitalism would clash head on with the plight of the everyday man.

"Is there a shooting competition in Leadville?"

The sunlight was burning on the window where Matthew had been staring but seeing nothing. His mind had its sights on Bathlott and how he might go about his killing.

He explained to Nola that he had been talking to a gambling syndicate in Leadville about sponsoring a competition. He'd put up the prize money for a piece of the action.

"Will you be leaving after that?" she said.

"Might spen' a while…See what kina oppatunities dare are for a go-getta."

"Do you have friends there?"

He said he could not exactly call them friends. Then he said, "How ya know Neihart?"

"The San Francisco Stock Exchange Massacre," she said.

"That musta been sumptin."

"It was something times ten," she said.

Her dark round eyes highlighted the gravest expression. "I got a taste of the world that day. And a perfect perspective on atrocity. I was there to interview of all people…Nathan Neihart. I had never met him. But who better than one of the architects of the speculation craze for mining stocks...that made millionaires out of paupers, and paupers out of millionaires? And where the phrase originated, '*A dollar's worth of greed will buy you ten dollars' worth of violence.*"

• • •

Neihart and Nola Dye had been on the mezzanine of the Mining Exchange in San Francisco that fateful day where a table had been set up so they could have coffee and talk cordially as the mercenary world of stock trading went on below.

She wrote on her notepad in phonography—*The trading floor is a world of well-dressed, ill mannered, money grubbing, exceedingly loud, get in first, get out fast, traders suffering some endless fever mania the world of speculative riches is moving on without them. I'm surprised they don't come to blows religiously.*

Neihart saw she was writing in some kind of shorthand. "You could be writing some terrible things and I would never know...until I read your article."

"That...is the idea," she said.

He put on the grin of a master pitchman. "I feel like the worm skewered by the grackle."

"And this coming from the man who practically invented the phrase—*Everything you say must exceed your expectations.*"

"It's not meant to be a term of art," said Nathan. "But a hard and fast reality. Otherwise it's a prescription for disaster."

"But it can drive up a stock price."

"It can't keep it there."

"But one can get rich along the way."

He swept an arm across the balustrade, taking in the trading floor with its tribal unlocked passions.

"That isn't just America down there. It is the flower of America, and the engine of America...It is the genesis known as speculation. How many stories people have told me. Only yesterday, a former waitress now owns the café where she worked, the building it is in, and the three story apartment next door with its dozen tenants."

"And I," said Nola, "interviewed a former shipyard owner who now works as a welder in the same yard."

"And tomorrow, with one stock buy, he could achieve…his wildest dream."

"Some say your engineers' true talent is subtly inflating the value of newly discovered veins of ore…and that your genius is knowing how and when to create 'rumors' about these new veins to manipulate the stock prices."

"Look down there," said Neihart. "Every fact that comes out down there is a rumor at one time or another. And every rumor that comes out down there is a fact at one time or another. And both are true…because the stock market is about speculation. And speculation is what fuels our wildest dreams."

"The stock market, in short, is gambling," she said.

"As is life."

"But the people who stay forever rich, curiously enough, in the market…are the brokers and financiers. Why is that? Are they just better when it comes to rumor and fact?"

Neihart had shifted in his seat. He leaned forward. He was deadly excited. "I invite you…No…I challenge you to come to Leadville and go down into the Americanus with the engineers and determine if what I claim as true is true…if my rumors are fact, or my facts just rumors. Write what you see. You'd be the first woman to go down into a mine like that."

CHAPTER 40

A cry for help from the trading floor cut into their conversation. From the mezzanine they could see the brokers below turning their gaze toward the entry. They both stood and leaned out from the balustrade for a better view.

There were two men that looked from their clothes to be laborers, maybe even tramps, and they were cuffing each hand of a stockbroker to one of theirs. And this was not the lone incident.

Across the trading floor, poorly dressed men were grabbing brokers by their suit coats and shirts and going through the same process. There was a spreading confusion and panic. Floor managers demanded answers only to find themselves cuffed. Brokers took flight from what they didn't know, flocking together, falling back from the entry toward doors that led to an alley.

Neihart quickly started for the stairs. Advised Nola to wait it out where she was. She raised her stare from the chaos below and regarded him as if he were mad.

The entry was swamped with people. Outside was even worse. Neihart disappeared into the melee that had become the floor of the trading exchange.

Nola went out into the street where the stairs were a wave of humanity. Most of the people out front were women, working women, who had formed one human chain after another, handcuffed together around the Greek columns that fronted the building.

There were police sprinting up the street, police trying to disperse the mob, get these women unhandcuffed. There were security guards for the Exchange trying to press back the crowd and they were not being polite or civil about how they did it, women or not.

But what, at first, looked like a flat out riot, was not. On the front steps of the Exchange, surrounded by a cohort of labor organizers, was Mary Jones, giving a speech to a barrage of reporters whose business was the Mining Exchange, and a boulevard that was now mobbed with citizenry.

As small as Mary Jones was, she wore the power of her beliefs like a force of nature in a plain black dress and wire rim glasses.

"We've handcuffed members of the Exchange to members of the labor force to make a dramatic point," she said. "Because in life, these two groups of men are handcuffed together and will rise and fall together. Those chains are the chains of the system that need to be overcome. For better or for worse those men and all of the men from here to our far shores, must be of a single mind that what is good for one must be good for all."

Then Mary Jones pointed from column to column where the women had chained themselves, and the police and security were trying to saw loose the cuffs because it seemed there were no keys to unlock them.

"And these women," said Mary Jones, "who handcuffed themselves to the Greek columns that support the building. These women who sew in factories, who cook in restaurants, who wait on tables in coffee shops, who plant in the fields and work as maids, who must raise their children in slums are the columns that support the system. And... and...do you know why buildings like this have columns? Do you know why so many courthouses have columns? How many banks have them? To symbolize these are the places where not only the rule of law, but the spirit of the law, and what is best about us as humankind is to be housed.

"So...is it true? Or is it a lie?"

Nola stood amidst the bedlam trying to keep from being overwhelmed. Police and security gangs were lashing out. Those who were protesting, passing out fliers, taking a stand and were not handcuffed were dragged off to the Black Marias that now started to line the street. Protestors fighting back, struggling to loose themselves, were beaten down. The line of civility had been severely crossed.

Women were being physically cast aside, shoved down the Exchange steps, dragged off and arrested. Some were bloody or hurt, others dazed and shrieking. One woman beside Nola sat on the steps holding her head, blood seeping from between her fingers where she had been gashed along the hairline.

As the woman tried to stand, to get her bearings, Nola reached out to keep her from toppling over, and a moment later, they both were swarmed by the Exchange security. To fight back proved futile, to assert she was a reporter meant nothing. She was shoved into the back of a Black Maria already packed with those arrested and when they slammed the cage gate shut and the latch took hold, Nola panicked.

CHAPTER 41

The gravity of life, Nola's childhood, of being orphaned, of being physically taken after her parents' death, being subjugated and stripped, keeping her eyes closed to try and escape it, pleading, begging, twisting her frailish body, feeling the wet grime of a man pressed against her thighs before she was old enough to know or understand. This day of being carted off to jail was all that—different—but the same. The tale of being trapped and powerless.

People in the street that passed the Black Maria, they spit at the protestors through the bars, defamed them, mocked them, threw dung at them.

She used all this to try to defend and empower herself against her naked fears. To remember she was there to give voice, not to give up.

At the jail they packed the women into cells, among them Mary Jones, who told the women to sing in protest because singing could be heard through the windows to the street below. The sheriffs demanded their silence, so they sang louder, and then a Pinkerton came up with a wily idea to bring them down.

A dozen men went out and came back with buckets and pails of water, filthy water from street troughs and gutter pools that they tossed through the bars. They soaked the women good and proper, and to get back at them the women sang louder so the men went out in shifts and brought back more pails and buckets, the water slopping over the tops. And so it went until the jail floor was a slippery and foul smelling soup and the women, shivering...but singing.

• • •

Nola wondered how to reach a person like those on the far sides of the battlefield. How to report what she had witnessed so it carried weight and measure.

After having been bailed out with the other women, she went to the little hotel where she stayed. Nola asked the night clerk if he might have a Bible she could borrow. From a drawer he took out a musty clothbound edition that he handed over. She sat in her room at a table and lit up a candle to read by.

She thumbed through frayed pages until she could find Luke 12:48.

CHAPTER 42

"Who was Ledru Drum?" said Nola. "The man you knew."

Matthew was a silent profile shaded beneath his hat. She had spoken out of nowhere. She stared quietly from the train seat facing him as the passenger car swayed and rattled on through the desert. This stillness in the face of the question bore a graceful defiance.

"That's exactly what I thought," she said.

He moved some in his seat, as if to look past her.

"Complete allegiance to the man," she said, "as heir to the Coffin Maker."

Matthew stood slowly, suddenly.

"It's something people would care to read about."

He started to walk right past her.

"It's something I'd care to write about."

He was looking out the window, but she did not notice. She put a hand on his forearm. "What do you think?"

He told her he thought there were things more...urgent...to write about.

He pressed past her. She watched him stride up the aisle and then out onto the car platform.

Matthew stood alone on the platform. Something had caught, or tricked, his eyes in the railcar and he wanted to see better whichever it was.

It had looked to be an indistinct line of dust moving through the seamless distance. Beyond a great patchwork of trees that covered the roughed out plain was hill after hill, each blanketing the next and blending together in the haze.

His vision was rarely wrong, and he held himself steady grasping the car grillwork, his stare deftly panning the country, for signs.

Then for a moment there it was again—dust—before disappearing into a cobble of ravines and before appearing again against a long hillface.

He could see now this was not the dust of nature, but of men on horseback, moving at a steady, even hard canter. From the way the dust clustered then stretched out he made it to be a hard dozen. And if they were following a true line to the west and kept to that as a marker, they would cross the northbound tracks somewhere about an hour ahead. He knew the country, he'd traveled the rail line. The water tower at Impossible Springs where the train would have to stop and refill the tender the most likely place.

"What did you mean back in there…about urgent?"

She had come out onto the platform but he did not turn and look at her, as he was intent on where the horizon lay flat and feathered with trees.

"Ta' who much is giv-in," he said, "ta' him shall much be requirt."

"You read my article on the 'Massacre'?"

"Luke…wha'ever."

She came to him and took hold of the railing and leaned forward to try and see his face.

"You're telling me this for a reason. Is it so we understand each other? Or is it something else?"

He turned to her now. And where her hand grasped the railing, he put his hand on hers. It was unexpected, and it affected her in a way she couldn't have anticipated. He told her to be careful. That he knew a "Coffin Maker" when he saw one, and so will others.

She was just starting to ask what he meant by that when the car door opened and there was Bathlott. He was so tall he had to stoop down to clear the doorframe.

Before he spoke, Bathlott seemed to turn his attention to Matthew. His gray fixed stare taking in the youth. Then he turned to Nola. "Miss… Mister Neihart would like you to join him in his private car."

She nodded. "Excuse me," she said to Matthew.

As she started off, Matthew said, "Remember wha' I tolt you."

She smiled privately. "It's etched in my mind."

As she passed around Bathlott, he said to Matthew, "You look familiar to me…We met?"

Nola turned. Matthew leaned back against the railing. His bad hand clipped up in his belt. He returned Bathlott's question with a stony fastness.

"Come on, kid. Help me out here."

"Maybe," said Matthew, "it wa' in a church sa'where."

"You're a clever kid," said Bathlott, "ain't you?"

"I taka wack at it, ebery now and ten."

CHAPTER 43

As far as Neihart was concerned Colonel Gheen was an ostentatious fool. Born into money, Gheen had achieved very little over the course of fifty years on his own merit or drive. He had been commissioned during the war, but that was the product of family solicitations. And he had never done a day of combat.

His talent was contacts—people with money, people of power, the lawyers and accountants of people with money or power, and the more corrupt, the better. His life now was a consortium of investors he headed that were the second largest voting block of shareholders in the Americanus Mine, behind Neihart.

The two men were in the midst of an intense discussion in Neihart's private car. Neihart had received a Western Union telegram in Albuquerque that three railroads, the Western Central, the Southern, and the Southern Pacific, had announced they were going to raise their shipping rates in thirty days on all ore and coal being transported out of Colorado.

"That's three cents on the dollar lost," said the Colonel.

"Stop being so judicious…it's gonna round out to four cents."

"And that Jones woman at the Exchange…she practically sunk the market single handed."

"The market will correct," said Neihart.

"Don't be so sure."

"The market is our aspirations…our roulette wheel to greater things. People can't live without it."

"But will it happen in time?"

"You're like plaster that's hardening."

"This anti-capitalism union crap is scaring off investors."

"Then we'll have to scare them all back," said Neihart.

"And how do we do that?"

"By being bigger and better braggarts. And poisoning the air with little words like 'socialists' and 'anarchists.' Because in the end every fool knows socialists and anarchists want your money…not their own. But yours."

"We need capital, Nathan. We're in a rough patch here. We need to upgrade equipment, get new equipment, there's tunnel expansion and—"

"You're not going to read off the whole shopping list to me?"

"My money people are avoiding me," said the Colonel, "or claiming they're tapped out."

"Like we haven't heard that before."

The Colonel jerked his thumb toward an imaginary spot. "And what's your idea asking that goddamn woman—"

"The reporter."

"You practically sounded like you were gonna put her on the board of directors."

"I hope to use her to our advantage at some point. Without her realizing it, of course. She's well connected."

"Did you read her article? She quoted the goddamn Bible."

"People have been quoting it for centuries…and what has it got them?"

The Colonel was running two fingers inside his collar. A nervous tell that Nathan well recognized.

"Writes about her time in jail with the other women. How the sheriffs treated them…"

"Mistreated," said Neihart.

"You know how many people have sent wires of protest? My desk is littered with them. They've been sending wires to the mine office. All the mines. And from people of influence—she wouldn't have that job if it wasn't for her father owning the newspaper."

"Her father wasn't in the cell…she was."

"Listen to you."

There was a gentle knock at the passenger car door. One of the security team opened it just enough to peer out.

"It's a lady," he said to his employer.

Neihart whispered to the Colonel to rack up his ire. "See if you can act the gentleman. Even for a minute."

Neihart motioned she be brought in, and that the guard then leave.

Neihart introduced the Colonel to Miss Dye.

"I know of and about the Colonel," she said.

She extended a hand to shake, but he was not having it.

"I read your article," he said. "Very biased, indeed. What you sacrilegiously called a protest was a vandalous and criminal act of violence. And it was a 'Massacre'…as millions of Americans lost money because of it."

"Some people will insinuate," she said, "that in America's present business state, millions of Americans are losing money every day."

"I'm going to get some air…and keep from jumping off the train."

"May I quote you on this?" said Miss Dye.

"I'll come back with a pail of water and you can quote me then."

He slammed the door behind him.

Miss Dye looked to Neihart. He had a caustic smile. "I think that went well…don't you?"

The car was not ostentatious like she'd suspected, but rather utilitarian. There was a sofa where Neihart had her sit near him. He offered her tea. He was trying to make her comfortable. She went right past all that and got right to the point.

"Why did you invite me? Is it to exploit or to impress?"

"Because we're very much alike," said Neihart.

"You mean it's not because the word is out your shareholders are in a state of panic that you can't deliver the dividend that you promised… which you blame on the 'Massacre.'"

"We'll deliver. And your getting right to that statement only proves how much alike we are. No wasted words. We're not like the Colonel. He was born and weaned on money, so he doesn't appreciate…the fight for its survival.

"You were an orphan. My father was a shabby hustler who made money, lost money, made money. And who died and left me broke."

"But rich in the ways of the hustle," said Nola.

"I'd like to think so. He made money out of thin air. Profits from a good pitch."

"A pitch like this one, you mean," said Nola.

"Exactly," Neihart said.

Neihart sat with his arms stretched out across the back of the sofa. Supremely true within himself, she thought, and more dangerous than the smoothest frauds, because he was out front with it.

"You'll be in Colorado covering the labor issue," he said. "Come to the Americanus. Go down in the mine. Freely talk to the workers, to my managers. Write what you want.

"And you know why I can do this?" he said. "Because in the end, you will see that unions destroy the American economy. Unions will hold the future hostage. They want the power of ownership without creating the wealth that makes ownership. People such as myself are the villains of political manifestos, but we are not villains in life. Not all of us…anyway."

There was an urgent knock at the door. Neihart called out. Bathlott looked in.

"Gunfire up ahead, sir."

CHAPTER 44

From the railroad car platform they could hear gunfire right away. It was far off, but quickly it became more intense. Nola was with Neihart and a number of the guards, who leaned out from the car, holding fast to the grillwork, trying to see what lay ahead because that's where the shooting was drawn.

But it was too far yet to see. The shots were being carried on dead air and the flatness of the country.

"Where are we exactly?" Neihart shouted over the heavy thunder of the train. "What's up there?"

"Impossible Springs," a guard shouted back. "Where we stop for water."

"We better go up front," said Neihart.

And so a line of neatly dressed gunmen followed Neihart from car to car, with Nola the last of them. They picked up the Colonel along the way. A nervous, bellicose, pain in the ass if ever there was one, and in dire fear for his overvalued life.

Passengers were pressed against the window glass. Some pushed their heads out into the breathless heat to see what devilment there was up country. Others were already hidden down in their seats, covering up their children, calling out to the conductor. In passing, Nola saw the seat where Matthew had sat was empty.

• • •

Far ahead in the ungodly heat, at the water tower and utility shack known as Impossible Springs, a violent skirmish was taking place.

There had been flatcars of railroad ties stacked up in the sand, left by the Southern Central for a siding that was to be constructed. The heavy, dried out timbers now formed a breastwork of sorts where about a hundred transients hid behind.

They were tramps and hobos and wayward youths and families with their carpetbags of meager goods who had been waiting for when the train stopped for water. Desperate they were to try and forcibly scale it and get to Colorado where there was the prayer of work. They were now under intense fire from the mounted riders Matthew had first seen. The distant men had dismounted and were out of range of the transients' weapons and were discharging pitiless rounds of fire into those pathetic itinerants who were crabbing sideways and crawling through the sand to keep from being slaughtered.

From where Matthew sat atop the railroad car with his bolt action Vetterli, he could make out the great puffs of smoke from the muzzles of their long guns and his eye told him they were not out of his range.

Matthew could look across the car and over the tender and down into the locomotive housing. The engineer was already slowing that iron monster. He would have run the Springs all right, but without water the boiler would lock up fast, and the engine stall, and where the hell would they be then? In the middle of some hard rock nowhere.

A pair of guards for Neihart were climbing over the tender, all weaponed up and ordering the engineer to brake.

He informed them in a rough and angered English he was no fuckin' fool and spat at the men because he meant to keep himself and his passengers out of shooting range. Though only God knew who those bastards were, and would they even fire at the train?

No one took notice of Matthew until he fired his first shot. Out there on that trace of scratch rock and sand the gunmen had formed a skirmish line. Two of their number kept back and remained mounted, holding fast the reins of the horses on the chance they might panic and scatter from all that gunfire.

The first man Matthew took aim at was upright and had his rifle mounted on a tripod. He had the brass to expose himself like that or was one of a special breed of arrogant fool. When Matthew fired, it took a count of three before blood and dust shot from the chest of the buckskin coat the fool wore. He was on the ground and rolling in anguish before those around him realized they had a devil in their midst.

Matthew lifted the weapon's bolt and pulled it back and another round chambered and he closed the bolt and shut her down and braced the soles of his hobnailed boots to the trim of the rooftop and took aim.

His next target was one of the bastards on horseback.

The men were crowding around their fallen comrade, trying to figure out from where the shot had come. They were dark shapes, thank God, against the bleached distance. Matthew could not see the first man trembling there in the sand with his coming death when the second shot exploded. The sound of it carried for seconds before the horseman was loosed from his saddle, the animal wheeling about on its back legs, round and round, like it was part of some crazed jamboree. The gunman had lost hold of the reins, and those mounts bolted, stricken as they were with fright. And the men now abandoned the cause they were hired for, or that was born from the pits of their political souls. They were just horseless scum now waving their hats, shouting, chasing the dust of their animals' hooves.

The stricken and desperate that had been hiding by the tracks had not dared chance making a run for the train. Too much of a waiting grave to cross. But now they rose up from behind the piled timbers and the utility shack in the shadow of the water tower like a patchwork of the passed over, resurrected out of the sand.

They were running now to the train, an exhausted rabble, but the security guards had fanned out in front of the locomotive with their weapons drawn and demanded they stay back or die.

Neihart came down the train steps to where Nola stood by the tracks deflecting the sun with the flat of her hand and looking up at the roof of the railroad car. There the youth stood, the sun framing his darkened shadow, a rifle slung over one shoulder.

"You, up there," said Neihart.

"Yes, sir."

CHAPTER 45

Neihart took in the scene around him. It was infected with desperation. The security guards were unable to keep back the sheer number of rabble racing toward the train and were awaiting Neihart's orders to open fire. But he gave no such order because about a dozen of these transients had reached the passenger car. Some were women, a few children. Ragged, dirty, and helpless they were, calling up to Matthew, waving to him, thanking him, pleading their cause to help them board the train and escape this hellhole. That all they wanted was a chance to get to Colorado and find work.

Neihart stood watching this happen just feet away, seething with private rage. He had been supplanted as the voice of authority by this lame youth who was staring down at the people mystified.

One of the women actually went to her knees and clasped her hands together as if Matthew was the fucking son of Jesus Christ, if not Billy the Kid himself.

And to make matters worse yet, there was the Dye woman with her anointed stare, taking mental notes for the story she'd write. Neihart could imagine the barbed discourse he'd have to read about if he didn't rewrite this goddamn moment.

At the front of the locomotive, Neihart stepped up onto the cowcatcher and grasped the headlamp. There he stood, the steam rising from the wheel wells and wreathing around his legs so he seemed, for those few moments, of the clouds.

"I'm going to take control of this train," he said. "We are going to board every person here. I will turn over my private car to the women and children and anyone who is ill, infirm, or wounded."

• • •

From where Nola stood in the shadow of Neihart's pledge, she could see past the tender. Matthew was still standing on the passenger car roof, the rifle slung over his shoulder.

He had been the one person who had not followed Neihart. He seemed distant, even disinterested. A man in some very private and meaningful world looking out into all that emptiness as if that is where his whole life was to be determined.

The moment spoke to her in ways she could not have foreseen. One life may hide another, this she knew because this she lived. And because she lived it, she could fathom it in others. There was such aloneness to him, and it was an aloneness she could feel inside her. Being of the world, but somehow outside it, ringside watching its changes and expressions, but excluded from that which is precious and dear.

She needed to talk with him about all this, but was intent on taking notes for the story she'd witnessed this day. While the tender was filled with water they boarded and carried on this homeless menagerie. There were so few cars, and so many itinerants. Not a seat was left, no space in the aisles, the air a soup of breathing sweat and tobacco, the platforms crowded, the most fit men left to ride the passenger car roofs, the sun burning so hot down on them you dare not touch anything made of iron with a bare hand.

It was something to behold. This spare little train draped in ragged humanity, bearing everything they owned, against a bleak and imposing landscape. It was—she noted—America.

In Neihart's private car, she began posing questions to the people, even children old enough to express a feeling or thought. She wrote these down on her notepad in shorthand. She called it—*A Journey of Hopes and Travails.*

Neihart had been watching her when they finally crossed paths in his crowded private car. She stopped him. He was without the Colonel or his security team.

"May I ask a question?" she said.

"Yes."

"What prompted you to do this?"

"This for your article?"

"Yes."

"What prompted me to do this. You mean all this?" he said, looking around him.

"I mean…all this."

"You should know," he said.

"What I believe, feel, assume, or guess is one thing. What I write about other people saying is quite another."

"Possibly," he said.

She picked up the cut in that statement.

"What prompted you?" she repeated.

"Why…you did, Miss Dye."

She was surprised. Not that she believed him.

"Believe it or not," he said, "you absolutely did."

She cocked her head back a bit. "And how is that, Mister Neihart?"

"Luke 12:48."

That is all he said. And it was enough. He dismissed her with the turn of a shoulder and, just like that, stepped his way through the packed weary that had taken up on the private car floor and joined that bloated son of wealth, the Colonel, in what quickly devolved into a heated conversation.

Mister Neihart—she would write in shorthand—had honed an act of goodness into a double edged sword.

CHAPTER 46

They had to switch trains in Santa Fe. The station was crowded, so most of that caravan of homeless gypsies had to wait along the tracks. Matthew sat alone on a bench in the dusky light of the station window. Nola watched him from a distance, through the passing of people, hunting for more clues about the person.

A boy came up to him with a scrap of paper and pencil. She recognized him as one of the children from the train. He and Matthew spoke for a bit, then the boy handed him the paper and pencil.

It was a slow process, Matthew placing the paper on the wooden bench arm and writing. He passed the scrap and pencil back to the boy and they shook hands.

Matthew was looking out the window to where the light fell across the tracks in long shadows, when Nola Dye suddenly stood before him.

"What was that boy's name?"

Surprised, Matthew said, "Homer Ward."

"I'll have to remember that for my article. What did you write?"

He told her it was something that had been written once before and meant for him.

"And what was that?" she said.

"...*It's up ta' God now...*"

What his look told her exceeded expectations.

"When Neihart was speaking, you paid him no mind," she said. "I watched. You were standing on the car roof staring into the desert. Why... What were you thinking?"

Matthew was leaning forward, his hands resting on his thighs. "Jus' watchin'."

"For what?"

"Ta see if ta bastards came back."

The answer was profoundly simple and made utter sense.

She came and sat next to him. They were very close. They remained this portrait in private silence with a noisy station all around them.

"When people came running up to you, thanking you, the way they looked at you. The other things they said. What did you feel?"

Matthew stared down at the floorboards by his feet, and scored as they were with endless wear, made him think of his own life.

"Matthew...what did you feel?"

"Feel?"

"Yes."

Almost whispering the word, he said, "Shame."

"Shame?"

"Dat I...me...was undizervin."

His bad hand was resting crooked on his leg, and she reached out and placed her hand on his in an act of unspoken kinship. Each of them well knew personal anguish, each was a storm brewing, each was trying to find a true place in the world, each saw in the other that flicker of themselves.

When she noticed Neihart making his way through the crowd toward them she pulled her hand away.

Neihart addressed Matthew, taking a moment. "Anytime you want a job," he said, "come find me."

"Hab a job, sir. But tanks."

Neihart nodded, his mouth opened slightly, showing teeth. "And... what job might that be?" He didn't wait for an answer, but said to Nola, "Can't wait to see what you write about."

• • •

A train came lumbering up through the yard to the station where it was switched onto a siding. It was an old copper firebox locomotive pulling three empty cattle cars. A present from Neihart for those wayfarers he'd picked up at Impossible Springs. It would be a slow and rugged passing on up into Colorado, but free all the way.

At the station, Nola overheard from a crew of Pinkertons waiting for the train that Mary Jones and the Western Federation of Miners committee were secreting into Pueblo to confront the managing directors of the Coal and Iron Works. The CIW, which was believed to be privately financed by Jay Gould, was the most formidable conglomerate in the West, and a frontline enemy to any form of unionization, and whenever necessary, would resort to violence.

She and Matthew were out on the station platform watching that line of ragtags board the cattle cars. It was a desperate looking company, that's for sure.

"I'll see you in Denver," she said. "Leave a letter for me at General Delivery telling me where you are."

She picked up her two carpetbags.

"I t'aut you takin' train ta' Denver?"

She started across the tracks.

"I'm going to Pueblo first."

"Why?"

She looked back as she labored along. "That's where the story is."

CHAPTER 47

After she was gone the world came crowding in. He could not keep from watching her until she'd joined that line of migrants being hoisted up into the slatted railcar. He had not felt this isolated and lost since the night all those years ago when they took him by force from the compound where the old woman and the dog lay murdered.

Outside the train depot a bar of sorts had been set up in the back of a wagon where a black man in a stovepipe hat played a rinky piano. Matthew bought a drink and went off by himself and sat on a crate, his belongings beside him. He was rolling a cigarette, alone with his thoughts, when a voice cut into the moment.

"I know who you are."

Matthew was staring at a pair of men's boots. He kept to his makings.

"You're that lame kid what lived with the Coffin Maker and the old woman."

Matthew finished rolling the cigarette. He licked the paper, then closed it up tight.

"You may be a hell raiser at three hundred yards but it's a lot different to hold court up close."

He slipped the cigarette into his mouth. Took out a match and scored it across the floorboards between the toes of the man's boots.

"How 'bout I put one of these boots down your fucking throat?"

The youth smoked, and rearranged himself slightly on the crate where he sat.

"Let's see you fire it up," the man shouted.

Matthew did not answer, and that was his answer.

People along the platform had taken notice. The black man playing the rascally piano slowed his tune then flat out stopped.

"You think you're gonna play Coffin Maker in Colorado? You sneak beat a man in the dark off his horse and leave a threat…I have one for you. Don't be on that train. Because you'll never reach Colorado alive."

Without ever lifting his glance, Matthew said, "Mista' Bathlott…Got no indenchon a comin' outta' Coloroto alive…You shoodin' eitha'.

• • •

Matthew boarded the train with his grip and rifles and Bathlott watching as he did so, cursing under his breath. He then went and talked to a couple of Pinkerton guards in the employ of the Leadville Mine Owners Alliance.

Matthew took up the backseat in the last car where he could be most alone and it would be impossible for him to be surrounded and beaten to death, for he had seen Bathlott talking to thugs and knew what the future would hold. When the train pulled out of the yard, he took a small piece of candle and a dynamite stick from his grip and kept them out of sight, but beside him. Then it was all about the waiting.

It was well into the night, the landscape they passed through black and moonless with reefs of dark mountain piling up in the distance. This was the perfect country for unmarked graves, for beings left to rot in the endless silence of the world's beginnings.

He did not sleep, but he kept his hat down low over his eyes and arms crossed as if he were. He watched the door to the car ahead knowing it would slowly open and sure enough Bathlott appeared with two men behind him.

There were a handful of people in the car, a woman and a child among them, asleep and unaware.

His head rose as the men shadowed in on him.

"We've come to visit," said Bathlott.

"So ya' say."

"You'll be leaving the train now."

"Alive…or dead?"

"We don't want to wake anybody, do we?"

Matthew held up the bit of lit candle. Bathlott had no idea what that meant. The youth sat there looking like someone in a church pew, then he held up the stick of dynamite showing off a fuse no longer than an eyelash.

Matthew could see their antagonism get a little soft around the edges. The two men behind Bathlott started to take a step back. Matthew moved the flame even closer to the fuse and motioned with his jaw the men not move at all. He told them it was they who would be leaving the train.

"Kill us, you kill yourself," said Bathlott.

Matthew told Bathlott in no uncertain terms his was a brilliant observation. Matthew stood. It was a chore in itself on a moving train, without having a lit candle and stick of dynamite to negotiate.

On sheer chance the conductor entered the car to make his nightly round and what does he see? He was not a young man or a brave one and became quickly pale. He tried to keep his voice calm, quiet, not to arouse a panic. Yet with a shaking voice he said, "What the fuck is going on here?"

Matthew initiated the conversation, saying these three men were getting off the train…And now. And could the conductor be so kind as to formally take them in tow, walk them out to the platform, and have them jump.

The conductor tried to beseech Matthew it was heartless country and the men could be badly hurt jumping from the train.

Matthew answered, "Hurt jes' tas bad here."

The conductor actually said, "Gentlemen…this way."

And off they went, cursing and enraged, promising hell as they ditched from the platform.

Matthew watched from the window. They were shadows in the light of the caboose one moment then lost in the void beyond the rumbling train wheels in the next.

When it was all done, the conductor reentered the car and said to Matthew, pointing, "What you gonna do now?"

Matthew blew out the candle. Then he turned over the stick of dynamite to show the conductor it was hollow, nothing more than a powderless casing.

The conductor had no idea what the hell to make of that. All he said was, "Wouldn't they feel the fools?"

CHAPTER 48

The ride to Pueblo in a cattle car brought back the black memories of the orphan trains and the myth of a glorious human race that was nothing more than a form of rape.

By day the journey was stifling with baked dust coming through the slats the awful topper. At night it turned bitchin' cold. Someone at the far end of the car had a guitar and played. It was hard to hear over the wind and the ever screeching iron of the undercarriage. Yet, there was tenderness to the music that she felt, and suddenly, she wished he were there. And the feeling was like protecting a secret for fear the world would find out and bring about some terrible downfall.

At Pueblo she went to a used men's clothing store and emptied out one of her carpetbags and packed it with trousers, work boots, plain blouses, a canvas hat more befitting the road, and a rubber Macintosh to face the rains.

• • •

The Coal and Iron Works—the CIW—stood alone on the plain outside of Pueblo. It was a black and filthy colossus that stretched near half a mile. The flames from the smelters and smoke breathing out the huge stacks made the whole of it look like some altar to a hellish deity.

Across the road from the entry to the works, there was a church made of adobe and shacks where the workers lived, all of it cordoned off by barbed wire.

That entrance is where Mary Jones and the Western Federation Committee set up camp and made speeches. There was a growing number of dissatisfied workers amassing at the protests that told the owners this was a cancer that needed to be reckoned with.

The superintendent was lashing the protestors with his speech and threats, reminding them that investors and inventiveness created the industries that created America and the jobs that Americans enjoyed. And the worker was "fortunate" to have a job. Mary Jones, standing in a flatbed wagon, flashed back at him that when the economy flourished with profit no profit passed into the pocket of the poor worker, but when stock prices fell, or there was the faintest hint of a recession, the worker was made to shoulder that reality. And prices for the worker never went down, only their standard of living…and hopes.

And if the worker did not obey, did not succumb, did not comply, if he fought against the shacks and barbed wire, what could he expect? Rifles, bayonets, and badges.

Nola was sitting by the wagon on a crate along the dusty road when Mary Jones pointed. Coming up from the corporate compound were a hundred men, it had to be that many—guards, Pinkertons, and workers for the CIW who were against the protest and union and they were bearing rifles, bayonets, and badges.

Nola suddenly envisioned the battlefield through Mary Jones' eyes. Lose that one night in jail and Nola only knew the woman from her speeches. But the speeches, her very presence—she was like the chorus in a Greek play, shedding light on the human drama that was unfolding. She was, by her presence—this plain looking woman with wire rim glasses— the conscience of a movement.

And Nola saw at work in that woman the long reach of time. She was building a social army, protest by protest, that had endured the humiliation, the beatings, and defeats. Because they all had value. The defeats especially, because defeats build character and courage if you continue on your course. She was, speech by speech, honing a generation by making them aware no good would come from their plight through complacency.

The men with the rifles, bayonets, and badges came forward and the protestors fell back from the blades and the bullets being fired into the air and the men of the CIW opened ranks and here came a cohort with the dogs. Dogs on heavy ropes, violent, angry beasts, teeth bared, straining at their leads, eyes bulging, kicking up dust, closing in, closing in, until the protestors broke rank.

The men attacked the wagon where the woman in the plain dress with wire rim glasses stood and they lifted the wheels. The protestors, outnumbered, could not tide back the assault. It was an easy task to overturn the wagon and when Mary Jones was thrown to the ground it was Nola who got to her just before the dogs.

CHAPTER 49

Bathlott and his two traveling partners, bitter and resentful at having been pulled into this crap ass predicament, followed the tracks where they could, then trudged across the pumice flats toward the Colorado border.

They were sun beat and desperate for water, searching the horizon for any sign of a tower that fed the rail line, and when they finally wiped the sweat and blur from their eyes and saw what looked like the rough frameworks of one rising up out of the fuming earth, their strides lengthened and their backs straightened and they cursed out loud with joy, then they stopped dead in their tracks and their voices strangled.

They stood there like misbegotten statues staring at a figure with a funny walk and a rifle hoisted up on his shoulder coming toward them through the heat of the desert floor.

One of the men said, "God can't be that much of a shit."

Whether God was a shit or not, it was Matthew. He had disembarked from the train at the Colorado border. He'd rented a mount from a livery in a one street town and started back from where he'd come, aiming to finish some of his business with the Committee.

The three stood packed together like playing cards, assessing the landscape around them for they knew the fight was coming. That lame bastard with his Vetterli and the three of them with five pistols, a derringer, and a couple of Bowie knives between them to face down a figure about three hundred yards away, carved out of sunlight and coming on.

When Matthew closed enough of that distance so they could hear him, he shouted that you can't hide for long behind your past injustices. And then to loosen up their bowels a bit he shouldered his weapon and they scattered, diving to the earth.

Matthew slowly kept on, walking his mount behind him. The men could have tried to make a run for it, but Matthew, having a mount, would have trained them down pretty quickly, so they decided to make a stand.

He saw them spread into a wide arc, so they could charge him from three angles. They were sprinting across that trackless flat doing their best to get into pistol range.

It was silent on the desert floor and then the wind kicked up creating sheets of dust. What it must have looked like from on high, men spent and desperate in thirst, pistols drawn, sweat burning their eyes, rushing toward one and all's death. The whole of existence nothing more than this forgettable tract of nothing.

Matthew stopped and from his saddle grip took out a picket pin. He bent clumsily and spiked it into the earth. He tied off the horse's reins to it, so it would be unable to flee when the firing started. He then marched out and away from the animal, tempting them even more. The animal would be "the all" to the last man standing, especially a thirsty man.

The wind blowing the dust had broken in the men's favor, buying them a chance. Matthew now stood his ground daring them to come to him. A shot from one of the pistols clipped the earth maybe fifty yards out from where Crippled Jack stood with his rifle stock positioned against his bad shoulder.

You could hear the crisp articulation of his shot through the dust hissing over the rocks.

The first charge missed, but Matthew chambered another shell, with eyes narrowing he fired.

The thigh of Bathlott's leather trouser leg was torn apart and blood smeared everywhere. His head made a stunned turn and his leg collapsed right out from under him.

The men were firing back and forth through a quaking haze and Matthew's horse reared and kicked trying to pull free of the picket. Bathlott was crawling toward the gunfire while the other men were on the move, hunched, silent, darting from spot to spot like feral dogs on the hunt.

One of them caught sight of a figure when the wind died a bit and he made a rush toward it, keeping his eyes marked on the spot for when the wind kicked back up, which it did and again he lost sight of the figure and then a moment later he was upon Matthew, who was chambering more shells.

The man fired but he had not counted his rounds well enough in the melee for his Walker pistol was empty and the hammer made a dead man's click.

Matthew heard it and turned toward the sound and then he saw and then he fired. His shot hit the man cold and clean going clear through the stomach and a wad of blood came spitting up the man's throat and out his mouth, and there was that terrible sound of death wrapped in the wind.

The one man left standing tried to run. But running was no better than dying. Escaping across that barren reef with the wind blowing, he did not hear the rifle shell chambered and then fire the round that separated his spine from his skull.

He fell to the earth paralyzed. And he would die within minutes, his body numb to the sun and the heat and the dust and the fact he had urinated helplessly or that Matthew walked right past him, giving the man his back, and chambering another shell.

Matthew fixed on one thing now—finding Bathlott. Out there somewhere, crawling close to the earth, as a rat would, bleeding badly because the bullet that had torn his leg apart had severed a vein and without realizing it Bathlott was going to die and nothing but God could change that.

Finally he sat up, wily enough to keep silent, not calling out, for the silence told him the men he'd come with were probably lying out there somewhere with all accounts settled.

A man can only look in one direction at a time and that is not even good enough when one's hand is pressed against the wound to stanch the blood and the pain. Bathlott did not hear Matthew step from the veiled dust, and he did not see the shadow of the gun arc like the long hand on a clock or the shadow of the man bending awkwardly just as he fired.

The round crushed the back of the shoulder that held his weapon. The concussion flattened Bathlott against the earth, the agony of the shattered bone froze him. The heel of the boot of Matthew's crooked leg ground the back of Bathlott's hand which still held the pistol until it came loose and Matthew kicked it away.

Then Matthew squatted down, posting the rifle stock against the earth, using it to keep his balance as he told Bathlott, "Ta Coffin Maka haz come for you."

CHAPTER 50

Matthew looked down at Bathlott's leg where the blood was darkening in the sand and Bathlott saw the youth coldly eyeing the fatal wound.

"Taking it all in, cripple?"

Matthew nodded, yes, that he was taking it all in.

Bathlott tried to rise up, jacking himself, using the elbow of his free arm, Matthew watching him grimly try but to no avail. And in his anger, Bathlott spit at Matthew, but he'd been so long without water there was nothing left of spittle in him.

Matthew then used a finger to sketch out a coffin in the dirt.

Matthew stood and leaned over Bathlott and went about the business of emptying the man's pockets of everything he carried—wallet, pocket watch, the makings for cigarettes, coins. These he tossed in a pile.

"Robbing the dead," said Bathlott. "What can you expect from a—"

Matthew grabbed up the loose coins and tossed them to the wind. The watch he glanced over to see if there was an inscription and when he saw there wasn't flung it as far as he could. He opened the wallet and peeled out the paper money which he tore to shreds and then sprinkled the pieces over Bathlott as if it were confetti.

But there was meaning to his actions. Matthew was searching as he went for something, anything he could use to prove the man Bathlott had been taken. But as life will, the places not marked on the map are the ones you have to most watch out for.

Matthew came upon a slip of paper, good writing paper, fine paper even, folded in half and then folded again. He went about the clumsy process of opening it out. The paper had dried wet spots and a few food stains, but what was written with ink in good, neat script:

Nola Dye

Matthew held up the paper. "Wha' dis?"

Bathlott saw, yes, he saw all too clearly, an apprehension engulfing the youth that was edging right into panic. Matthew demanded an answer, only this time more forcefully.

"The tables have turned," said Bathlott. "Haven't they…cripple?"

Matthew leaned over and shook Bathlott, who grimaced with pain. Matthew wanted to know what it meant. Why her name was written down and who had written it?

Bathlott swung at Matthew and caught him with a slap on the side of his face with a bloody palm. Matthew sat back. His cheek streaked with blood. He wiped at it with the sleeve of his jacket.

"You been marked now, boy," said Bathlott.

There was a nest of shadows in that dying man's expression. And a devil lurking in the glinty stare and grin. "You'll ruin just thinking about what it means. And remember this, you ain't no ministering angel. You're just a rat ass viper of a kid who can shoot. You're just a shit pile trying to pass himself off as a Billy the Kid."

Matthew told Bathlott he would bury him before he died if he didn't answer.

"You can't dig the hole fast enough," said Bathlott. "But there's another hole out there." He then reached out with the bloody hand and touched the tiny coffin Matthew had scratched into the dirt.

"Who's the Coffin Maker now?"

With a last run of contempt Bathlott gave Matthew the finger. Matthew grabbed him by that bloody hand, then shoved the hand into the dirt. He pressed the rifle barrel against the guilty finger and blew it the hell off.

PART THREE

CHAPTER 51

When she saw the headlines Nola knew it had to be him. News of the incident on the train had gotten around, but this:

MESSAGE FROM THE COFFIN MAKER

The message was simple enough. A blood stained wallet that belonged to the late Charlie Bathlott, who had been, according to the article, unceremoniously buried in the desert, had mysteriously appeared at the offices of the *Denver Times*.

The wallet came wrapped in cloth and with an attached note, marking this murder as the work of the "Coffin Maker."

The fact that Bathlott had been in the employ of the Americanus as part of a security team opened doors of questions, none of which could, or would, be answered. Of one fact you could be sure, a growing litany of events was leading to an ultimate and violent conclusion where the good and the bad would be cancelling each other out.

She'd left a letter for Matthew at General Delivery. She crossed the river and walked past the Denver Smelter Works to the outskirts of town. The imposing flames from the furnaces burned against the black of the night.

There was an old two story house that had fallen on hard times after years of being a maison de joie. That's where Mary Jones and members of the Western Federation took up temporary residence while in the city.

Along the county road no one took much notice of Nola being a woman. With her coat collar up and hat pulled down low, she was just another ragged stranger.

The house was up a long wagon track and the woods it passed through grew darker and heavier. As the silence deepened the noises she picked up took on more menacing tones. She was beginning to suffer a new shade of fear. Innocent sounds of the night now hid a dark history of danger and threat.

Her courage was being tested, her will being threatened. The dark shadows crossing before her very eyes was she herself. Having been taken by force as a little girl became foremost in her consciousness, because that sinful act was one and the same as the sinful acts going on in the world around her. They were called different things, but they were the same.

The poor, the jobless and desperate, were the same as the child she had been when taken. And those who ruled, those who set the table of life through power and force, were liken to the man who had taken her.

What made her consumed with fear for her life at that moment? Was there something suddenly in the silence that reached out and took a stranglehold on her heart?

She ran all the way, looking behind her, and the darker it remained and the more silent it remained the more afraid she became till she could not even breathe.

She reached the lights of the house pale and shaking. There were men on the porch from the Western Federation who now stood as this woman came rushing out of the dark. They were not without weapons and stood at the ready and one of them said, "What's out there, miss?"

A shake of the head was all she could manage.

She showed Mary Jones the newspaper story.

Mary took in the words with the look of one who has seen it all. The two women were alone in a little room off the parlor that served as an office and place for Mary to sleep.

"You don't have to stay," said the older woman. "And it may be better if you don't. The closer we get, the more killing is promised."

"I can't know what to write, until I come to know it."

Nola glanced out through the curtains and past the lights from the house on into the darkness. "Are you ever afraid they will just come and kill you?"

"It took me years to become friends with death," said Mary. "I have come to learn that death is not always my enemy, but a valiant ally, for just as the good will die or be killed, so will the bad."

She held up the newspaper and said, "For endless reasons and all kinds of causes."

She passed the newspaper back to Nola. "It's your friend, is it not?"

Nola was intentionally hesitant to answer. "I don't know that...for a fact."

"We all have friends like that," said Mary. "It's the nature of our world, as we all are conceived in conflict...and all the way to where our lives are packed up and put in the ground for safekeeping."

She saw Nola was intent on the window, and the breeze touched curtains, and what might be out there in the night. The fear, it was all flushed out in that young woman's downy features.

Then Mary Jones just opened up to Nola about her life. Of her girlhood in Ireland, she said, "My first memories are of the food riots in Ireland. The landowners had given the farmers pitifully small parcels of land, barely enough to plant to make the payments, and unless they thrived on starving were eventually run off, to be replaced by another wave of desperate farmers. And when they finally revolted they were put down by thugs the landowners hired. Trash with a badge…like here."

The older woman removed her glasses and with a steady and studied look went off into the world from where she'd come.

"What I see most from my past is being in the back of a cart with our family's possessions making our way through village after village, on muddy paths, and seeing cottages on fire…and the sight of men hung. Men beaten, and then hung, as a warning.

"To this day when I smell burning ash or timbers ablaze my stomach turns sick. The corpses come to me in nightmares of remembering. They were there on my wedding night, when my first was born, when all finally died, and when I stood alone in the world with the sweat on my skin thick as syrup and only God there to wipe it away."

"Does it ever…?" said Nola. "Did they—"

"It is always with me, girl. But I cherish it now. I drink from the cup of my wounds and sufferings, because they not only strengthen me, they sanctify me. And they assure me on my march toward progress."

CHAPTER 52

His first instinct was to blow the goddamn building to kingdom come. He stood across a busy street studying the small, neat brick structure just off Market that was the corporate headquarters of the Americanus.

When Matthew had arrived in Denver he went first to General Delivery. There was a letter from Nola Dye telling him where she was staying, and how to get there.

He sat on the sidewalk outside the post office and read the letter a number of times, because some of what she'd written expressed a soul in conflict, and gave him pause.

In her own way, Nola suggested it might be best if the two did not meet again, so as not to allow a personal intimacy develop between them.

She was honest enough to admit:

> *...If certain facts come to my attention that prove you are the person I believe you are, I would be forced, ethically, to expose you...And a "deepening" friendship will not only make that morally treacherous but emotionally devastating...*

Each sentence seemed to cloak the one that had come before it in pure human conflict and she could only close with:

> *...come at your own risk...or should I say, at both our risks...*

He closed the letter and slipped it between the flaps of his wallet and beside the scrap of paper he had taken from a dying Bathlott.

Matthew had determined the offices of the Americanus were the best place to lay in wait and watch. He did this for a day and a night, playing the gypsy shadow at the entrance to a faceless alley.

He had seen Colonel Gheen come and go in a constant state of flux. He had watched the fat man, framed by an upper office window, in a pointed argument with Neihart. It had to be, at least in part, about the killing of Bathlott, since the Colonel held up a rumpled copy of the newspaper in one hand and defiantly slapped at it with the other.

What Matthew did not know, could not know, was that the heart of this heated go round was one unimpeachable fact—the Americanus was on the verge of bankruptcy. That a most secret evaluation done by Neihart's personal engineer showed the mine to be a tapped out shell. And even a massive infusion of cash to get at the deeper veins of ore might not be enough to save it.

That was a stretch of conversation where Matthew saw the Colonel grow so visibly shaken he had to sit. He undid his starched collar and tried to gather in as much air as possible. He swilled down a drink Neihart handed him, and then the grown man began to cry.

Matthew found it impossible to believe this reaction had anything to do with the engineered demise of dear Mister Bathlott.

The two men spent hours talking after that, their conversation punctuated with long bouts of silence and drinking. This went on well into the night and good thing, too—

The street was pretty dark by then. There was a tavern still in full swing. You could hear a piano and drunks singing. Matthew was just an alley cat, smoking, eating crackers from a tin, when there came the slow approach of horsemen appearing in a halo of street lamps along Market.

Four men to be exact.

He couldn't truly make them out until the men reined in their mounts at the offices of the Americanus. Vandel, he recognized, and McSorley. The other two he did not know or remember. He took out the writing paper "The Cook" had given him with the names of the members of the Committee that had hunted Ledru. The last two names were Adolphus Tobin and Percy Fry.

From deep in the darkness, Matthew called out, "Hey, Percy."

One of the two men turned immediately. Well, if that was Percy Fry, the other was sure to be Adolphus Tobin.

Fry walked out into the street, looking up and down Market to see who might have been calling out. Tobin joined him.

"Forget it," said Tobin. "Could have been just some drunk down by that bar."

"No…it didn't come from there."

Fry and Tobin were cut from the same cast of street trash. Men who had a few bucks in their pocket and wore a better brand of hat and coat, but who never shaved or took a bath, and whose pants had that gluey feel of sweat and urine to them. Matthew gave them a studied going over. They were hale and hearty and not a chance of a please or thank you between them. And best to kill them with the first shot, otherwise they would come tearing up your ass with a knife and fork.

CHAPTER 53

The four men entered the Americanus building and began what looked to be a long night of drinking and hard talk with Neihart and the Colonel… but Gheen did not stay long. He climbed into a waiting carriage and disappeared down Market Street. He looked to be drowned in misery and what Matthew wondered, had he left of his own devices or for some reason was he sent packing? Were there uncertain aspects of Americanus business that Neihart kept Gheen walled off from?

Matthew went to the livery where he'd stalled his mount and grip. He decided from his vantage point in the alley he could kill at least one of them and get away. But when he returned the building was pitch dark and the horses out front nowhere to be seen. Luck had crossed the men's path, only they did not know it.

Matthew followed the directions in Nola's letter to where she was staying with members of the Federation. He took the county road and crossed the river. It was heavily treed out that far, and not a light anywhere. He found the path off the county road that led up in the house by a marked tree. A hundred empty whiskey bottles had been hung from its branches by chicken wire and with the slightest breeze the bottles started tipsy dancing that sounded like the faintest music.

He rested there and studied the letter. He read and reread what she had written by the light of a match. He considered what he could do, should do, might do or not do, but he always ended up in the same place. He had stumbled out of the dark back there on the road and right into the woman's life. As he started up the path he did not hope what he was doing was right, only that it did not breathe of disaster.

• • •

There were two men on the porch, still talking hard times and the burn to end them, when one was suddenly drawn to the silvery darkness where the road filed off into the trees. He waved a hand for the other to hush.

"What?"

The first man stood. "Something out there."

The other got up and pushed open the front door. "We need you out here, people. We might have visitors."

Nola was with Mary Jones in her room off the parlor and they joined the rush of men to the porch.

"I don't see anything," one said.

She wasn't the first to see him, but she was the first to know who it was. He was leading his mount, his walk a cumbrous grace you could not mistake. "It's the young man from the train at Impossible Springs," she said quietly.

He was stepping into patches of light cast from the windows upon the earth. One of the men on the porch said, "You ain't hiding any dynamite on you?"

A wave of laughter from among the men as the story had already gotten around.

Matthew acknowledged her with a slight nod of the head. She, like him, knew the world of themselves was awaiting. She watched from the parlor while he led his horse to the barn, with no idea how to shed what she was feeling.

He stood in the hallway with his sheathed rifles and grip and watched Nola and Mary Jones in the lamplit parlor talking together in whispers. Nola came to him with a candle and closing the parlor doors behind her, said, "Come with me."

They started up the stairs, with him behind her. "I knew you'd come," she said softly.

His boots made scarred sounds on the stairs as they climbed their way to her room in the attic.

"Maybe ya' shudent a written ta' letter."

She opened the door to what had been no more than a crib for a prostitute when this building had its day as a whorehouse.

"I tried my best not to," she said. "But I just couldn't stop myself."

CHAPTER 54

The room was spare and musty. A bed of wood slats and a cloth mattress stuffed with straw took up one pitched wall, a table where she placed the candle and a lonely chair took up the other. He set his rifles and grip down by a window no larger than a human face.

He told her how he thought about tossing her letter in the road and being on his way, but he knew he'd go back for it.

He was taking out his wallet while telling her this. And then he held out the slip of paper with her name written on it.

"If it's about Bathlott, I can't know," she said. "Because if I know, I will have to act. I will have to tell the world you killed those men…that you are the Coffin Maker."

There was no holding check on her emotions.

"I'd suffer too much for that," she said.

The breeze came through the poorly constructed clapboard wall causing the candle flame to lift then lilt. He sat on the edge of the bed but her refusal notwithstanding he kept his arm with the paper held out for her to take. "Look," he said.

She reached out and reluctantly took the strip of writing paper from his hands, their fingers brushing. She looked it over, trying to understand, to decipher its meaning.

"What is this?" she said. "What does it mean?"

He told her, in no uncertain terms, it meant she should leave Colorado.

"Leave Colorado," she said. "How do I explain an act like that to myself?"

How could he answer?

She demanded he answer.

"Have ta' lie ta' convins ya'self."

It was a dismal reality that aroused her anger. She sat on the bed practically beside him.

"If they can weaken you a little today," she said, "what can you look forward to tomorrow?"

She was still holding the paper with her name on it. He saw her hands were trembling slightly. He reached out with his good hand and took the paper from her and let it drop to the floor, all the while holding her hands with his other. They remained just so in that dingy, claustrophobic cell until he said to her that she could write about what she had seen.

"What have I seen? Just a name on a piece of good writing paper. It's not a story…until it is a story. And I intend to be there when it happens."

Matthew then openly expressed that he would not hold it against her if she did expose him for who he was. That it would be all right. That it would not change or diminish his feelings for her.

"That alone," she said, "would break my heart. And I have only so much to break."

In a moment of clear eyed transparency he admitted he knew who he was, and what he was, and what he'd done and what he intended to do, and that he would get what he deserved…fairly or unfairly. And death's meaning wouldn't change it.

"I stand by ta' blood I shed," and that was the last he said.

There was something in the wracked soul of this boy and man that touched her most private suffering in a way no one ever had. He was there within her, like a shadow moving from feeling to feeling, from memory to memory, casting out the hurts and the horrors. And suddenly she recaptured this place in her being before misery, before loneliness, before being orphaned and put on the road, before being raped. This place, safe from weeping, safe from grieving, safe from pain, this place that haunts us all because it is undeserved and pure and is forever out there on the frontiers of our existence, defying everything that means to destroy us, waiting to make us well, to make us whole, to make us be again. It has a thousand names it seems, and yet no name at all. But it is the last and best of us. And she wanted it through him, and him through it.

CHAPTER 55

She stood and stepped to the table. She licked her thumb and index finger and snuffed out the flame between them. "A poor candle," she said quietly.

Matthew had not quite heard her.

"A poor candle...you know what a poor candle is?"

"I do."

"That's what we are...poor candles."

She stood by the table now in the dark. A lonely figure to say the least. He sensed something in her silence, something that clearly concerned her, or maybe even overwhelmed her. He let her have her time by keeping quiet. Her fingers were rubbing the plain wood tabletop with a slow intensity.

"I was taken as a girl," she said, quite out of nowhere. "Against my will. I was taken by the man in charge of the orphan train I was on. He ran the orphanage where I lived. He took me... more...much more...than once."

She stood quietly now in a place she never had before. A place where you are exposed to the enormity of what you have just confessed.

Matthew did not know what to say. He just watched the smoke from the wick gathering on the window in a ghostly fashion.

"I've never spoken of this to anyone," she said. "I carry too much shame."

Matthew cupped her face in his hands. "I know one thin'," he said.

"Yes?"

"I know—"

"Know what?"

"Shame is a cos'ly enemy. It haz defeated me...many times."

"Yes," she said. "I understand. That...has been me."

A world that held her in its grip was suddenly weakening enough so she was no longer prisoner of its dark streets and narrow alleys. She felt a surge of courage and desire that led her to sit on the bed beside him.

He thought to himself – she is braver than I am, bolder. And this filled him with resolve and freed him from himself so he could take his arm and use it to ease her toward him so her head would rest upon his shoulder.

They were silent and still as children in the deepest realms of sleep, peaceful, and beautiful and filled with a want. But he also knew what she also knew—they were now on a path together that led through a tangled world that was long on hate and short on mercy.

• • •

Somewhere in the pit of sleep he was seized by a stark and fleeting presence that awakened him.

He sat up, Nola there under the blanket beside him. Once he slipped out of the bed, she stirred. It was still dark, that hour before the softs of daylight come stealing in.

He was staring out the tiny window when she rose. "What is it?" she said.

He was already getting his trousers on. "Dress…an' quick."

"What's wrong?"

"Don' know."

He grabbed his rifle scabbards and grips and placed them on the bed. She stood naked to peer out the window. "Did you see something?"

"In here," he said, pointing to the side of his head.

He told her to take everything and keep close to Mary Jones, that they would most likely be separated and that he would meet her in Leadville… if he was alive.

He came downstairs. He was carrying his rifles. A few men were already stirring in the darkness and had taken up positions at the windows with weapons in hand. Mary Jones stood behind them with her arms crossed. She saw Matthew coming through the shadows with Nola not far behind him.

The men with Mary were whispering among themselves—if a threat was out there, would it be best to make a stand in the house, or manage an escape out back, through the woods, on a path they had already plotted out?

A decision had to be made, and it had to be made soon and it had to be determined by someone secreting out into the night to figure out the lay of things. A couple of men offered themselves up but Matthew said he would be the best choice, because the best choice had to have the best eyes and from a coat pocket he took out one of the sights to his rifles.

A few quiet nods and he was elected. One of the Federation men opened the front door just a slit, enough anyway for Matthew to get down and snake out onto the porch with the door easing closed behind him.

CHAPTER 56

He inched along silently. At the edge of the steps he rested on his elbows. He began to line up the telescopic sight so as to search the woods when he noticed an open hand pressed against the parlor window. Beside it the faint image of Nola, the glass becoming misty where she breathed. She mouthed the words, "Be careful."

He scanned the cool dark world of the trees. He was sweating with nerves and the breeze made the back of his neck chill. The gun sight was trembling a bit when he picked up a sudden flutter of motion in the heavy brush.

He held his position and watched and he waited tirelessly. The darkness murky, shrouded, dimensionless, and still. So utterly still.

Then he caught sight of something. A sliver of movement at the edge of the cart path. How he caught sight of it—a touch of moonlight glimmering off what had to be one thing—glass. And then he knew.

Lying there on the porch he grabbed for his rifle and inside the house you could hear the sharp metallic clicks of the bolt as Matthew chambered a shell. His whisper was flush with panic, warning everyone inside to get out back…to get out now.

When he saw a fist sized ball of flame he knew they were going to firebomb the building. Kerosene or naphtha in a whiskey bottle, most probably. He could see the flame begin to arc back and he fired as it was about to be thrown.

He heard the shell shearing through the brush, and the one throwing the bottle was hit just as he flung it. The flame cometed off at a skewed angle and must have hit a tree because it exploded at the edge of the woods and the darkness lit up like the inside of a fuckin' church at Christmas.

It was a state of pure panic after that, not a lick of sense or organization. Just confusion, screaming, and stupidity. Federation men were trampling out the kitchen screen door making for the barn or woods. Some were already mounted and firing back over their shoulders with pistols, scattering into the trees, Mary Jones and Nola Dye among them.

A bottle with a burning cloth tucked into its neck exploded against the barn roof. The horses in the corral tried to launch themselves over the fencing to escape a rain of fiery ash pouring down on them. And for a few moments a scene of dust and gunfire was playing out in a hellish unreal light.

Matthew ended up alone just off the county road crouched in the high weeds for his own protection with the dawn stirring all around him. He had gone back into the house for his other rifle and grip and smashed out a side window with the barrel and then disappeared past the dead and wounded and on into the trees.

There were birds calling out and those tinkly bottles that hung from the branches as he started back to Denver. He kept parallel to the county road but just off it enough to not be seen, traveling like he had in those first days with Ledru Drum…who was very much on his mind.

If Ledru were alive, there was plenty Matthew wanted to ask him, as he walked in the same footprints as the man who'd saved him. Ledru was more the father than his own father had been. Yet each had their profound effect upon his life. Each was one outstretched arm of the world.

Eat the bread of love, and you will not starve. He had heard Ledru speak this, and it seemed incongruous being the killer that he was. But yet—

Because of his feelings for the girl, Matthew was now living out some uncharted existence.

Where the cost of your actions is rising, the value of your actions must rise with them, or what are you? This came from Missus Drum.

Matthew was an assassin, heir to the man who'd saved him, who meant to bring a reckoning to those who had enacted their own form of reckoning upon the world.

On the road behind Matthew, there was only his own death to confront. His life would leave behind no grief, no sorrow for others. Like the grief, like the sorrow he felt over Ledru and Missus Drum and Corporal Billy.

Should he abandon the girl? Should he take a vow of loneliness, like the devouts take vows of poverty and silence?

Were these thoughts, he wondered, the province of his private shame? That he could feel unworthy of being grieved over, like he himself grieved, disguised the fact he felt unworthy of being loved at all?

There was a black mark of smoke in the distant sky from the barn which had burned to the ground.

It was Vandel who'd led the attack on the house and whose orders were to make sure none of the men under him were left at the scene. Vandel was hoping among the bodies he'd come upon the cripple, but it didn't matter. There was bloodletting enough ahead of them.

CHAPTER 57

"You've grown into a game fuck, ain't you?"

Matthew turned to see who had spoken. It was Vandel.

"That's right, Crippled Jack. It's me."

They were at the Denver fairgrounds. It was the day following the violence in the hills, of which much had been written in the newspapers. Matthew had originally come to Denver to be part of the shooting match that was scheduled. There were over a hundred contestants, and around three thousand spectators, who until the match began, were crowding the food and liquor stands or listening to the city's foremost high school band. The day was hot and the sky a near jewel of cloudless blue. And the music echoed on the still air. A robust marching tune.

"Do you miss Sugarland?" said Vandel. "I'll bet you got quite an education there."

Matthew was signing a few autographs as Crippled Jack. He did not answer Vandel. He knew better. Let the bastard slither, he thought.

"A silence is best," said Vandel. "Especially in your case."

Vandel had grown a beard to cover up the devastating injury the old woman had inflicted upon him with a single shot. His jaw and lower mouth had become a wound that never rightfully healed. There was always a discolored spittle dripping into his beard that Vandel endlessly dried with a handkerchief.

"I thought I saw you last night, Jack."

By now McSorley and the two other members of their corporate rat-pack had gathered up behind Vandel.

"We were at an old whorehouse just out the County Road. Quite a get together. You probably read about it. And I swore I saw your ass skittering off into the trees. Maybe I was wrong? Was I wrong?"

Matthew stood mute.

"Like the prisoner in the docket," said Vandel.

Matthew glanced at the rifle that Vandel was carrying.

"That's right, Coffin Maker," said Vandel, and he reached out with the barrel of his gun and tapped the barrel of the rifle Matthew had slung up on his shoulder.

• • •

As they moved the targets two hundred and seventy-five yards out, Matthew asked himself why had Vandel chosen this act as a point of confrontation. Was he looking for a tangible means to test Matthew's mettle as a marksman?

At this distance, it was the best two out of three shots. Twice the men tied. At three hundred yards they tied again. The crowd responded to every shot, from anguish to applause. And each time the targets were moved the band drummed out a heightening cadence.

At three hundred and twenty-five yards it wasn't just about one's abilities to maintain accuracy as a marksman, but to evaluate wind direction, weight of the air, the diminishing power of your cartridge in flight.

Matthew took his own sweet time reloading, catching glimpses of Vandel as he could. He was being studied by the man as if he were a bug or a butterfly. What's hiding in the mind behind that look, Matthew kept asking himself.

Matthew missed his first shot, just managed the second, and came up short on the last. His best shooting had run its course and the crowds tempered applause pretty well said as much.

It was Vandel's turn. He wiped the crusty spit off his chin with a handkerchief. Poised, steady, eyes like thumbscrews, he aimed and fired. His first failed, as did the second. At this point it was tie or die and the crowd was silent and still as a photograph of a summer day. Vandel leaned into the shot with the sound geometry of the well seasoned murderer... only to miss.

The crowd erupted, the band followed suit. Hats were thrown into the air, parasols spun with delight. The fairgrounds were aswim in cheering and applause, but none of it matched the hatred Vandel expressed. He was not the good sport and silenced the crowd by smashing his rifle stock again and again against the Judge's stand and then flinging it away.

He moved through the crowd like a malefic cavalier, his men following, leaving a wake of shocked spectators behind him.

• • •

If only Matthew knew, or could guess, how Vandel was privately laughing over the whole matter.

"What happened back there?" said McSorley.

"Back there?"

"Back there," McSorley said, aggravated.

"What do you think happened?"

"I've seen you make those shots—"

"A thousand times."

"Damn right," said McSorley.

"Might have made it a thousand and one…but I didn't. Did I?"

"No…you didn't."

"And you know why I didn't?"

"I do not damn well know."

"Would you like to know?"

"I'd like to get out of this conversation a lot less confused than I am going in."

"Because I missed…on purpose."

CHAPTER 58

When Matthew passed through the exit from the fairgrounds there was Vandel and his cohort. Whether they were about to press a conflict amidst the congratulations, the back slapping and autograph seekers, a hard rock character strode up alongside Matthew. He thought he recognized the man who spoke before the youth could pose the thought.

"Yeah, kid...last night. I'm with the Federation. Name's Joe Sweeny."

He had a croaky voice and packed shoulders and he turned his sleet gray eyes upon Vandel.

"You here to start trouble with the boy?"

"Who the fuck are you?" said McSorley.

"I'm the guy what's gonna shit in your soup, that's who I am."

Right after that, a half a dozen men djinned out of the crowd. Federation men from the night before, their clothes still stained with ash.

"Me and this kid are leaving here," said Sweeny. "You understand, Vandel? We know who you are. And you four shits aren't following... unless you want to trade bloodshed."

• • •

"I got an invite for you," said Joe Sweeny. "From Mary Jones."

Sweeny was now Matthew's armed escort to a beautiful brick home in Hartman's Addition. The labor leader was the invited guest of a wealthy Neapolitan businessman who had made his bones as an importer. He was also considered a dangerous foreigner who believed the eight hour workday and livable wage were legitimate claims.

It was a stately neighborhood of Phaetons and gentle ladies with their well dressed tots. So you can imagine the neighbors when they saw the house guarded by whiskey swizzling, tobacco spitting workingmen of the Western Federation, who eyed these women like they were something to be served up for lunch.

Matthew had to wait while Mary Jones conducted a meeting on a screened-in porch with half a dozen well suited gentlemen. He watched the women and there was no doubt who was in command of that meeting. He was witness to a new type of fire in the way she pounded one fist into the other palm to make her points.

When the men retired, Matthew was called in. Mary Jones put out her hand to shake and he offered his left, which was his good hand, but she reached out and took the other.

"I want the hand that made you."

He looked down at the twisty mass that was his fingers.

"God gave you that hand," she said. "And that body. It is part of the blessing, like so many others who crawled out of the womb, broken… but who answered the call. And by their actions bear witness and so make others believe."

She stood with arms crossed, waiting to see what, if anything, he might say, but he was still in many ways a boy.

"Why'm I here?" he said.

"Here," she answered. "As in this world? Or in this room? You are here…in this world for the same reason I am. You are here…in this room for the same reason I am."

"Got no ideer, ma'am. Wha' ya' mean?" he said.

She stood with arms crossed. This tiny birdlike woman who was all sinew and steel.

"Matthew…we are here to raise hell. You, in your way. Me, in mine.

"I knew before the telling. I knew Ledru Drum. I knew that beast dog of his. I knew the old Missus Drum. Knew her like one sister knows another. Shared sufferings and joys, we did. And not in equal measure. And I was born with a special sense to know what I see, before I even see it."

She came right up to Matthew. He could see himself reflected in the glass of her spectacles. A shy, wild eyed stranger.

"And when I see you, Crippled Jack, I see someone who means to carry the fight to them. To whoever 'them' is. You got heaven locked up in one hand, and hell in the other. Like me. And we don't need any lectures on goddamn grief from anyone, do we?"

"No, ma'am."

She reached out and tugged at his shoulders." She held him by the coat sleeves. "I have a quest for you, Matthew."

He did not know what a quest was, and he told her so.

"I want you to join up with the Western Federation. We are going to Leadville. That's where the real fight will take place for the heart of the state, and the soul of the country."

He did not know what use he could be to her.

"It's a bloodthirsty place of unmitigated wealth as you know. The most powerful mines in the country are there…and home to the men hired to kill you."

All the injustices he'd faced were leaning against him now like a weighted pillar. How best to settle all this, he was not sure.

"Nola Dye is on her way there," said Mary Jones. "She will be there for the duration. For we intend to shut down that mountain of riches."

She saw the conflicts, the personal turmoil, fanning across the boy's expression.

"It's all right. In your own good time, you'll decide," said the woman. "But…I have a favor to ask that will just take no more than today."

CHAPTER 59

Her request was simple enough. She wanted Matthew to scour the city and collect up to a hundred children. Poor children, urchins living on the street, those abandoned by their parents for want of a job, sickly children, desperate children left alone, children who had worked in the mines, at the smelters, with the railroad, who had been cut loose because of physical injury.

"Children who were like you," she said. "The gutter and alley children."

"Wha' I do wit 'em?"

"Ah!" she said. And she leaned in close to him as if in confidence. "Tell them they're going to have a fine dinner and then attend the theatre."

Matthew took to the street with his Vetterli slung over a shoulder and Joe Sweeny on his flank smoking a chipped and battered pipe.

The first children they approached were street wise and listened skeptically. "What's the catch?" was usually the first thing out of their mouths.

This is where Joe Sweeny stepped in and pointed his pipe at Matthew. "Do you know who this is? It's Crippled Jack…the marksman. He just won the shooting match at the fairgrounds today. You want to come along. Fine… What do you got to lose? You're hungry and dirty and not a cent between you."

After Matthew acquired a small entourage of cast asides following him it got a lot easier. They moved along at a slow pace as two of their number were on crutches and one in a three wheeled wheelchair.

Sweeny played harmonica, and he took the instrument from his coat pocket and tapped out the saliva, and from there on he riffed up flashy tunes. They were eye grabbers all right liting through the Denver downtown and children came up to them flush with curiosity about where they were marching off to.

Matthew knew the best street corners for begging, the best for scaring up a few pennies by running errands for storekeepers, or loading a wagon, maybe carrying some woman's packages…even where youthful thieves and pickpockets worked their trade. He found children there. And he knew the alleys where poor black kids like those he suffered alongside at Sugarland worked at their survival. These were all the streets of his own past, where he was reprising the tragic dreams of his boyhood that left him heartstricken and empty. But no matter now. Today was all about this little ragtag army of human grievances that knew too well about anguish and mortality.

• • •

On the street behind the Denver theatre was a vacant lot where Mary Jones and the Federation brought food and set blankets on the ground for the children to sit and eat. Mary Jones moved among them, asking about their lives, then she had Matthew follow her to the theatre where they entered through a stage door. There, a white haired attendant silently nodded to her.

She whispered to Matthew, "He's Federation."

She asked Matthew to wait, and she disappeared into a darkness of stage flats and props where a small crew of men awaited.

Once alone, Matthew edged out past the curtains where he could look into the vast interior of the theatre. He had never been in a theatre before. Not a real theatre, anyway. He'd never been close to such beautiful velvet seats and intricately painted scrollwork, never stood beneath a hand carved ceiling and awe worthy chandeliers.

His first thought, oddly enough, was that his clothes were too filthy for those seats. It was then Mary came up alongside him. She was cleaning her glasses with a white cloth and spoke to him cautiously so as not to be overheard.

"You're to have the children at the stage door at seven. That attendant will guide you in. You and Joe must be quick and steady."

Matthew nodded.

"A number of theatre hands will guard the stage. If something or anything should befall me...I want you to take my place."

To say Matthew looked shocked would be an understatement.

"You know what has to be said...Do so for as long as you can."

"I'm na' able ta'."

"I don't give a tinker's curse about being able...it's being willing that matters."

CHAPTER 60

After the children were fed, Mary gathered them up and explained what were her intentions, and how they may be able to help their own cause.

Things happened quickly after that. Matthew led them across the street to the stage door with Sweeny herding up the stragglers. This night was special and the theatre would be flush with newspapermen. It was a political fundraiser for the mayor, who was an anti-union advocate of the first order. The evening's entertainment was to be a burlesque of *The Pirates of Penzance* titled *Beadle's Pirates for Ten Cents*. It was based on Beadle's western dime novel series of the same name. And so the costuming, for that evening's show, was western attire.

Having seen the costumed cast of characters milling about backstage Matthew understood clearly why Mary Jones had chosen this night, this show, for her assault on the system. It would give her and the children a fighting chance to get to and on the stage, and to make her case before the powers that be brought her down.

The white haired attendant gave Matthew the nod and here he came through the stage door, the children filing along behind him like God's own little troopers.

Matthew heard the stage manager say to the attendant, "Who the hell are these kids?"

And the attendant, calm of purpose, answered, "Guests of the mayor, for a few words he means to say to the audience...before the show."

Before tomorrow came dawning up, that old man would be without a job...for sure, so thought Matthew.

Matthew and Sweeny got the children lined up and packed in behind the curtain. Mary Jones appeared from the shadowy flats of bygone plays and took her place with the children. She motioned for the stagehands who were with her to begin their task.

Matthew could hear the call of those creaking rope pulleys as the heavy cloth drapes began to slowly spread apart, and he was suddenly looking beyond the footlights and into a world of finery, wealth, and prominence. The theatergoers had been politely whispering among themselves up to then, but when the curtain was fully open to expose this cast of impover-ished children it was as if they had been all struck mute at the same thorny moment.

"Dear Ladies and Gentlemen of America," said Mary Jones. "I'd like to introduce you to the children of another America. One that lives and dies in the shadows of your good fortune."

There was a growing murmur among the audience. People now stood to see better, to try and understand how this could have happened. They were as much enraged as they were shocked.

"These children are in desperate need of help...and why?" said the woman. "Because their families are in desperate need of help."

Matthew saw a man running up the aisle toward the entrance and knew the mayor was in the lobby lording his achievements to a cadre of the press. It wouldn't be long now before the stage would be overwhelmed with police and security.

Mary Jones held up a piece of rich cloth.

"This cloth that makes the beautiful dresses and fine coats that you wear was woven in the mills here, built alongside the mines and the found-ries. It was woven by children like these. And do you know why they work in the mills instead of going to school and being educated? Because their fathers, who work in the mines and the mills and the smelters, are not given a livable wage. And do you know who owns those mines—"

There were now boos and catcalls from the seats. People standing, demanding she get off stage. There was applause and someone in the bal-cony cupped her hands around her mouth and shouted, "Let her speak!"

Mary Jones walked over to one of the children—a little girl—and led her to the edge of the footlights. "This girl, this child, helped make that cloth until she was maimed in an accident."

She held up the girl's hand that was missing three fingers. "She was then put to the street," said Mary Jones. "Where she can beg...or prosti-tute herself."

Matthew saw the theatregoers had had enough. Those in the front seats were already standing and starting out, their comments now more derogatory, their expressions more sullen, vexed, exasperated.

The mayor had entered the theatre, followed by members of the Denver police and a string of newspapermen scrambling to get as close to the stage as possible.

"You can walk out, you can walk away," shouted Mary Jones. "But these children will still be here. You are creating an underclass of destitution."

Someone just beyond the footlights shouted Mary Jones was an agitator and fanatic.

"I am both," she said. "And remember this. Your heritage or hard work may have gotten you as far as those seats, but you will need a soul to get any further."

The Denver police muscled their way up the stage steps, arresting workmen who were silently with the Federation and who had been holding them at bay. Backstage was chaos. Actors everywhere, in costume and confusion, being herded like sheep by hard case officers of the law while pleading innocence. The Mayor's private security team took Mary Jones by force but she kept right on fighting the cause, defying their attempts to silence her, or the theatregoers denouncing her. She was a fever nowhere near breaking.

And in those seconds, only a few seconds as it turned out, watching this slight woman manhandled then handcuffed, Matthew stepped forward, leaving the children to Sweeny, pressing through the mob of stagehands and sheriffs… And choking on his own reticence, did as Mary Jones had requested.

He walked to the edge of the stage and stood in the hard glow of the footlights, its shadows breaking over his cheekbones, eyes looking like liquid glass. Feeling naked and exposed he entered into the story of his own life, shouting toward the aisles that were packed with theatregoers who had come by invitation and were done with the whole damn spectacle, but who could not help but stop and take in this threatening eyesore with his halting speech and rifle slung over a shoulder. Who in raw detail told the people how he'd been tied up as a child by his poverty stricken parents and left in the desert as a child to die…because he refused to beg.

He said much more than that, and much worse, at one point calling the people there leeches because they had, with all their finery and wealth, come to this—whatever they wanted to call it—to grab a little gratis from the mayor by playing the part of his loyal and dedicated servants, while those children on the stage were left to rot.

Matthew remembered little that followed his harsh condemnations, as he was beaten over the head with the barrel of a policeman's pistol until he was left unconscious and bleeding by the footlights.

PART FOUR

PART FOUR

CHAPTER 61

Nola stepped from the train in Leadville in her filthy men's clothes and was greeted with bad news. A handful of troops from the state militia were stationed on the platform.

She went up to a young recruit and excused herself. "What is going on?" she said.

"Agitators," he said, as if it were a secret. "We're watching for agitators."

He was staring her up and down as he said this.

"Really," she said. "And if I might ask…what does an agitator look like?"

• • •

Chestnut Street was at the heart of downtown Leadville. Busy, dusty, with a long run of shops and businesses and from there you could see all the way up to Fryer Hill, where the mines were hammered into the earth. There was a lot of sidewalk traffic along Chestnut and endless freight wagons. The address Nola hunted for was where Chestnut mated up with Harrison Street.

The house was well back from the wide slat sidewalk and a wall of honeysuckle. They too were heavily powdered with road dust. The two story clapboard wasn't much to look at, but it had been recently whitewashed and it had a friendly looking screen porch. One other thing about it—it was a mere hundred yards or so from a slight rise of ground where there was a smelter. The goddamn smoke the stacks kicked out turned the air black and the runoff down the hillface looked like blood that had rusted over.

Nola knocked on the door and waited for what seemed an eternity. She half caught some movement out of the corner of an eye—the closed window curtain most probably. It wasn't much after that the front door opened and there stood a woman with a hard straight face and arched black eyebrows. She wore a simple dark frock and Nola guessed her age to be somewhere in her late thirties.

The woman looked over the girl who stood before her in those grubby clothes and bearing a carpetbag.

"What, may I ask," said the woman, "are you?"

Nola offered the woman an envelope as a way of answering.

"If you're Harriet Bloom...this is for you."

The woman looked at the envelope with an aloof stare and took in the matter.

"Good tidings...or bad?" said Harriet.

"You'll have to judge that for yourself," said Nola.

Harriet Bloom opened the letter with long, slender fingers and her eyebrows expressively rose as she read.

"It appears to be both," said Harriet. And folding up the letter, she said, "Come in."

The two women sat at a table on the screened porch and drank coffee. Harriet Bloom seemed a very composed woman and spoke with a life informed manner.

"You know, around here I'm called the Jew."

"Yes," said Nola.

"And it isn't a form of endearment."

Nola said she knew that also. Mary Jones had given the girl a pretty complete history of the Blooms. The father had been a prospector, a drunken scrapper and a gambler. He had made a fortune and would have lost it all, but for a wife who served as his accountant. She had enough sense to buy up most of the property on Chestnut Street and put it in trust for their daughter. The father had died in a drunken fall from a brothel rooftop. And the mother—

"My mother is in a Denver madhouse," said Harriet. "You know that, I'm sure."

Nola nodded slightly that she did.

"She was a sparrow in a world of hawks, Mother was." Harriet reached for a whiskey bottle on the table and laced her coffee good and proper with it. "They say the madhouse is where I'm headed. But not soon enough for the bastards around here that have to pay me rent. But I intend to fool them all."

She drank down that coffee without pausing for a breath.

"You can have the bedroom on this floor," she said. "It's back behind the kitchen. Privacy...Unfortunately you'll have to wake up to that loud and filthy scene." She was pointing at the smelter. "The Harrison Reduction Works. When Harrison put up that excrescence, he made this city. Made it…and ruined it."

Harriet grew quiet. Contemplative. Took to looking out the screen toward that industrial monstrosity.

"Are you the type of person that suffers themselves?" Harriet said.

"I don't believe so," said Nola. "I hope not anyway."

A couple of men were coming from the smelter and decided to shortcut it through Harriet's backyard. They weren't laborers. Too nattily dressed. Management, maybe. Maybe salesmen or corporate reps.

"Keep off my goddamn property," Harriet shouted. "You prissy bastards. You hear me?!"

Her tone was ugly. The men looked about to see where this tirade was coming from and finally settled on the screen porch.

"That's right. It's 'the Jew.' 'The madwoman.' Now get off my property you weak willed shits."

One of the men actually gave her the finger and what she shot back at them, Nola, in her life, had never heard from a woman, and hardly even from a man. Harriet threatened their lives with one bloodthirsty scenario after another and she sounded in a way one might mistake for madness.

When the men were finally gone Harriet turned to her guest and winked.

"They'll be talking me up tonight in the bars," said Harriet. "I can promise you that."

CHAPTER 62

Nola Dye was to meet with Neihart the following day. She sat at a desk in the tiny bedroom where she would sleep. She was jotting down notes and questions to be asked but her mind was unwilling. She had received a wire at Western Union about the "incident" at the Palace Theatre, and the beatings and arrests of members of the Federation. Mary Jones' name was mentioned, along with one other—the marksman known as Crippled Jack.

Nola stared out into the night to where the smelter furnaces looked like huge open mouths of fire, ready and willing to feed on you.

She began to cry because she could not escape feelings that had power and authority over her. Her humanity was in a struggle with hard moments, and how this would play out she could barely imagine.

Then, there was a knock at the door. Quiet and gentle as it had been, it nonetheless startled Nola.

"Come in," she said.

She was wiping her eyes as the door opened and there in the backwash of the hallway light stood a shadowed Harriet.

"I knew it," said the woman.

"Knew what?"

"You *are* one of those people that suffers themselves."

Harriet stepped into the room, looked at the desk with its sheets of paper and a notebook spread out, floating there almost in a sea of candlelight. But what caught her eye? A strip of fine writing paper with Nola Dye's name written on it in script.

"What is this?" said Harriet.

"I don't know."

"Well said," said Harriet. "You want to speak out on what's got you?"

Nola dragged a bit before answering. "There is nothing more helpless than feeling helpless."

"Except," said Harriet, "actually being helpless. And I have something for that."

From her robe, Harriet took out a pistol and set it on the desk. It was a pocket Colt with a spur trigger. A nickel plated .22 with a pearl handle.

166

A present from her father long ago.

"Perfect for a purse, or frock pocket," said Harriet. "Every woman should carry one…especially here, especially now…especially you."

• • •

Officers of the mining companies, the handful of major operations that dominated the scene, had organized to meet at the Clarendon Hotel. It was a three story frame structure on Harrison Street. Some of the owners kept suites there for parties and assignations, and also because the building was beside Western Union and the A.T. & S.F. Railroad freight and ticket office.

They took over the entire dining room, shut the doors and stationed a Pinkerton security team at each entry. Representatives for the Little Pittsburg were there, the Little Chief, the Robert E. Lee, the Morning Star, the Americanus. Most of the smaller mining operations had sold out because of the recession, or what they most feared—a long strike that would cause a catastrophic tumble in stock prices.

The discussion went pretty much as Neihart expected. Miners working above ground were pulling in just under two dollars a day. Go underground, and it was three bucks plus change. And that was for a ten hour workday. Rumor had it what Mary Jones and the Federation might push for was a twenty percent bump in pay and a workday that was eight hours.

The owners were not afraid of the miners, or the Federation, or Mary Jones for that matter. They could, and would, wipe them off the face of the map if it came down to that. What they were afraid of was a prolonged shutdown and how that might damage their stock prices in what was rapidly becoming a recession.

There was no consensus on how best to handle the situation. A delegation would have to be enlisted to at least sit with the Federation and go through the motions of conciliation.

After having sat there silently for so long Neihart offered a thought, one that was at the back of everyone's tongue, "Decrease wages…increase hours…across the board. And do so…immediately."

The Colonel could not fathom he was hearing what he had. Neihart wanted to put the owners immediately on war footing. That was a place everyone was prepared to get to, but only if every other means of destroying the workman's will had been played out. Neihart was walking the plank alone pushing for such immediate action, and with his own future about to go belly up.

Or was it?

The Colonel had no chance for a private moment and when he left the hotel with Neihart they faced a mob of off shift laborers from the mines, foundries, and smelters. Their language and insults were "colorful" to say the least. As for the threats—

But outside the hotel there were Pinkertons who went about the wholesale business of stilling the mob with stark efficiency.

Watching the crowd be dispersed from the quiet distance was Nola Dye. Neihart saw her, but did not acknowledge her. She was there, as he knew she would be. The fool clothed as the well meaning reporter.

CHAPTER 63

After the meeting at the hotel, Neihart and Gheen were driven back to the mine in the company Phaeton. Neihart had a steadfast rule of never talking business where faceless employees could eavesdrop. At Fryer Hill, he ordered the driver to pull over. The two men stood alone by the side of the road where the ground had been turned to mush over years of horse and wagon tracks.

From where they stood, the men could look out upon the hills, covered as they were with an armada of mine structures. Monolithic beasts and their smaller progeny, born of rain and sun ruined boards, the earth all around them carved up for its ore, and where long funnels of black smoke from the stacks marked its passing.

"Go ahead," said Neihart. "I see you've been burning to get it off your chest."

"What were you thinking back there?"

"About how to save the Americanus."

"And you intend to by—"

"Starting a war?" said Neihart. "Absolutely."

"I'm exhausted, Nathan. Living with our investors grinding me about money and stock prices and the dividend that never arrives and having to try and explain your secretive and outrageous ideas."

"I can explain myself, thank you very much. But I have an even more satisfactory idea. I will buy them and you…out."

The Colonel was uncertain over this turn. He moved around a bit, almost lost. He stared out into the littered landscape that had bled profit for years.

Neihart could see that beady little brain in operation.

"Why would you do that?" said the Colonel.

Neihart glared at him. He repeated what the Colonel had said, and he was absolutely condescending.

"I can't be sure if you're being serious," said the Colonel. "But…let's suppose for a moment you are. What…what would be the price?"

"You're not even good at being obvious."

"I don't need to be insulted."

"Oh, but you do, Colonel. You need to be insulted very definitely. The price...wherever the market is at the close of the day we agree to the deal. So, you have some wiggle room."

The Colonel ran his fingers along the rim of his short collar. A wagon passed, loaded down with ore for the smelter. Its passing was loud and heavy with strain. "Today," he said, "the market closed at nine dollars a share, down two from its high water mark at eleven and change."

"And six dollars and forty plus cents a share above our initial public offering price. Or simply put...where even an idiot can pass for a king."

The Colonel was utterly resentful, because he knew he was being handled by a master manipulator.

"I can list all the questions," said Neihart, "that you're asking yourself. Would he really do this? And why? Where will he get the money? Does he have it? Can he secure a line of credit or a loan from some silent partner? Does he just want us out? Or...is there some scheme behind him wanting us out?"

Neihart pushed his hands down into his pockets and looked out at all the mines.

"You'd like to stay in," said Neihart, "on the chance there's something...but you want to get out before the collapse of a dying mine. There's just one issue. By what standard do you measure your own greed?"

Neihart was about to start back over to the Phaeton, but one last thought came to him. "If...you notify our partners...don't go through Western Union. They've got telegraphers in that office that have gotten rich leaking information like this."

CHAPTER 64

Mary Jones was released from jail that very evening with all charges dropped. She and members of the Federation were escorted out of town by deputy sheriffs and put on the road west. This was by order of the mayor, and more about just plain old-fashioned self preservation than an act of social justice. Newspapermen followed the entourage to the city limits where Mary Jones addressed the press with a few choice words.

Her destination was Leadville, home to the bare knuckle fight that was about to take place, that could turn the West into the killing capital of the world. She went on to tell them that American social history had many facets, and endless faces. And that the unionization of the West was much the same as the classic battles between the homesteader and the big ranches. The mine worker, the foundry hand, the day laborer—they were the homesteader. And the Lords of Industry, they were the big ranchers. The battle was not over grazing land and barbed wire fences, but the hourly wage and length of the workday, child labor laws and health insurance.

And there were two other things they had in common—bloodshed and injustice.

Matthew was detained in jail overnight on charges of disturbing the peace, assaulting a deputized official, brandishing a weapon in a public theatre, and inciting a riot. He had to face a judge the following morning. He should have been made to serve a short jail term, but the mayor sent word a fine and release would best serve the city. Sweeny had been left behind to pay the fines and make sure Matthew exited Denver in one piece.

Matthew did not understand why he had been freed until he stepped out into all that Denver sunshine. There was quite a crowd out front. Not only a few hundred poor street kids and curious adults to see the strange creature who had been written about known as Crippled Jack, but there were also dozens of black members of the United Brotherhood of Friendship.

Knowingly or not, Matthew had made news because a number of the raggedy homeless children he had brought on stage were black.

And that in and of itself was a shocking act. Denver, like most towns in the West, had racist mood swings. The good citizenry, in one of those transforming moments, had burned down their Chinatown. Destroyed its homes and businesses. And there was also a little matter of a lynching. The blacks, in turn, were made to live out on Cherokee Creek, where they could entertain a view of the city dump.

The United Brotherhood was led by a black gentleman named Reverend Titus. He had organized to have his photograph taken on the courthouse steps of himself and Matthew shaking hands with the United Brotherhood allied behind them. While the photographer got his shot, they were laid into with endless insults and threats that were not just limited to male members of the citizenry.

And while all this went on the good Reverend told Matthew, "I, like yourself, have survived the hospitality of Sugarland. I was there after you. And endless times have I heard the story of the fire and escape and Red… and the incident on the road with the Brotherhood."

"Reverin'… God got one lon' reach."

"He's reaching out now, son…Word is out on you."

• • •

It was true, all right, as Reverend Titus could attest. A janitor at the courthouse had thankfully picked up a scrap of conversation coming from one of the mayor's private offices, that if there was an attempt on the cripple's life, it must happen outside the city limits, otherwise it might prove to be too political. Word was that he was heading west to Leadville to join the rest of those America haters. Corporate spies would be watching the ticket offices and train depot, but that the County Road was also a likely route of exit and that any murder should be made to look like the work of road agents.

Matthew and Sweeny were brought out to the black neighborhood along Cherokee Creek for their protection and were given a good meal while a plan was put together to send them on their way.

They were in sight and smell of the city dump and what looked to Sweeny's sorely poor vision like the flight of fleeting birds was actually nothing more than trash being carried on the wind across the rooftops. This told Matthew that Sweeny would be of little help in anything beyond a street brawl.

From across the creek Vandel watched through field glasses the comings and goings of the good Reverend and his flock of black sheep. The cripple and that beer keg of a miner with him being treated like genuine gents pissed him off capital. McSorley was practically breathing down Vandel's neck with another pair of field glasses and the smell of garbage a misery all its own. Tobin and Fry were spread out behind them, searching out any sign their prey was kicking it out of there.

Vandel was sure they wouldn't leave Denver by train or coach, so the others knew better than dare to disagree as Vandel had a habit of being right, even when he was wrong.

It got to be close of day. Those cool shadows taking over, stripping away every detail, except that which was at the heart of a hanging lamp, or table lantern.

Blacks came, blacks went. On horseback, by buckboard or flatbed. Among them a few whites, to their social disgrace.

The four kept watching, that was until Vandel spoke out. "Notice anything? Any of you?" He set aside the field glasses and eyed the men critically. "The silence of stupidity," he said.

The men looked among themselves, trying not to seem like they'd come up short.

"The gypsy wagon that just left," he said.

The photographer who had taken the pictures on the courthouse steps. He drove a gypsy wagon, with gaudy advertisements hand-painted on the sides of it. A kind of wooden boxy thing you could travel in, live in, and would serve as a darkroom.

Vandel pointed. There it was, on a road that cut through the city dump, being pulled by two large draft horses. You could barely make out the wagon with the dusk dying off the way it was, and the trash swirling around it.

CHAPTER 65

"They're in the fuckin' wagon," said Vandel.

"You saw them?" said McSorley.

"I don't need to see them. I see the fuckin' wagon."

They mounted up and followed off into the night the gypsy wagon at a distance. It trundled over the railroad tracks, then turned off the County Road and started southwest toward Bear Creek with only the moonlight now and the stars and the dark half wild mountains, and they knew Vandel had been right. And what sewed it up, the back door of the wagon opened and there in the light of a swaying lantern and standing on the top step was Crippled Jack. He was undoing his trousers with Sweeny clasping the back of the kid's coat so he wouldn't fall into the sand roadway while he took a piss.

Vandel knew the country well and pressed his men hard after that. The hooves of their mounts clattering down through rocky switchbacks and across traces of hard scrabble and along pined hillsides. He meant to get well ahead of the wagon and lay into it at a place of his own choosing.

He had in mind a stretch of road just beyond a covered bridge that crossed Bear Creek at the county line. A dark and isolated place and deeply treed, where gunshots could not be heard by any living man for miles.

They forded the creek down from the bridge and came up shoshing over the rocks, their horses trying to snort and shake the wet from their muzzles. Vandel had his men dismount. Tobin was to take the horses well back into the woods and keep them damn well quiet. McSorley and Fry would cover one side of the road, Vandel the other.

The moonshine shadows had barely moved before they heard the slow approach of harness metal and the wheels of the gypsy wagon and hooves of the draft horses on the bridge planking. The rhythm of those sounds changed as the wagon slowed before it passed through the bridge archway and into the night.

It had come up the road a short piece before the driver reined in his team. Vandel's men, now hidden behind bandanas, were to take no action until Vandel ordered them to do so.

The driver was a little man of faded youth carrying a bucket filled with water, and while he let the animals drink, a pistol was suddenly pressed against the base of his skull.

Vandel whispered, "Keep silent now or I'll separate you from your spine. And hold these damn leads tight to keep your animals still."

Vandel motioned to his men to surround the gypsy wagon on three sides. Vandel got down into a kneeling position facing the wagon door and aiming his Winchester, he called out, "You got visitors, boy."

He opened fire. And his men followed suit.

It was a full-throated barrage of rifle fire and shotgun blasts. The gypsy wagon being torn apart, the boarding splintered, the windows blown out. The air around the wagon a gray dense smoke of endless round after round, until the board slats were a pox of holes.

And when the shooting finally stilled and the gypsy wagon barely hung together, Vandel walked through the smoke and kicked the door from the last hinge that held it dangling.

He peered inside and was greeted with a world of ruined emptiness.

"They're not in here," he shouted.

He came rushing around the wagon to confront the driver, but he was nowhere to be seen. Vandel yelled for Tobin to bring on the horses.

CHAPTER 66

The night there on the road took a predacious turn. Vandel had his men stay still and within the boundaries of smoke that drifted on the air. Tobin joined them, leading the horses on foot. McSorley whispered to Vandel, "They coulda got out of the wagon anywhere."

Vandel thought back to those few moments when he heard the wheels slow down on the bridge considerably. He ordered his men to fan out and keep to the trees.

He fired off a handful of rounds at the bridge with his Winchester. The gunshots carried, and then all he was left with was a covered bridge, quiet and motionless as a coffin.

He got Fry's attention with the wave of his rifle and pointed the barrel toward the bridge. Fry started down one side of the road while Vandel took the other. He whispered to McSorley as he passed him to watch for flashes of gunfire.

The bridge was old and sagged a bit at the shoulders and was missing slats in the boarding and roof where slivers of moonlight slipped through. The closer the men got to the structure the more ghostly it felt, as if this were some gateway for the nameless and dead.

Fry had just passed into the frame of the archway when there came one punishing strike from a rifle. The shot wrenched him about and Vandel yelled for his men to scatter, and that they did, firing wildly as they went.

Fry tried to stand and was shot again and went to his knees trying to grit away the pain as he retrieved a pistol from his gun belt.

Vandel yelled to McSorley, "Where are the shots coming from?"

"Don't know," said McSorley.

Vandel shouted over the gunfire, "Useless fool."

Fry was on his knees when he was shot again, a shot that drove him face down onto the roadway. The gun that he held lost from his grasp. He was pleading for help now and trying to crawl. But crawling was useless as he was too badly wounded, and as far as pleading, what good it did was none at all. He would die there alone in the company of men who claimed him a friend but could not give a damn.

Once Fry had pleaded out the last of his blood and his own people saw him there decorating the roadway, from somewhere in the pall that had fallen over Bear Creek there came the willful tune on a harmonica playing, of all things, "Silent Night."

Vandel and the others started throwing shots in the direction they thought from where the music came. Flashes of gunfire fell upon the landscape and like bitter magic it was all silent suddenly.

That pall settled in again. Vandel and his men hung back by the gypsy wagon ever watchful and waiting. Then there was that harmonica, only this time it was a jaunty rendition of "Blow the Man Down." Gunfire frayed the trees along the creek and by the covered bridge, but to no avail.

The music finally stopped. And again that pall settled in.

"Why you grubby, detestable little shits," said Vandel.

He scanned the darkness with the care of a cat.

"You crippled nightshooter."

His eyes fell upon a patch of cottonwoods. Maybe there? He kept watching, but no trace of shadows broke his way.

Staring into a world of baleful trees and wild brush, he shouted, "Come on, boy...You and me...Coffin Maker to Coffin Maker. Yeah... That's right. I know...You know...We all know who you are."

Vandel started for his mount. The other two fell in line behind him. Vandel's mouth burned. All that was deadly in man exacerbated what was physically wrong with him from the wound. He spit a foul tasting pus mixture away. He wiped his beard with a dirty rag, then mounted his horse.

He looked back toward the bridge. He was staring into a world of dark misgivings, and the soul of it was staring back at him.

You could hear the creek now, the strands of it running over the rocks. Making its way, but to where?

"You're a dead man, Crippled Jack...only you don't know it yet." Vandel's mount began to anxiously turn, sniffing at something in the air. Vandel had to hold the animal still, as he was not yet finished. "You can hear me, Jack. And I want you to know. You came too late, boy...and you stayed too long."

CHAPTER 67

Nola was asleep, yet not asleep. She felt something she could not place. Even with the room dark and the shades drawn a slip of light from the smelters was creeping in through a crease around the edges of the shade.

Something was wrong, something unexplainable closing in. By the time she realized someone had entered her room it was too late. A nest of shadows became two, no, three men she could not place. Yet she had seen them before, or so she thought.

A hand pinned against her mouth. She was being bound and gagged. She struggled with fury, a fury she did not know she possessed.

But it did nothing to stay what was happening to her. She fought her way upright for a moment before she was hit across the face.

She felt she was smothering. She was being carried on someone's shoulder through the night. She could sense the cool damp air. She was being taken up a hill. She could hear the heavy breathing of the man carrying her. Or was that her own breathing?

In the next moment she felt this incredible wave of heat that was like a terrible omen of some kind. She could feel the force of the heat climbing up her back and wrapping around her throat. She struggled like a dying person struggles to escape her death and in doing so saw the heat was coming from an open blast furnace in the smelter. The flames so hot, so bright, one had to close their eyes and turn away or be blinded. And then a man's voice said, "Throw her in."

• • •

Nola sat on the porch in the dark, drinking coffee. She could not clear her mind of the dream. She did not try to put the dream out of her mind… because the dream was part of her. It was in part her past, and in part her future.

"He's dangerous."

Nola turned to see Harriet coming into the room in her nightslip.

"Who?" said Nola.

Harriet touched the coffee pot, felt it was hot, got a mug and poured herself some.

"Who?" Nola repeated.

"You always get up this early?"

"Only when I can't sleep."

Harriet sipped from the steaming mug, looked out toward the hilltop smelter. The dawn edging up behind it was beautiful and made what she was looking at even more of a lie.

"Makes you rich, makes you sick," said Harriet.

"What?"

"All of it out there," she said. "It's like going from a wedding to a funeral in the same dress, and on the same day."

"That's awfully cynical of you."

"You haven't seen cynical…yet."

"You didn't answer my question."

"I thought it obvious."

"I'd like you to be more obvious…if you please."

"Neihart, of course."

"Really?"

"Even when he's being charming and decent. Particularly then."

"In all cases, in all situations?"

"Beyond all civility."

"How are you so sure?"

Harriet took another sip of coffee and with pure dispassion, said, "I used to fuck him."

This earned Nola's silence.

"That crass enough for you?" said Harriet.

"As compared to what?"

"You can never be crass enough when crass is the subject."

Nola had dressed in her shabby men's clothes since she was going down into the Americanus as a guest of Nathan Neihart. An offer, she had been told, afforded to no other reporter, and certainly not another woman.

When she left the house Harriet was standing at the edge of the sidewalk. She was watching about two dozen women slowly marching up the street and passing out fliers. They were led by a man beating a drum he had slung from a strap over his shoulder. Two women carried a banner made of sheet cloth on long posts. On it was written: *SHE IS COMING!*

179

Most of the citizens in Leadville knew who "*SHE*" was, and what that meant. They knew so well, in fact, one gent with a horn toad face came out into the street from an alley carrying a bucket of slop and doused the women with that foul mixture of excrements. He then tipped his hat and wished them well.

"You know what they say up here on the Hill?"

Nola did not.

"How soon before the water barrels fill with blood?"

"Will it get that bad?"

Harriet answered with a gruff and cold hearted laugh. Then she offered Nola one last little bit of advice before the girl trudged off on her quest.

"Make sure Neihart doesn't have you accidentally killed down there."

After that remark, Nola said, "Could I pose you a question?"

"For certain," said Harriet.

"How come Mary Jones sent me to you?"

"Charm...I ooze charm and good humor."

"I see."

"She sent you here because there's only two people that Nathan fears might do him in. One is Gould, of the railroad...the other is me."

CHAPTER 68

The mines on Fryer Hill looked like fortress slums of boarding and tin sheets. One structure heaped up on the backs of the last. The earth stripped bare from a distance was now the color of shit from the tailings. The smoke coming out of the building stacks bitter and gritty. The Americanus was a few hills' walk and the manager's office just spitting distance from the hoist house.

From the filthy office window Neihart watched the miners coming on and off shift give Nola a looking over, and not all of it good. She was a curious specimen trudging along in those grubby clothes to become the brunt of stale wise cracks.

"Our guest is approaching," said Neihart.

"Nathan...do you think this prudent?"

Nathan glared at his Operations Chief, who sat at his desk, ever the gentleman.

"Well, Jonah," said Neihart, "prudent means to show care and thought for the future. Which is what I am doing."

The Colonel could not contain his anxiety and rose from his seat by the window. "Why don't you just tell her you've changed your mind. That it isn't safe."

"Won't that sound like exactly what it sounds like?"

"And what is that?"

"We don't want her going down in the mine."

"Nathan...I picked up a rumor," said Jonah. "There is to be a massive selloff of stock...that we are having trouble raising money."

Nathan looked to the Colonel. "Can you believe that?" he said. Then addressing Jonah, "That's just so much competitors' sleight of hand to try and damage us. Especially in this market."

"And if she starts asking questions about that?" said the Colonel.

"You defer all such matters to me."

"What about this?" said the Operations Chief, holding a draft of a letter to the workers, that management had to take a compulsory dollar a month from their wages to pay for insurance.

"They're always screaming for insurance," said Neihart.

"Not with them paying," said the Colonel.

"I don't feel this is the right time," said Jonah. "Not with that woman coming to Leadville. And the Federation. What's going on in the street. You don't want to trigger a fight."

The door opened and Nola entered. The men had become curiously silent, and that she picked up on.

Neihart made the introductions. Nola had already met Colonel Gheen, much to her dissatisfaction, and he was wearing the same expression.

"And this," said Neihart, "is my Chief of Operations...Jonah Smalls."

The man politely stood. He was white haired with a thick moustache just as white. He was sixty with a faded white shirt and vest, the image of a gentleman on the tired outside of life.

Neihart ran through Smalls' curriculum vitae, which she thought strange at first, but finally understood.

"Jonah is Harvard," said Neihart. "Law degree. Degree from Yale... Engineering. Taught there. But all that was back in the seventeen hundreds. He's had every job in the mining industry. Started below ground... Owned his own mine, once upon a time...But as luck and skill would have it. People say he's the most accomplished man on the Hill...Can you believe that...And that I am lucky to have him working for me."

Neihart was praising Jonah and demeaning him at the same time. Shaming him in a most profound way. For whatever reason, she could only guess. Maybe the one thing Neihart felt he had over Smalls was money.

She followed Neihart into the head frame tower as a crew of miners at end of the shift were coming out the corrugated doors. Exhausted and filthy men who could not help but stare to be sure of what they saw.

Inside the hollow structure was a large cage that hung from steel cables up to a pulley system. The cage sat over a hole, a dark cored out cavity that went deep, deep into the earth. The machinery in the housing was very loud and Neihart had to get close to Nola to be heard.

"It's a long, long way down," he said. "The cage rattles. The cage gets stuck sometimes. In places it can be very, very dark. And the air is dusty and thin, and it becomes hard to breathe. And I would be lying if I said you can't die down there, because you can."

CHAPTER 69

She tried to prepare herself for the fear. She had posed the full arc of imaginary dangers, facing them with quiet conviction. But standing there, confronting the cage and that bleak hole for her descent, she was stripped of all strength. Her head swam, her body shook with anxiety. She wanted to run, to escape this self-imposed threat. This moment was the dream, just as it was parts of other dreams that had been and were yet to be.

And there was Neihart in the cage, waiting patiently. He wanted her down there for a reason and she reasoned it was to exploit her somehow. And she hoped God would do her one little right—that she be able to keep her utter distress to herself.

She stepped into the cage and when Neihart set it in motion the enclosure made this clumsy jerk and as she grabbed for the wire meshing Neihart said, "It's all right."

She was quickly engulfed in dark and an air growing more oppressive and the odd sounds the machinery made, and on all sides of her the tomb-like bowels of the earth. Earth you could smell and taste.

Then a sudden rush of light and they passed the first tunnel. She could see into it for yards. Dust and ore wagons and men picking away at the stone. You could hear the steely chiseling of those hard rock men.

And then it was dark again and you were going deeper, the dense air pressing against her chest and the cage shaking. They passed the skip hoist weight, pulling the cage down as it rose. Another bloom of light and they were down on the second level of the mine. The dust thicker, harsher, men waiting for their turn at the cage. A mule there the color of a ghost from so much dust. Its eyelids weary with dust. The purity of the animal gone forever.

Again the dark.

Neihart handed her a bandana. "Put this on," he said.

She did as he said.

There was another swash of light and the cage slowed, and then the light opened like a dusky fog and the cage came to an abrupt stop and she could feel the bile flood up into her throat.

"We're here," said Neihart.

He opened the cage door and stepped into the last and deepest of the tunnels. She followed him down a long passage of stone and earth buttressed by timbers. Dust dripping in fine columns from the roof like sands in the hourglass.

She passed ore wagons pulled by mules and the endless chisel and hammer of men so beyond self-regard, dark eyed and cadaverous who could only gaze at this passing woman as if she were something otherworldly.

After that, the tunnel got smaller, tighter. There were just eyelets of floating lanterns at the entries to hives where children chiseled away the rock.

Neihart explained, "New tunnels. Too small yet for full grown men."

She could see the boys were little bigger than the picks they carried. They would be old and used up before they'd even tasted manhood.

Neihart came to a place at the end of the tunnel that had been boarded off. He pointed to where Nola could see between the slats. There were cutaways in the rock, small sections burrowed out where a man could just crawl in.

"An engineer next week comes to evaluate what kind of ore deposits there are. Then we'll know if the Americanus has a future or not. I'm sure you'd like to be here for that moment."

"Yes," she said, through her bandana. "I would appreciate that opportunity."

"You can write what you will about what you've seen. But I have a question I'd like you to address, any way that you want."

"Ask," she said.

"The unions want power to decide the fate of their workers…and the industry. If they get such power, who is to watch over them? Who is to see they are not corrupt, corrupted, or corrupting? It isn't their money that built the system, created the jobs, they just want the system to treat them as if it was."

He started away, but one more thought was lurking there.

"Who is to watch over you, Miss Dye? And reporters like you? Who is to keep you in check? Whose moral imperative do you really serve?"

CHAPTER 70

When she stepped out into the sunlight it was like a Bible camp out there. The workers above ground and those coming off shift were gathered up and their anger and outrage was no secret and directed at the operations office. They all had fliers that seemed to be at the heart of the matter and Nola asked if she might see one.

It was an issuance from management that one dollar per month would be garnished from the miners' wages to pay for health insurance. It was, in effect, a de facto wage cut, and those working above ground, who were paid less, would be losing a greater percentage of their wage. An act that even a child understood seeded disharmony among the workers.

"I saw you with Neihart."

Nola turned to face a short chinned laborer with this murky stare.

"You were down in the mine with that bastard. What's he got some woman being down there?"

"I'm a reporter," she said.

This netted the men's interest who were around her. A declaratory hand pointed at her. A voice raised, "This one was down in the mine with Neihart."

A voice behind her said, "What's he let a reporter down there for?"

"I want to tell people what it's like to work in a mine. So they'll have a better—"

"And Neihart allowed this? Bullshit!"

Uncertainty was now feeding ire. Voices escalating in revolt. A brick was thrown at the operations office and a window shattered. Mine security came hustling out of the office door carrying cudgels and batons.

She was being called a spy for management.

"I am nothing of the sort," she said.

She was told to leave. She did not move fast enough. The miner with the murky stare shoved her and she ended up on the ground.

A couple of men stepped in to stop what was about to become a miscarriage of strength and size. She was advised to go, then flatly ordered.

She was a portrait of baffled innocence. "I only want to—"

She was warned, then threatened. Called a whore for management. She started away. She had become, in effect, the enemy.

CHAPTER 71

Mary Jones and members of the Federation were secreted into Leadville by private stagecoach. Agents for the mine owners knew something was in the works when pro-union forces were gathering at dusk outside the Board of Trade Saloon on Harrison Street. This was one of the city's most prestigious gambling halls and was never short of the town's monied well-to-dos.

There was also an unusual number of reporters milling about. Who had put the word out to them was unclear, as both sides now were in the press warfare business.

When Mary Jones arrived at nightfall she faced a rush of newspapermen with her diehard presence. She was told the infamous Doc Holliday had arrived this same night by train and was in the Board of Trade at that very moment gambling. And did this portend some kind of omen?

"The well known Mister Holliday and I do have something in common," said the labor leader. "We're both bettors. He bets on a set of cards, while I bet on a set of principles."

She stepped up onto the sidewalk, stood before the saloon, and pressed forth on her cause.

"I stand before this gambling hall to show you by way of example… Tonight…here…more money will pass through the hands of patrons than the wages of all the mine workers in Leadville."

She held up a flier. "This flier says that the Americanus intends to charge the already exploited worker for health insurance. Well…I and the Federation are here to tear down the wall of indifference that separates the American worker from a living wage. And that fight begins here."

A reporter shouted, "Where did you get the money that passed through your hands so you can travel by private stagecoach?"

"And so it begins," said Mary Jones. "This is no ordinary knock on the door," she told the mob around her. "What this man means to suggest is that I am corrupt.

"Well…we scrambled and pleaded for donations. We went with hands out. And why? Because we were told of threats made against us by the railroad and the mine owner. And what does that tell you, when such high and mighty men are afraid of a widowed seamstress with bad eyes?"

• • •

Nola had watched quietly from the crowd with Harriet at her side. She had intentionally kept back as she did not want to instigate animosity like that aroused against her at the Americanus.

Mary Jones and the Federation men were getting back into the coach to be taken to a miners' camp near the crest of the hill. They made it known that tomorrow they would lock horns with the Americanus.

Before the coach could clear the crowd a fight broke out in the street. Full-fledged and violent, the kind of fight that could blow an ill wind over the lives of the innocent as well as the guilty.

It got bloody and fast. Men with cudgels, with badges, poor look-ing roughs wielding knives. They were all mixing it up in the throw of streetlamps and store front windows. Neatly dressed women trying to escape this degradation in their heavy dresses were shown no consider-ation. A man was being half kicked to death as he was curled up in the street, another was hit in the face with a bottle, another's hand that held a pistol was being bitten. Someone leapt at the coach door to get in, but was punched and pounded and fell away only to have the coach go over his arm and crush it. Patrons from the gaming hall came streaming out onto the sidewalk to see the melee up close. Some say the whole episode was witnessed by a coolly smiling Doc Holliday, his sickly, frail figure back in the shadows with arms crossed.

Nola knew the truth of this bloodletting, it was all there bold as print. No one would ever be able to actually say who was at fault here. Whose madness came first, whose madness instigated the madness that followed. Each side would entrench in their own rightness, each side would exploit the other for their own practical, political purposes.

And then there was the script of a gunshot and a man's racked cry, and it all took a turn for the worst.

Nola pressed into the crowd where the body lay. People were asking, who fired the shot? Where had the shot come from? Nola saw it was the reporter who had pressed Mary Jones with that singular question. The wound on the side of his head looked like a scoop of bone and brain matter. And the face, too, stained with its own blood. Blood that had leaked over the teeth which were visible because of lips that were pulled back with death.

The man kneeling over the body was a Denver sheriff as far as Nola could tell from the badge.

"It wasn't a pistol shot," he said. "That hole was made from a rifle."

No sooner had the words come out of his mouth than she was stricken by one singular black thought—he's done it.

CHAPTER 72

An uncertain world and its utmost consequences had brought you here, and look what here had become. The boundaries of the story you're reporting on had changed, and so changed how the world sees you, which is as it should be, because you are of the world.

The reporter's death just minutes after asking one question felt of premonition.

Why was he killed?

And what about Matthew?

Will I emerge from this alive?

As the two women walked back to the house they could hear a trail of voices a block over shouting about the murdered newspaperman.

"It will go on like that all night," said Harriet.

"There'll be no peace here now, will there?"

"Sure…after they burn this place to the ground."

Someone yelled their way, "Hey you—"

There was a gang of ruffians carrying whiskey bottles. They were drunk and in a dark mood. One of their number was pointing at Nola.

"I saw you at the mine today. You're one of Neihart's shit bearers."

Nola kept silent.

One of the men flung his bottle at Nola. It missed her barely and shattered against a storefront wall.

"You filthy drunken bastards," said Harriet.

"We come over there, we'll show you how filthy we can be."

"No need," said Harriet. "You hole diggers are all alike. You get drunk, you get angry, you get malicious, then you piss on yourselves and pass out. And I don't think any fuckin' union is gonna help you with that."

If they were going to spew out vulgarities or cross the street and get violent, a half dozen random claps of gunfire quieted them down considerably. They stood there now trying to gauge from where the shots had come, when a man's voice shouting a block or two over served as a marker.

The two women could see the men take off running as they passed under a streetlamp and through an empty lot. They waited on the sidewalk in front of Harriet's house looking up into the quiet menace of the street.

"What do you think?" said Nola.

"I think it best we keep the side of the house that faces the street very dark. After all, honey, they know where you live now, don't they?"

• • •

Nola was cocooned at the writing desk in her room. She had sent off her article—A WOMAN'S JOURNEY INTO A NOTORIOUS MINE—by way of Western Union. Knowing full well that the copy would be in the hands of Neihart by now. And that Western Union may mysteriously lose it in transit. So, as a precaution, she had mailed off one copy, and another went by private courier that Harriet had recommended.

She was drafting an article—THE MURDER OF A LEADVILLE REPORTER—posing the question *Who did it and Why?* An answer she felt in her heart was close at hand when there came a gentle knocking at her bedroom door.

"Come in," said Nola.

Harriet entered, barefoot and in nightclothes. In one hand her fingers clasped a pint bottle of whiskey and two glasses. In the other was a folded up letter. Nola could see the woman had indulged herself already. Harriet set the bottle and glasses on the desk, making sure they were clear of the writings spread out there.

"If you care to," said Harriet. She then poured herself a suitable drink. She saw Nola was eyeing the letter.

"We'll get to that," said Harriet.

Harriet glanced at the curtains, noted they were just a sliver open, and closed them completely.

"I know what the shooting was about," said Harriet.

Nola straightened up in her seat.

"People on the sidewalk. I overheard them."

Harriet scanned Nola's writing as she spoke.

"The shots were fired out front of the *Leadville Pioneer*. A note was left for the managing editor. It was about the murder of the reporter."

She took a drink.

"You're making me wait intentionally."

The woman grinned. "Yes…the note said… 'The Coffin Maker.'"

191

Harriet didn't bother to look at Nola. She did not need to digest her reaction. She knew what it would be. And besides, she was more intent on reading over Nola's notes.

"You wrote down what I told those miners," said Harriet.

"That's right."

"Why?"

"I write down such moments so I might learn about people."

"Did I really say all this?"

"I pride myself on my memory. Which is not always a good thing."

"I'm a nasty soul." She handed Nola the letter she'd brought. "Let's see what you learn from this."

CHAPTER 73

Nola read over the letter. It was a gentlemanly defense of what might well have been a confidence man's exploit. It dealt with the property on the Hill that had become known as the Americanus Mine.

"Your father owned the original shaft?" said Nola.

"Which he sold to Neihart. Who at the time was engaged to his daughter. Somewhere along the way the terms of sale…or partnership… seem to have legally changed. We lost the suit in the courts. But that's not why I'm showing you the letter."

"No…what then?"

"Your powers of observation need sharpening," said Harriet.

She looked over the desk until she found the scrap of writing with Nola's name written on it. She then placed it beside the letter, which Nola had set down.

"What can you learn from that?"

It was there in the candlelight. True enough for even a blind man. The handwriting…the fine bonded paper. The handwriting the same…the writing paper the same. Right down to the watermark.

"Now you know who," said Harriet.

Nola kept looking from one to the other.

"And that's not all," said Harriet.

Nola looked up.

"No…? What then…?"

"I am going to leave the room. You will wait a few minutes, then you will turn off the light as if you are going to bed. But you will get the gun that I gave you and we'll—"

Nola grabbed Harriet's hand.

"Don't look at the window."

Her eyes wanted to, but she fought the impulse.

"Yes…we're being watched."

Harriet left the room without a trace of sound.

Left there, Nola felt like a creature ensnared, that no sureness of movement could overcome. That every answer posed a new question, and every question after that posed a new danger, and every danger posed a new question that had to be answered. An endless hiding one behind the other, lying in wait, like whatever it was out there in the starless overcast night.

She had known a professor in college who had one phrase, one over-riding statement on the laws of the universe he felt bore repeating, under-standing, and believing... *A stalwart grave is all you can expect from this world, even for all the grace you put into it.*

On that quiet note, she blew out the candle on the desk and the smoke curled and wisped, then died. She retrieved the revolver from her purse that Harriet had given her.

• • •

Harriet was waiting in the hallway with a House revolver at her side. She heard the floorboards make that menacing creak, and she softly called out, "I'm here."

Nola joined her in the dark. They stood shadow to shadow. Harriet wearing a black cape over her nightclothes. She carried an extra which she passed to Nola.

"Wear this," she said. "The harder to see you with."

Nola slipped on the cape and Harriet had her sidle up to a window. She pointed to where the girl should look out the ripplish glass to a treed darkness at the base of the hill that could just be made out because of the glowing light of the smelter furnace.

"I mean, you should know something," said Harriet, "right here and now. If I wanted Neihart dead, I would damn well do it myself. No qualms, no questions, no remorse, no plea for forgiveness. But I would rather see him taken down, exposed for the confidence man he really is, and so ruined. Do we understand each other?"

"If he is what you say...I hope to oblige."

"Well...let's go chase the bejesus out of whoever the hell is out there."

They slipped out onto the street side of the house. They could see over the honeysuckle that hedged the sidewalk. Two members of the state mili-tia walking Chestnut, keeping watch, rifles slung lazily over their shoul-ders, talking to each other, smoking, a light laugh from one of them. It had happened that quickly—Leadville was being put under a state of alert. No saving grace in and of itself, as everyone knew the militia would be in concert with the mine owners. Because they were the political force behind the powers that be, who'd ordered them there in the first fuckin' place.

Nola followed along behind Harriet around her storage shed and covered stable and down into one of the endless wallows, born of hideous mixtures of chemical refuse. Their heavy walking boots clinging to the earth made this loud sucking sound, so the women were forced to proceed more slowly, more lightly.

When they reached the edge of the trees they stopped and stood together. Nola took in a deep swig of air to relieve her fear. The pistol she bore in one hand was small and somewhat light, but it felt as large and heavy as an anvil. There was no point in her questioning why she was there, because she was.

They entered that soundless world staying close together so they could whisper and be heard. The slight wind blowing their capes like the wings of great birds. Gray smoke lingering above them from the night shifts working the mines.

Something skittled through the twisty brush, fallen leaves flying apart. Startled, the two women just stood there like misplaced statues until they knew for sure it was not something that would steal their lives. They then pressed on. The slow tread of their footsteps to where the trees began to thin out and images of the smelter began to fill in the slender vacant openings, and soon that was all there was.

Nola looked to Harriet.

"There *was* someone here," said Harriet.

Nola's silence, to Harriet, felt of doubt, if not outright disbelief.

CHAPTER 74

They returned to the house. Together, but solitary. Unsettled, unsure.

"There was someone out there watching," said Harriet.

They crossed the unlit room.

Harriet practically shouted, "Answer me, goddamn it."

A broken voice from the shadows answered.

"She betta…cause der' waz."

Harriet had just begun to scream when Nola covered her mouth. "Shut up," she said.

Clipped footsteps on the wood floor. A lean and hobbly outline with a rifle slung over its shoulder.

"Matthew?" said Nola. "It was you?"

"Me."

Nola took her hand from Harriet's mouth.

"Harriet, this is—"

"Yes," she said.

They were not shadows now, but edges of detail. He put a hand out to shake.

"So…I'm not mad," said Harriet.

"Ya' might be," said Matthew. "Don' know."

Nola went to turn up a lantern. But Matthew grabbed her hand.

"Not safe."

You could hear his boots now track to the parlor window.

"Is it—"

"Yea'," he said.

"You saw them? In Leadville?"

"In Lettville."

Harriet crossed the room. "I'll get whiskey…cause this sounds like a long night ahead of us."

When she was gone, Nola said, "A reporter was killed earlier."

"Saw it," said Matthew.

"Saw it? You were there?"

"Yea."

"You know what the word is?"

He was peering out the window, studying every shadow, any stillness that might prove to pose a threat, while he told her how they'd tried to kill him outside of Denver at Bear Creek Bridge.

Harriet was returning with the whiskey bottle and glasses when she thought she heard Nola say something like... "It was 'the Committee'"... and Matthew answer that it was.

Harriet set the bottle and glasses down on a sideboard as she said, "Who...or what...are 'the Committee'?"

Matthew looked to Nola to see who would answer.

"They mean to kill Matthew," she said.

"No..." he said. "Mean ta' kill us both."

"Well," said Harriet. She poured a drink and handed the glass to Matthew. "Why don't I keep watch then?"

Nola led Matthew to her room and as she closed the door he set the glass of whiskey down on her desk and slipped the rifle from his shoulder.

"You should not have come here," she said.

"I came fa' you."

"It's terrible," she said, "to love someone for doing something you don' want them to do."

He understood.

"What happened at the bridge?" she said.

He told her hard detail after detail, and how Vandel even said, "From one Coffin Maker to another."

"They're hunting you out."

He lifted the glass of whiskey to toast the veracity of her statement.

She sat on the edge of the bed and began to cry. It was a gentle crying and not just for herself and Matthew, but for humanity itself. A troubled, lost, desperate, and needful humanity under the full weight of its plight.

He put his arm around her and whispered of all he felt, hoping to soothe her, but whatever it was that had her suffering was too deep and true.

Pressed against his chest like she was a part of him, she said quietly, "Well...if it's a fight they want...it's a fight they'll get."

The hours they spent that night in the dark grew more impassioned because they knew the world was closing in and laying claim to them. Even as they exorcised the suffering and loneliness inflicted on them, life was coming on fast and it meant to hammer their souls to the ground. And no matter how real it was in the blue black darkness of that tiny room, the shadow of the mines meant to impose its will.

PART FIVE

CHAPTER 75

Matthew explained how after the Bear Creek shootout, they had slipped off into the night on foot. At the settlement of Morrison, members of the Brotherhood were waiting with fresh mounts. Vandel and his men had passed through the town earlier, and the red rock formations, so beautiful by day, now looked like immense inky black ocean waves breaking toward the sky.

Members of the state militia had set up patrol stations on the roads and rail lines west to Leadville under the governor's orders. And anyone who looked or acted suspicious, who gave off the impression of trouble-making, which meant any worker or caravan of the poor and unemployed heading to that mining town for the massive confrontation Mary Jones was organizing, were to be arrested and detained.

There were passages in the hills where the sheer weight of time and effort would make it an impossible misery to get past the roadblocks. At one such station, a collection of the poor and ragged sat huddled around a series of fires. Swaddled in blankets and old tarps they were watched over by a motley crew of militia.

Among the detained were an inordinate number of blacks who were chased from the road for little more than being who they were.

The country did not want them, the law did not want them, even the workers who wanted to unionize for fairness didn't want them among their number. Only the mine owner wanted them as strike breakers.

Matthew and Sweeny were crouched among the rocks like wolves deciding on how best to make their break.

Ledru Drum was always one to throw around advice—outthink your opposition with simplicity—he'd told the boy.

And so the two men approached the guards under the dark of silence. The only sounds announcing them, the harness metal and steamy broth of their snorting mounts.

The guards numbered four and one shouted out, "Announce yourselves."

"We're Pink'tons," Matthew shouted back.

They reined in and were soon sidled by the four and Matthew and Sweeny presented papers and badges—taken from the killed, first by Ledru, and after that, by Matthew—and shown as their rightful identification.

"Half a mile down the road," Sweeny said, "labor radicals up to mischief are being hunted by you fellas. We were asked to tell you they need you down there."

The guards looked to the man in charge, who seemed no more suited to command than a worm, and who pointed to that potluck of homeless around the fires.

"But we've been ordered to—"

An explosion cut the mountain night far down that track. The last stick of working dynamite in Matthew's possession had been neatly placed among a cluster of trees and piled brush. And when it blew, everything went up like one of God's own precious torches.

You could see it marking the landscape like a stylus and the guards hustled to their mounts with Sweeny proclaiming that they would watch the riffraff.

Once that backwater conglomeration of misfits had disappeared into the night, Matthew got his horse around, waved his hat, and shouted, "Git now...b'fore ta' bastads come back."

CHAPTER 76

Matthew had crossed a sea of unanswered questions well before dawn, before Nola said, "How do you know they are the ones who killed the reporter? Vandel and McSorley, I mean?"

Upon reaching Leadville, Sweeny went to the camp being set up on the hill for Mary Jones, to report that he and Matthew had gotten there alive, hungry, and sober.

Matthew went about the business of hunting out Neihart, which was easy enough. He believed the mine owner would eventually lead him to Vandel, but that did not come to pass. And again he was crossing a sea of unanswered questions.

Neihart had left his mine office and walked all the way out Hemlock Street. On the way he took this most peculiar action. He removed an envelope from his coat pocket and slipped it between the pages of a folded up newspaper he was carrying. Not much later, he met a man outside of Saint Vincent's Hospital. He was well dressed, youthful, a civilized looking gent.

A conversation ensued. It was brief, cordial, one might even suggest it to be innocuous. It ended with the men shaking hands, and then, of all things, Neihart passed him the newspaper, which the man took with hardly an acknowledgement. He slipped the folded up newspaper, with its tucked away envelope, under his arm and strode off down Hemlock Street, a picture of gentlemanly quiet.

Of all possible names given to that particular street and what took place there in the summer of that year would prove to be cruelly fateful and questioned up to this very day.

• • •

Matthew had been at the Board of Trade when Mary Jones arrived that night to make her speech. He was, by now, seasoned at the art of remaining faceless in a crowd. Of knowing where and how to linger to arouse little, if no, attention. He had even finessed his hobbled gait enough when covering very short passages of ground so one would not easily recognize him as a cripple. He had added to all that distinction by not carrying his rifle that night.

He had seen Nola arrive. He had watched her from the shadows pass the gambling hall windows that burned with light. He was just part of a handful of poorly dressed cutouts taking in this political scene.

And when the reporter came forth from the crowd and scored Mary Jones with the question, "Where do you get your money?", Matthew recognized him right off as the youth on Hemlock who had walked away with the folded up newspaper.

Wrapped in nothing more than a thin blanket, Nola paced that little room of hers. "What was in the envelope? Why was he shot down? Who shot him?"

"Vandel," said Matthew.

"For sure?"

"Ya' taut it wa' me?"

"I did at that."

The years of marksmanship had tuned his hearing, and Matthew felt right off that shot came from a rifle somewhere down Harrison Street. The reporter would have been in the flow of light from the gambling hall and a reasonable target. Matthew had wandered down Harrison right off and who should he see crossing the street but Vandel, with McSorley just paces behind. Vandel was carrying a rifle scabbard and he and McSorley slipped into an alleyway. They were too quick for the lame young man and Matthew lost them in a maze of dark, squat buildings.

Nola sat at the foot of the bed, thinking through their situation, and of those around her.

"They're a quick lot," she said. "They'll fix blame of the reporter's murder on this Coffin Maker to use against Mary Jones and the Federation. It's right there to be seen."

He was sitting in a chair, close to her, slumped a bit. He admitted to her, then and there, he was sorry he had not foreseen this. And that he would admit his own culpability. That she could name him, and he would sign an affidavit to that effect, even if it meant indicting himself. And anything that would help destroy those bastards he would do.

She reached out and put a hand over his lips to see him quiet.

"Don't," she said. "If you admit it…I'll have to report it."

He slipped his fingers around hers and removed the hand and then kissed it.

He got up and walked over to the window. He leaned against the wall, naked in that twisted body, running his fingers along the edges of the shade, where dawn was slipping through. He was unfairly weathered for a boy his age, like something patched together from mismatched parts. He was, she thought, the country. He was the image of a generation on the cusp of the brutal life they were trying to come through.

"I cud go ta' summen else. Notha' reporter."

"I won't have it," she said. "When...no, *if*...that action allows them to be exposed and taken down, I will put the words to it. I will bear, broken-hearted, that responsibility. That way you know I'll be standing right there alongside you on the gallows."

CHAPTER 77

Matthew left when there was still dew on the ground. His arms draped over the rifle which rested on the back of his shoulders. Both women were asleep, or so he thought, until Harriet called to him from an upstairs window.

"Good luck with hell raising."

Later she sat at the kitchen table, smoking, her father's open pocket watch there beside an empty coffee cup. She was already worn out from too damn much thinking.

Nola entered the room wearing that frock the older woman had lent her.

"You get some sleep?" said Nola.

"Sleep is only for the living…there's coffee."

Nola went to the shelf for a mug and checked to see what bug or spider might be lurking there.

"You going up the hill?" said Harriet.

"I am…And you?"

"I never miss a disaster. I feel it's my honor bound duty to attend."

"Do you think there'll be violence?"

"You mean there hasn't been so far?"

Nola poured the coffee and set the pot back down on the stove. "I see what you mean," said Nola.

"I don't think you do," said Harriet. "I really don't."

Nola blew away the steam rising from that roily brew. She was facing a very pointed stare. "I don't feel good about the way you said that," said Nola.

"Nor should you, if you're smart."

"I don't think your manner is ever going to be confused with gentility."

Harriet took a draw on her cigarette. "Gentility is shit. It's a chance to hide behind weakness and manners."

"Are you insinuating—?"

"It isn't Matthew that Neihart wants. That boy could walk out into the world at this very minute and admit to killing Christ and little of consequence would come of it. He could kill every one of these 'Committee' bastards and it will have no effect on what happens here. And God knows that ruffian trash working for the owners need killing, then burning."

Nola had set the cup down listening through this. She had stiffened up, and now she pointed toward her bedroom.

"You were—"

Harriet took another draw on her cigarette. She was fiddling a bit with her father's pocket watch case.

"Damn right I was. Silent as a cat at it, too. In my house, I want to know where the guests keep their poison. There's people want to carve that boy up like Christmas supper. So I mean to be well appointed with the situation."

She flicked the ash into her empty coffee cup. She was looking at the watchcase. Nola noticed there was no watch in there. Only what looked to be a photo.

"There's a difference between being an ally and a fool," said Harriet. "In one, I have the right to choose."

Nola folded her hands. The woman sitting across from her looked like she could bull her way through about anything. And Nola suddenly, quietly admired her.

"I would have told you, if you asked," said Nola.

"Not all of it, sweetheart. Not all of it. No one can afford to be that honest...though you already have too much honesty for my taste."

"Is that an insult...or a warning?"

"Both...And it's not Matthew that Neihart would be after. He would rather that boy was alive causing turmoil. Neihart thrives on turmoil. He is at his best behind a veneer of turmoil.

"It's someone like you he's got his sights on. You are at risk."

Harriet took another draw on her cigarette, then started to prod the air with it. "He has a plan. He never does anything without a long term plan. And my guess is he means to compromise you in some way."

Nola stood, angry, flustered. "He's not going to compromise me."

"You won't do it willingly...or even knowingly. He's pure confidence man. Even when he's being honest...that's when he's at his most dangerous."

CHAPTER 78

Harriet slid the watchcase across the table. There was no timepiece in it, as Nola had noted earlier. There was a crinkled photo in the frontpiece of a man and woman somewhere on the frontiers of their life. A couple not unlike the forgotten in endless scarred frontpieces, gone to the roadside or to death.

"Your parents?" said Nola.

"The timepiece broke years ago," said Harriet. "It was not important anyway. Time means nothing. Time does not heal all wounds. It just furthers one's cause."

Nola set the watchcase down. "I did not know my true parents. But to at least have a picture of them…If nothing else…is to create memories over."

"You're worse than I even thought," said Harriet.

"Thank you," said Nola.

Harriet stubbed the cigarette out in her coffee cup.

"What I tell you now," said Harriet, "is in the strictest of confidence… Agreed?"

Nola was flush with uncertainty over this sudden question, but agreed.

"You cannot use it in an article…at this point. Agreed?"

Again, Nola reluctantly agreed.

"Colonel Gheen and his investors will be selling off a huge block of stock. And that Neihart himself, possibly through a front company, is buying it himself."

"How did you come by this?"

"I have a source on the inside who despises Neihart. This is why you can't use it…yet. Neihart would assume you got the information from me. And that I got it in turn from someone on the inside. That would put them unfairly at risk."

"Why were you told this?"

"I have shares in that mine."

"But you want it—"

"I want Neihart taken down. The mine will stand or fall on its worth."

"If," said Nola, "they are selling out—"

Harriet rose from the table. There was a tin plate on the counter where she kept her rolled cigarettes. She lit another. She stood with her back against the counter, her arms trussed up against her chest.

"The Americanus," she said, "may well be running out of ore."

"Then why is Neihart buying up stock through a front company?"

Harriet made a grotesque laugh.

"And what's all that nonsense on the Hill? Meetings between Neihart and the Federation over insurance and the union?"

"This is where Neihart is a master."

"He invited me down into the mine. To be there when he brings in engineers to test new tunnels for ore."

"When you go down there for that," said Harriet, "bring a sack."

"A sack...Why?"

"So you can catch your own head when he chops the damn thing off." She started out of the room. "I got to dress. I have my own hell to raise."

Harriet stopped in the doorway. Nola was totally flooded in her own thoughts so Harriet snapped her fingers. Nola looked up.

"It could be Neihart is fronting for the other major mine owners in a drive to ruin the Federation. Because everyone up here understands, if the union breaks one major mine on the hill, it puts a crack in them all. You put a crack in them all, the crack expands across the state. You crack a state, the country is not far behind. And the mine owners, like the railroad and oil barons, live by one truism...*It's best to kill the horse with the first shot.*"

CHAPTER 79

The road up the hill was trampled with everything from the townspeople to derelict strangers. There were those for and those against the hard politics of labor, and all the taunts and threats that go with it. And there were those who didn't give a damn but just wanted to be there on the chance something violent or terrible was to be witnessed.

A city of the penniless now camped on the hill near the Americanus, and everywhere fires smoked for their beggar's breakfast.

A large bell tent that had seen use during the Civil War had been pitched in the shadow of the Americanus headframe. There Neihart and his executive team were in discussions with Mary Jones and delegates from the Federation. The tent was ringed by enough heavily armed Pinkertons to put down an organized assault and to make negotiations.

Matthew found himself a strategic spot at the edge of the camp where he could sit on an old tree stump and keep watch on the bell tent. Back in Denver, just before the march on the theatre, Mary Jones had taken the youth aside for what amounted to a clandestine request. She wanted him in Leadville, where he could serve as a lone set of eyes watching for any plots of sabotage or violence against the Federation. And he was to tell no one of this, for fear it might leak out.

A calliope wagon had been set up on the hill and you could hear that gaudy steam whistle a long ways off knocking out its circus tunes. There were food vendors moving among the crowd, and it was a crowd all right. Must have been over a thousand people wandering those ravaged acres around the mine. And stalls had been set up for ice cream and soda pop and treats, and there were makeshift bars where you could get all liquored up and strut your politics, as if empowered by the very hand of God. All of this courtesy of Nathan Neihart, but no one could prove it at the time. It was mostly just well grounded guessing that he meant to change what was a serious negotiation into a nonsense sideshow.

The people Matthew watched pass before him he felt he could greet by name. He had seen the wretched toil in their faces so often, the misery compounded by hunger that still tormented his sleep. The shoeless children clinging to their mothers' shoddy dresses following in their parents' wake.

A boy came along with his hand out, asking if Matthew might spare a penny, and there Matthew was staring at a vision of himself all those years ago. The crippled hand, the twisted leg. It never goes away, does it? The stark shock you are what you are, even if you overcome it. That…is your connection to the world.

He was looking at the boy's face and just past his face was the crowd, and just past the crowd was the tent, and past the tent was the mine, and past the mine the rest of Fryer Hill, and past that…What?

He pressed some paper money into the boy's hand and squeezed the hand and told him about his carrying rocks in a sack to make the damaged shoulder stronger and the walk straighter…And to hate begging with all your soul, because it cheats you.

And when the boy walked away, Matthew saw he had attracted visitors. The bone and leather faces that had tracked him over the years.

"Well," said Vandel, "look who landed in Leadville."

Matthew sat with hands folded in his lap. The rifle on the stump beside him, helpless.

"You ready to have it out?" said Vandel.

They were deeply grimed from hard travel. Vandel, as always, was wiping at the curse that was his mouth with a bandana that looked as if it had not been washed since the days of Julius Caesar.

The boy had to squint a bit because of the sun, but did little else.

McSorley hit the bowl of his pipe against his belt buckle to see if and how the boy would react.

The boy did nothing.

"I'm paz baitin," he said.

Would they shoot him down where he sat? He thought how he might slip that possible obscenity.

Then came a flurry of reedy chords from a mouth organ. And there was Sweeny, shucking out a tune with half a dozen heavily armed miners behind him. And all of them leaning toward drunkenness.

"Young Mister Crippled Jack here," said Sweeny, "may be past baiting. But me and my friends aren't. We'll match you, pizzle to pizzle."

Matthew reminded Sweeny of what Mary Jones had been righteous about. No warfare on the Hill. Nothing that could be used against the

Federation. Matthew took up his rifle and stood and as he labored off to join Sweeny and the miners, Vandel tossed a remark at his back.

"I'm gonna send you a photograph one day," Vandel said. "It just came into my head what it's gonna be of."

And if that wasn't enough, Vandel shouted, "The drums are calling, boy."

Matthew stopped and looked back. The comment had the desired effect because Matthew knew what the bastard really meant.

CHAPTER 80

Mary Jones knew what Nathan Neihart knew. They could go eye to eye with each other until one keeled over or one was killed. Also, this was no negotiation, and it was not about insurance and who would pay. This was about the unquestioned superiority of Goliath and the neglected existence of David. And it would not be a one slingshot fight like in the Bible. In the Bible it was too fuckin' easy.

During a break in the discussions, when each side went off to their appointed corners, one of the Federation delegates said, "I have a sense Neihart is going to yield to our insurance demand to keep from striking."

"Yes," said Mary Jones, "I agree. And that, gentlemen, is what should worry us."

By end of day, an agreement had been hammered out—the Americanus would pay health insurance for its employees. Out front of the bell tent, Mary Jones and Nathan Neihart would stand side by side and she would read from a prepared text. Among the shabby multitude there to witness were an army of newspapermen that had flocked in from across the state. In their number was Nola Dye, who had already been passed a handwritten note from Nathan Neihart.

There was also a photographer there to capture the agreement signing. The very same gentleman with a now patched up gypsy wagon, that had been part of the shooting on Bear Creek. It was an ironic counterpart to the scene, and a symbol of the inherent dishonesty in that handshake between the mine owner and lady labor leader. As this would be the last peaceful moment before the bitter and unrelenting violence that would take them from the mines of Fryer Hill, all the way to the mountains outside of Leadville, to the place known as the Bold Face Stripe.

• • •

The note was from Neihart, in his own hand. He requested Nola Dye be at the field office at daybreak, the day after tomorrow. That she join him, a crew, and an engineer who would make a geologic survey of the new shafts and determine their value—*I think you should find it fascinating to be present at the moment a mine is to live or die. And what that will mean for all concerned.*

The note was on the same bonded paper and in the same script as the scrap she carried.

Matthew, who met up with her on the Hill after the signing, read the note, and believed something was very wrong with all this. And Nola agreed. But there was only one way to find out and that would not be by waiting for some grand wisdom to be imparted, but to take that fate collecting first step.

Mary Jones said very much the same thing, that very same evening, in the tent set up in the miners' camp that now served as home and headquarters. She sat at a table hunched over a lantern, the light glistening off her glasses as she read the letter. Looking up, she issued forth with, "They mean to use you somehow."

"They can't use me if I don't agree to be used. They could be testing me...baiting me...possibly."

"They have spies on the Hill," said Mary. "They know at this very moment you are speaking with me."

"All the better," said Nola. "And I have a question that Neihart once asked that I ask."

"Indeed," said the woman.

"If the union gets power to negotiate, to demand, to...in effect have a central say in what happens everywhere...what is to stop the union from becoming just as corrupt as the people you're fighting now?"

"It is a thought I live with all the time. And the answer is always the same."

"And that is?"

"The only way to stop them is with people like you...and people like me." She swept open the canvas to the night. "And people like those poor bastards around all those fires. Because if the union gains power and goes corrupt, there will always be a generation of newly poor, newly disenfranchised, and newly exploited to fight them."

She let the canvas drop away.

"Miss Dye, I hope you didn't actually think the fight can be won for all time. Only youth believes such nonsense exists. Life is much more egregious and demands relentless dedication. And understands that failure and defeat are as essential to success as goodwill and honesty."

CHAPTER 81

The announcement of health insurance for the miners caused only a few percent drop in the Americanus stock price—less than anticipated. This, of course, was a day to day, hour by hour financial climate that would change with one flash of news, and become like planets spinning out of orbit and into oblivion. It did give Colonel Gheen and his investors a window in which to sell off their shares, and still walk away with a hefty profit. But they did not sell all their shares, mind you. They retained a small percentage, as their own insurance policy. On the chance Neihart proved to be providence itself, and had plotted out a scheme for the greater glory of his own good—and so, theirs also.

The next morning, the hammer fell. All shift bosses at the Americanus were notified by corporate flier—For THEIR OWN SAFETY, THERE IS TO BE NO SMOKING OR TALKING DURING AN EMPLOYEE'S WORK SHIFT.

Mary Jones was in her tent writing letters to labor leaders across the United States that an organized plan of attack was absolutely necessary for their success, when Nola Dye brought her the flier. She had just come from the Americanus field office, letting Jonah Smalls know that she would be going down into the mine the following morning. He had given her the flier while it was being first passed out.

Mary Jones read it with resentment, because she not only knew the intentions behind it, but that Neihart invariably had this in the works well before the Federation had sat for negotiations.

"I should thank that bastard for being so quick to the draw. I will send a copy of this with each letter I'm writing, to fan the fires of discontent."

"By the way," said Nola, "I told them I'd be going down into the mine tomorrow."

"You're down in it right now, young lady. In case you didn't yet realize. We all are."

Mary Jones stepped out of her tent and into a hard wind that blew across the Hill, and made the canvas tent flaps flutter like battle flags. There she addressed a crowded half moon of the angry and concerned. Miners and newspapermen alike, infected with urgency, is how Nola saw it, and would report it. Because they too had heard the news, it had spread that quickly across the Hill. And they knew what the older woman's response would be, but needed to hear the words from her own mouth so the reign of humanity could begin.

The small white haired woman with the shawl around her shoulders, and a cupped hand shielding the wind side of her face, spoke out, "Gentleman…and ladies…The Federation's response to this…outrageous and uncalled for demand…is that the fight for the country is joined…."

• • •

The Hill was the universe after that, where word spread with fierce resilience that the Federation would ask the afternoon shift to not go underground until the order was rescinded.

Mary Jones gathered up a hundred hard rock miners and had them join her on a stretch of free land upon the Hill. They would fan out behind her with their picks and axes in the shadow of the Americanus hoist house and head frame. This rough, unwashed, uneducated, foul mouthed coarse crew of working stiffs and human beings would pose in defiance and contempt. And that same photographer at the handshaking would take the picture.

Mary Jones already had it in mind, from the moment she saw the flier, she would have this picture taken and copies made and sent out across the country to newspapers, politicians, religious organizations, and zealots of all kinds because she knew, as she told Nola later that day, that pictures would replace words. That everything people thought and felt would be stripped down to the vivid brilliance of an image—a deplorable reality that we would be the better and worse for.

In the far back corner of the frame you could make Sweeny out with his boulder chest and huge sweaty head. And there was Matthew beside him. Sweeny had dragged the reluctant kid into the shot and kept him there with an iron grasp. It would turn out to be the only known extant photograph of the youth called Crippled Jack taken while he was alive.

• • •

Neihart watched all this from the field office window in spite of the sneers and snide remarks hurled at him from people passing. People, mind you, who did not work in the mine. He was intoxicated by his own sharp wittedness at how all this was proceeding.

Everything the woman did had moral significance, which worked to her disadvantage. He studied how she organized that lot of donkeys.

"She should have been a mine owner," said Neihart.

Jonah looked up from his daily worksheet. Tired and tired out, living a life at arm's length from everything that was valuable. A man who willingly and neatly would be forgotten.

"Who, sir?"

"The Jones woman."

"Yes, sir..."

"She'll make a charged adversary...thank God."

Smalls had been in many a "delicate" affair for his employer, but this—

"I want to issue another order."

"Today?" said Jonah.

"Right now."

Smalls thought it unwise, but more unwise to disagree. He set aside his workbook and prepared pen and paper.

"Here's how it is to read...If any shift boss captain fails to completely comply with said flier sent out this morning...they will be immediately terminated."

CHAPTER 82

By dusk they had to board up the Americanus field office windows and post more security. There came random gunshots from indistinct quarters of the Hill. The afternoon shift had been less than half manned. Signs of an impending catastrophe were everywhere. Miners who lived through hopeless squalor were being browbeaten for attempting to shut down the city's economy. For as the miners went, so went the businessman, and so went his profit and so went the rents he paid and the rent he collected, and so went the value of the land, and so went the taxes, and so went the politician who did not act.

All along the roadside at the crest of the Hill, the Federation set up posts to protect their camp. After dark in the distance a firebomb birthed a burning stand of trees. Like candles, they were at the altar of a diseased and disenfranchised America.

• • •

Nola was sitting on the screened in porch in the dark, her arms crossed against her chest, when Harriet appeared in the doorway, drunk as could be. Nola had been waiting all night for Matthew to come to the house, but it took Harriet to finally say, "You're wasting your time sitting there. He won't come."

"Why?" said Nola.

"You goddamn know as well as I do. Because he's straightforward and honest...and he can smell blood in the air."

She wasn't having it like that. Nola wrapped an old cape around her and walked to the Hill. On the road patches of workmen everywhere passing around pints of whiskey, groups of townsfolk on the cusp of misery, voices in anguished proselytizing over their plight. More men than usual were packing revolvers, this too she noticed and noted.

She walked the miners' camp an hour at least, up and down the rows of tents and wagons in the smokey darkness. A wraithlike figure, with a touch of the fugitive, hunting out faces around the oil lamps and campfires. Faces that stared back in uncertainty.

She finally found him at the edge of the Hill by a ragged assembly of miners. Music played by banjo and fiddle was carried away toward the stars. There was a rowdy tension in the air, and he was just off alone enough where he could scan the distance in peace when she eased up beside him. She had not taken a breath till she said, "What are you doing?"

"Watchin'."

"Why didn't you come to the house tonight?"

"I can't brin' harm ta' ya' dat way."

The answer was too painfully on point.

"What are you watching for?"

"Fa' word."

"There are different kinds of harm, you know."

Well, he knew.

"Like the harm of not coming to the house tonight." She saw how what she'd said affected him. Even darkness cannot always hide heartbreak.

"Coming up the hill," she said, "I saw so many men with guns. There's going to be violence here like they never saw before."

He wondered aloud if she had any idea what Neihart's intentions were. Had she picked up some scrap of information or rumor?

"All I know," she said, "is Harriet keeps warning me I should make sure the cage is safe."

"Sab'togue…"

"Or we're dynamited when down below."

He told her there would be no morning shift in the mines.

"Is it a complete walkout?"

He pointed to Mary Jones' tent. From the light within a host of busy shadows moved about the canvas.

"Is that the word you're watching for?"

He answered by barely shaking his head—no.

She knew now what—"waiting fa' word"—meant. It meant separation, it meant being cheated, having no illusions, existing in a constant state of hope and fear, need and silence, anticipation and denial, all the while clinging to a fancied dream you can hang your unquestionable affections on.

It wasn't fair of life, and not fair for her to say it.

CHAPTER 83

Matthew was alone another hour before he saw, far off in the western night, a shining, passing first to the left, then to the right, and back again. He was mounted and on the move through a moonless night where he left the faintest shadow. He caught up with Sweeny at a crossroads. The burly man was with a half breed miner who at one time had tracked for the Army, the same Army that had run his people into the ground. He was known as Johnny Dog, because he was as fast as one and about as small. Matthew pressed paper money into the tracker's hand.

"If there's gonna be killing tonight," said Sweeny, "count the Dog in. He's labor…and has a special hatred for Pinkertons."

They followed Johnny Dog out toward Turquoise Lake. The air got thinner at that altitude. The breathing more strained. A spidery mule trail followed the shoreline. The water like black cut glass and probably cold as hell. The night out there, at the edge of the Rockies, was pure silence, pure solace. Back from the lake long inclines with great stands of aspens.

Johnny Dog rode them into the trees to where they eventually dismounted. They crawled out along a sandy ridge, lay with bellies to the earth. There was a house far out in a glade, an extended cabin with corral and stable. Large enough for a dozen men, and there was about that number.

Matthew asked Johnny Dog if all three were down there.

"Vandel and that other one…" he flitted two fingers toward Leadville. "Comin' back?"

"That depends on their dicks," said Johnny.

"What about Tobin?"

"Gone. He serves as some kind of messenger for the owners. Heard him say he'll be back just after dawn."

Matthew asked what this place was. Johnny Dog explained how he'd bellied his way to the house earlier that evening. He'd squatted in the high weeds peeling and eating an orange as he listened to idle chatter. This was where strikebreakers were recruited, organized, and where Pinkerton security chiefs for the miners came with orders…and money.

"Big fight coming," said Johnny. "These fellas paid well to knock heads." Johnny Dog was a grubby runt of the litter with a deeply scarred face from the pox, but he was hell on wheels. He dramatically pointed his pipe toward the glade. "Burn 'em out…Kill 'em…Urinate on 'em."

"We could end a lot of them," said Sweeny. "Some would scatter… Escape."

It was left for Matthew to decide.

. . .

There was an earthen causeway for the train entering Leadville where it swept below the mountain to the west. Tobin crossed there with the dawn firmly on his back. It was the quickest and cleanest passage to Turquoise Lake. By the empty roadside a couple of hobo cowboys shared a pint of whiskey. Laughing like fools, Tobin thought them harmless enough until he was facing a couple of "Come to Jesus" pared down shotguns. Johnny Dog got quick hold of the reins while Sweeny stuffed his double barrel into the padding of Tobin's back. They asked him to dismount and then they deprived him of his weapons, which they tossed into the brush. All except his Winchester, that Sweeny held onto.

Tobin raised his arms. "I'm not worth robbing, gents. But have at it."

"You're worth killing," said Sweeny.

Sweeny emptied Tobin's Winchester. Johnny flashed his weapon to signal someone up the road. There was Crippled Jack, rifle at his side, about a healthy seventy yards away.

Tobin looked down. The beginnings of his shadow had just begun to stretch out before him. "Christ," he said.

"Christ always comes up at moments like this," said Sweeny. "You notice?"

"Second only to a pair of fast legs," said Johnny.

Sweeny loaded one shell into the Winchester. He offered the weapon back to the shaken youth, barrel first.

"You get one shot, boy. Crippled Jack gets one shot. Which is a lot better than the soup you served up for us at Bear Creek."

Tobin's eyes shifted from man to man. His situation was hopeless at best. He was standing at the headwaters of two shotguns, first light glistening up those gun barrels, and Johnny Dog offering, "Come on, scum swallower. Have at it. We're late for breakfast."

Tobin took the gun. His hands were sweating. He rubbed them on his trousers. He turned the weapon and slipped his fingers into the lever.

"How do I know that kid up there's only got one shot?"

"If he doesn't kill you with it," said Sweeny, "you'll know."

Tobin stepped out into the road. The Winchester stock squared up against his ribs. He could smell the morning, feel the sunlight. It did nothing for the terror he felt. He started to come forward cautiously to try and close the distance, whatever he could.

Matthew took but one step forward. His body made that painful hitch. Tobin had the rifle up faster and he fired.

The bullet must have carried as far as its echo, as Matthew stood there, untouched. He didn't get off a shot, he didn't even try. He raised the rifle and Tobin flinched, but Matthew only rested the barrel on his shoulder. Tobin turned to the two men in the road behind him. There was a look on his face that Sweeny noted—the shallow son of a bitch actually thought he was gonna survive this.

That's when Sweeny fired off his belly gun and blew Tobin right out of the road and onto his back in the brush. He and Johnny Dog were standing over the gasping youth when Matthew slipped between them.

"Thanks," said Sweeny.

Matthew nodded.

"He's still alive," said Johnny.

He was, at that. Tobin had a parcel of bloody wounds and he hissed as he breathed. His nostrils flared and closed rapidly. His window was narrowing.

"It's gonna take a little while yet for him to die," said Johnny Dog.

"We ga' time," said Matthew.

CHAPTER 84

The road up to the Hill was becoming an impassable ruin with trash and overturned wagons where ore had spilled out and lay in large piles like burial mounds. Cooking fires lined the road. People kept arriving, ready for conflict. The first sleepy hour of coming light had passed. The sun was stealing into the dark corners and crevices of the grim structure that was the mine.

The rutted track to the Americanus had been cut off with long shanks of steel and hacked up wagon parts, corrugated tin, packing crates, heavy pieces of machinery that had been dragged by crews using ropes from the trash bin that the hillface had become over time.

To get to the field office you had to pass through a barricade of strikers. And trying to get through you had to face pleas for support, questions about motive and loyalty, insults if you dare not comply, resentments, and worse if you pressed on. You were cursed at and spit on for your defiance.

Nola tried to explain she was a reporter there to cover a story—a story about their aspirations—only to have excrement thrown on her. A half dozen women—the mothers, wives, daughters, sisters of those homeless and unemployed—were carrying sacks of shit and wearing heavy work gloves and greeted anyone who crossed the line with a fistful of foul smelling feces. Animal feces, human feces.

After all, Nola Dye, in their eyes, was nothing more than a corporate shill. A lackey for big business, and a lying, stinking spy. And how did they know this? They were blessed with the fervor of the moment.

A battery of security guards and Pinkertons ringed the field office. They were badged, holstered, and carried cudgels. When Nola presented her letter from Neihart and was allowed entry she was roundly booed by the miners.

Neihart was at his desk smoking, the picture of calm. Two filthy boys silently shared a bench off against one wall. Jonah Smalls was there, and a man he introduced—Ben Stapp. Youthful, plain looking, he would more easily pass for a barber or clerk rather than a graduate of the Rensselaer Polytechnic Institute and the Colorado School of Mines.

"Well," said Neihart. "Let's begin."

Guards flanked them on the walk from the field office to the head frame. Beyond the insults, the boys were viciously called traitors.

As they climbed into the cage for the descent, Neihart told his security people, "Take care of the cage, boys. Otherwise, there won't be anybody to sign your paycheck."

Smalls was carrying a kerosene lamp, as were the boys. In that bare light, faces bore a stark glow. For Nola this trip was more difficult. The first time it had been a hive of noise and dust. Now it was a soundless and seemingly bottomless hole with only that iron tremor of the cage which Nola would describe in her article as—the death rattle.

The cage came to the bottom tunnel with a bleak thud. The gate opened into perpetual dark. Neihart with raised lantern led the way into that stony bowel.

While Neihart, Stapp, and the boys slipped through the slatted timbers into a new excavation, Nola waited with Smalls.

"Mineral determination and feasibility," she said.

"You've done your homework."

"Why can't I go in there?"

"We wouldn't want it suggested we colluded with the press in any way."

"I understand completely," she said.

"I hope you do…For all our sakes."

She was about to press the issue, as his answer was all things and nothing at the same time when she heard, or thought she'd heard, something, and from the unsettled look on Smalls' face at the same time, he too might have heard.

"Was that a gunshot?" she said.

He walked to the shaft entrance holding the light and listened. The air was still and heavy and they were so far underground the pitch of a gunshot would die quickly.

Behind him the two boys squirreled back through breaches in that lattice of tunnel boards, one lantern swinging crazily, the other left behind in the breaches.

"Everything all right?" said Smalls.

Out of breath, one of the boys said, "They were done with us crawling around and collecting samples, so Mister Neihart ordered us out."

Nola could hear a conversation far down that craggy bowel of tunnels, with its hazy light. She could not understand the unquestionable stream of words, it was too far for that. But the highlights of emotion—that yes, she could tell. Touches of shock and surprise, that too. Then a long even voiced declaration she was certain to be Stapp. A flurry of back and forths between the two men followed, and then Neihart cursed out loud, but it wasn't a vile epithet of defeat or despair, but of something much more vivid.

CHAPTER 85

Neihart appeared carrying the lantern with Stapp a few steps behind. He passed the light to Smalls and the two men slipped through breeches in the boarding. "Let's head back up," said Neihart.

They started for the shaft and Nola asked Neihart what he had discovered, but all the while her eyes were on Stapp.

"Mister Stapp will have a fully detailed report within forty-eight hours, which I will pass to you for release."

As they entered the cage, she was curious. "Why me?"

"Because, Miss Dye…who better to trust with the facts than someone who is honestly after your hide?"

He pulled the cage lever and so began the long lift.

She tried to read Stapp's expression, but it was no easy task when she heard that sound once again and looked over at Smalls. He'd heard it as well as did everyone else.

"Was that a gunshot?" said Stapp.

Before anyone answered, there was a furry of gunfire up through the shaft and screams coming out of the dark.

Then the cage froze there in place. It shifted slightly but did not move. Neihart flexed the lever, but the cage did not move.

They were all looking up, trying to see past that sifty light from the kerosene lamps, hoping God lent a hand before long. Sweating through their clothes from the fear and stony tight heat. You could feel the fullness of death in that tomb, enough to chase the soul right out of your body, when something came crashing down on the cage.

Everyone was thrown, or accordioned where they stood. One lamp was shattered, another wheeled across the cage floor leaving a spindly trail of flames that had to be stomped out before the planking caught fire.

Neihart held the one lamp that kept them from complete darkness, and he rose up and reached with it to see what had fallen on the cage. There was a body pressed to the grating, blood dripping from the crushed bones of its face. The badge he wore shiny with light.

It was a casket of panic now. The boys pressed up against Nola, and she covered their eyes without even thinking. She felt she would retch, but fought it. She began to cry, but clenched her teeth so not a sound came out of her. There was more gunfire and the thrashing of men and cries of the wounded and that's when Stapp broke.

He began to scream out for help, to be gotten out, saved. He grabbed at the cage and shook it like some out of his mind thing. He tried to open the gate and get out—but go where? It was less than a foot to the sheer rock facing.

Neihart passed Smalls the lantern and grabbed Stapp by the coat and tried to calm him, but he only got worse. His face contorted, eyes stricken, he tried to climb up the caging as if there were some invisible means of escape that dead man might know about. Neihart began to slap Stapp into submission, but when that wasn't enough, when Stapp was crawling in the blood that had dripped onto the planking, Neihart resorted to his fists.

He beat that engineer about the head until he was curled up in the corner like a whimpering child.

"Even those boys," said an out of breath Neihart, "are more fuckin' man."

To hear Stapp weeping, to hear it carry away in the depths of all that darkness, was something she would never forget. And it spoke to the fact that in one's life there were only moments.

"I have no intention of dying down here," Neihart shouted. He went from one to the next. The boys he shook both by their shoulders. "We'll get out." Even Nola, he held her face. "We'll get out." He then leaned over Stapp and screamed. "You fuckin' hear me?"

Stapp, exhausted and beaten, nodded his head, for whatever that was worth.

CHAPTER 86

After living hours of nightmare, the cage was brought to the surface in a slow and tortured rattling. The sight of dead bodies lying on the pitted earth in the mine's shadow pretty much told Nola a crude assault had been attempted.

Dizzy and disheveled, Nola stepped into the sunlight. A sunlight unlike any she had ever been promised. It was the glorious light when one has just escaped death that made the sky more enormous, the Rockies just outside the city the chiseled bounty of God, and their faint toppings of snow even in summer perfect for bringing one to tears for their beauty. She wished she could scoop a handful of that snow and put it to her dried lips and sweated out face. Then swallow chunks of that cold ice to cool her sanded throat, cool everything inside her that burned with death. Then she looked about, and there was the greater disappointment known as the world.

There was violence everywhere across the Hill. Packets of men from both sides of the political battlefield squabbling, lashing out at each other, mob like cat and mouse fistfights, security police charging the ranks of protesting miners.

But order was being reinstated—militant, corporate, state run order.

And from the length of the line of troops marching up the Hill, that stretched all the way back to the rail depot, looked to Nola to be at least a thousand men.

At the crest of the Hill officers were directing companies of troops to each mine. They were organizing crews to clear the road for passage. Guards were being posted on the slopes along that road up to the Hill, with orders to arrest, and if necessary, shoot, anyone who did not comply with the cease-and-desist orders. A curfew would be put in place within hours, and for all practical purposes Leadville would be under martial law.

Mary Jones and an array of miners, their wives, children, and members of the Federation were at the crest of the Hill, trying to block the advance of the militia only to be pressed back by that shoulder to shoulder army of ill-trained troops.

Nola stood outside the Americanus field office and watched these newly uniformed companies pass, row after row of them. Many looked like little more than children themselves. As for the rest, what number she wondered were lost souls, hobos, vagrants, refugees from the homeless camps, maybe former miners, itinerants, foreigners, sharecroppers, day laborers, who'd signed on in desperation as a means to three meals a day and a place to sleep? How many were now part of an Army fighting against their own self interests? It was the tale of a disjointed and tragic America, thought Nola. An America trying to pull itself up by the bootstraps of another man's boots.

A hand clasped Nola by the arm and spun here around. It was an angry and unbridled Neihart and he was not alone. At his side stood a thickly mustached and gnawed out Pinkerton who served as security chief.

"Please tell Miss Dye what you told me," said Neihart.

The Pinkerton spoke with a heavy Russian accent. "Assault dis morning on mine," he said, "was planned act in sabotage. Meant to blow headframe with Mister Neihart below."

Once the Pinkerton finished, Nola understood immediately the significance of his statement.

"How did they know you—"

"That's right, Miss Dye. How did they know I'd be going down there this morning?"

"Someone," she said, "leaked the—"

"Right again, Miss Dye. It was a planned assassination. I want you to write about this today. And why do I entrust you with this? Because you were down in the mine with me. And maybe you should ask that angelic, miracle voiced firebrand and phony, Mary Jones, what she knows about it."

"It might be one of your own that leaked it," said Nola. "Or it could have been someone you told...someone who doesn't give a rat's ass about your life."

That finished it. Neihart brushed past Nola, then pressed his way through that line of passing troops to the remains of a toppled derrick. He scaled the rusting monolith to where he would tower over the harassing miners.

"If you meant me dead...it's your bad luck," Neihart shouted.

The crowd was rabid in their hatred. He was beyond the grasp of their rage, beyond where they could throw rocks and reach him. And as for the miners themselves, none had the will, the audacity, or the skill to shoot him down. Especially where there was a line of rifled troops ready to bear down on them—man, woman, and child alike.

A fraudulent legion of the unwashed, is what he shouted down at them. He was unlike other owners in that he was not a coward, he was not a dilettante that pouted, or a brilliant gentleman who hated the common man. He was a common man, and a common shit, who had climbed higher, and climbed better, faster. He was imperfect and proud of it. And he told them, warned them really, if it came down to where he had to concede to their orders or demands, he'd blow the fuckin' mine up himself. And that he could…because it was his to do with as he wanted.

PART SIX

PART SIX

CHAPTER 87

The late Mister Tobin was given quite the sendoff that morning down in what was known as Vulture Alley. It was a notorious half street of the shoddiest saloons and whorehouses in Leadville. The standard joke—You could smell the whores a mile away.

Not long after dawn, the late Mister Tobin was discovered propped up in a chair outside the CRACK A LOO Saloon. He was tied to it so as not to tip over. A bottle of whiskey was wedged down between his legs. A note had been pinned to his fancy Dan hat that read:

Poor Mister Tobin
He's had one travesty too many
The Coffin Maker

Vulture Alley was popular with the hired thugs and security teams for the mines, and where they could get rancid and not worry about being poisoned by some prolabor bartender.

Pretty quick word got to Vandel and when he and McSorley arrived, the alley was crowded with gawkers and whores. Tobin was a pretty bloodied up mess. Vandel tore the note from his hat, read it, showed it to McSorley. A reporter who happened on the scene pressed Vandel about what was obviously a murder.

Vandel showed him the note, but his attentions were elsewhere. "Anyone here," shouted Vandel, "seen this man's horse? Listen up." He whistled to get everyone's attention. "I said, anyone here seen this man's horse?"

It wasn't the horse he gave a crap about, it was the packet carrying all correspondence from the Americanus.

• • •

They were lying among the trees on the ridge well above the cabin at Turquoise Lake. Sweeny rested in the high grass rooting about like a hog.

Johnny Dog was watching the road from town with field glasses while Matthew went through the packet of dispatches he had discovered among Tobin's belongings.

Most were perfunctory correspondence, others bore the pitchman's mark of braggadocio. But one drew Matthew's deep curiosity. It was addressed to Jay Gould, the railroad Czar. It, in part, read:

> *Gheen is an offal headed fool and to be ignored. Within twenty-four hours of date above will release a statement that will shake the rooftops. I'm sure it will only increase the Federation's drive to break me. But I've always known it would come to this. All future correspondence, regarding said matter, will be through Mister Smalls.*

All the dispatches, useless or not, but especially the one to Gould, he returned to the packet with every intention of passing them onto Nola.

"Men coming," said Johnny Dog, and he kicked Sweeny in the side to rouse him.

Matthew got out his field glasses. The three men hovered at the edge of the high grass, necks lengthened. A handful of riders coming on slow through the midmorning light. Wavery horsemen in the windless distance taking their own sweet time.

"Na' him," said Matthew. "Na' McSorley."

"How long do we wait?" said Sweeny.

"Ni' fall," said Matthew.

Johnny took Matthew by the shoulder. "Wanna show you...so if it's a fight and we have to get over the willows...." He lifted his field glasses to his eyes. "Beyond the lake...straight across...a mule path into the hills all the way up."

Matthew followed the sightline of Johnny Dog's field glasses. He scanned the far shore first, and there it was, a trodden path that snaked its way up into low smooth hills that were spare with sage and browning brittle grass. At the edge of the uplands the trail passed through long windrows of cottonwood and quaking aspen. Skyward the trail went until it came to the first rising pitch of the Rockies themselves and there it was—the goddamndest sight.

A long strip of rock across the mountain face was black and shined like something polished. It made a sheer drop across the breadth of the rising mountain.

"Wha' is that?" Matthew wondered.

Johnny Dog named it in his native tongue. Then said in English, "Means... Bold Face Stripe...old time trappers and miners called it...the Stripe...like war paint on a face."

The sun against the black stone caused Matthew's eyes to crinkle, the glare burned so.

Sweeny had taken up his field glasses. "How'd it get like that?"

"Engineers from college, I heard say that something from far out in the sky might have struck the earth in times back."

Matthew lost sight of the mule trail.

"It's there," said Johnny Dog. "Winds up to the peak then over the other side."

There were still a few patches of snow blanketing the crest.

"It would take days to get around that fuckin' place," said Sweeny.

"We fight here...escape," said Johnny. "Go up Stripe...No catch, no way."

CHAPTER 88

Mary Jones was arrested that evening. She was taken into custody at her tent, by two companies of state militia. The charges were inciting violence and conspiracy to commit murder.

As they lorded her away, she ordered her people not to follow, and to do nothing that might undermine the Federation. She was on the road down from the Hill, flanked by troops with lanterns when Nola Dye arrived on the scene.

She had been in her room most of that day after escaping catastrophe at the Americanus. She'd been updating her notes, expanding them, refining them, on the chance a more ill wind blew her away.

She had filed a secure copy of her articles with the private courier arranged for by Harriet. She was just returning from Western Union where she had fired off another copy when she saw the troops marching Mary Jones out to Fourteenth Street.

She wondered where they could be taking the woman in handcuffs, as there was not much out that way except for the rail yards.

Nola followed at a safe distance until she knew more. She questioned the people after that squad and their prisoner passed, to see if they knew what was going on. Some of the responses defied repeating. Their livelihoods lived and died with the Leadville economy. And that was more important than the safety of some self-promoting fanatic and her followers, who had tried to bomb the mines.

This small procession of lanterns trooped Mary Jones out to the railyard where a locomotive pulling a lone box car awaited. Two of the soldiers climbed into the car and then the older woman was hoisted on board.

That is when Nola crossed the tracks and into their light.

"Where are you taking this woman?" she said.

Caught off guard, the commanding officer's mouth momentarily dropped open.

"Do you know who I am?" said Nola.

Neither the commanding officer nor those with him were much older or more experienced than Nola.

"Do you know who—"

"No, ma'am. I don't. And I don't care to—"

"I am a reporter who has been working with Nathan Neihart…of the Americanus. And I need to know where you are taking this woman…and why?"

Nola saw that Mary Jones was being seated on a plain wood chair in the middle of the box car and immediately handcuffed to it.

"I'm getting on this train," said Nola.

The officer stepped in front of her.

"If I don't get on this train I will find out each and every one of your names." She began to point from one to the next to the next. "I will see they are published in the newspapers when I write about this. And every member of the Federation will know who you are."

It was a dark and cynical threat that was meant to leave no fear unturned, and she was appalled to be voicing it, but voice it she did. The commander gathered his men together and they talked among themselves in whispers, looking over their shoulders at what they could only describe as a crazy woman.

When they ceased their little secret talk, the officer waved to the engineer to move. Then he grabbed Nola by the back of her coat and flung her toward the box car door. The troops handled her like a grain sack and up she went. Then there she was on the box car floor at the feet of Mary Jones.

"You should not have done this, child."

CHAPTER 89

Outside the open box car door the night was black with long runners of steam from the engine that swept past.

"Where are you taking her?" said Nola. "You're being used. You know that, don't you?"

The car rattled and swayed. The troops sat with their backs against the slatting. There was a terrible sense of apprehension that Nola could chart in their expressions.

Mary Jones began to sing. Not very loud. Was it to keep her mind off whatever lay ahead? To make a point, to mock her captors? Was it an indictment of some kind, or to just prove she was in command of her own fate?

> *The judge he has spoken and the hangman stands ready*
> *And Maggie Shepherd is soon to join those that are rotting*
> *For she killed her traitor husband who was no more than a boy*
> *And she don't regret it a droppin'*
> *The Pinkertons came to the place where she lived*
> *And thought takin' the girl would be easy*
> *But a handgun she hid, beneath the music box lid*
> *And left two of these like trash in the doorway...*

Before she was done the train slowed, then stopped. Mary Jones was uncuffed. Both women were taken from the box car and into the emptiness of the high frontier away from the tracks. Four of the militia were already digging a grave. They worked with great speed. The women were close together when Mary Jones whispered, "Do nothing, say nothing. No matter."

With the hole dug, it took less than moments for the officers to place Mary Jones before it.

"Step down and sit in the grave," said the officer.

"I prefer to die standing up, if you don't mind," she answered.

The four men that dug the grave formed the firing squad.

The older woman wore her contempt and defiance that only comes with an exactness of conscience.

The severe huffs of the locomotive like the breathing of some ungodly beast as the officer said…"READY…AIM…FIRE."

And fire they did.

A gasp came out of Nola.

But the older woman did not fall. Her body shuddered for a moment, but she did not fall.

The soldiers turned and started back to the train.

The officer told Mary Jones, "Let this be a warning to you."

He waved to the engineer and the train began to move, leaving the two women there in the dry desert darkness, come what may.

CHAPTER 90

They were maybe two miles out of Leadville and of all things, Sweeny was about the business of entertaining Matthew and Johnny Dog with ditties on his harmonica, when there came this terrible pronouncement from a heavy bore pistol lurking out there in the darkness.

Sweeny's horse reared and he fell to the earth in a great roar of pain. Matthew and Johnny Dog were quick to return fire. The shooter was thrashing through the brush to escape as Matthew fired at the flash from the pistol barrel. While he dismounted to see about Sweeny, it was left to Johnny Dog to lay chase.

It was a horrible scene there in the road. The big man writhing, kicking his legs about. The open palms of his hands pressed against the gushing wound that was at the center of his chest.

"I've been executed in the fuckin' road," he said.

The words carried the weight of his absolute agony.

Matthew could see there was no lying that might convince the big man otherwise.

"Take my hand, will you?" Sweeny pleaded.

Matthew took his hand.

"Say a prayer for me after I go."

"Yes, sir."

"You know some prayers, don't you?"

"I rekal' makin' some, from time ta' time."

"And don't bury me."

"No?"

Sweeny grabbed the youth's shirt.

"No...I'm afraid of being underground."

And that was the last of it.

Matthew knew pieces of different prayers and strung them together. He thought they may have made a pretty pitiful invocation, but he knew his intentions were true and right, and he apologized to whoever the Almighty was out there in the darkness, for being such a poor messenger.

He lugged Sweeny to a brushy ditch just off the road, barely up to the physical task, apologizing all the way for his clumsiness, when Johnny Dog returned with his rope around the neck of the shooter he was unmercifully dragging.

It turned out to be a boy, not much older than Matthew himself. They got him upright and he was crying and begging for his life. Johnny Dog exclaimed how this "little shit" was street trash hired by Vandel to watch the roads for the "Coffin Maker," who traveled with a "slob of a thug" who "fancied himself a harmonica player."

Johnny Dog slapped the little shit across the face a couple of times. "So you just shot him," he said. "Not even a hello to be sure."

Matthew had been staring at the youth. They'd come out of the same hole, most probably. Poverty Road. Always looking over your shoulder to see if any of those terrible omens you'd been witness to were catching up. Keeping that one step ahead of life's worst captivities.

Johnny Dog took a coin from his pocket.

"I'll toss ya," he said.

They couldn't let the boy go. Mercy was out of the question. He had been looking down the barrel of both their faces.

"Hetz," said Matthew.

Johnny tossed the coin into the air. He bent over where it landed in the dust. As he rose up, he removed his knife from its sheath. "Sorry," he said to Matthew. He took the boy by the hair and bent his head sideways. He then used the tip of the knife to puncture the vein in the youth's throat. Arterial blood shot out a good two feet.

They then went to the task of stacking brush and desiccated branches around Sweeny's body and turning that ditch into a funeral pyre. Most of the way to Leadville, they could look back and see this one wild, slewing flame in the starred upcountry from where they'd come.

"You know what I was thinking?" said Johnny Dog.

Matthew had no damn idea.

"We shoulda' kept his fucking harmonica."

CHAPTER 91

Harriet had dozed off on an old sofa on the screened in porch with a revolver at the ready in her lap, on the chance the bad news she had heard proved true. Her answer came when she felt a presence pass over her. She came up in a sudden lurch, choking on her own breath. She was grabbing for her revolver when Nola put a hand on hers.

"It's me," she said.

"Dear God, girl," said the woman sitting up. "I was keepin' watch till I fell off. Word was the militia took Mary out into the desert and you with her and they killed you both."

"She is alive as you and me."

"What happened?"

"Trooped us to nowhere. Dug a grave. Put her before a firing squad… and fired. It was a warning."

"Was she sufficiently warned?"

"I think both sides are sufficiently warned."

Harriet sat up rubbing the exhaustion and stress from her face. "I have a drink around here someplace…see if you can find it."

On a table sat a glass with dregs of liquor in it that Nola passed to the woman.

"I have a question," said Nola.

"Who doesn't?"

"Do you have a wedding dress?"

This crimped Harriet getting that drink down. "What?"

"Do you have a wedding dress?"

"What the hell are you talking about?"

"A wedding dress…do you have one?"

"Get me a cigarette from the kitchen, will you?"

Nola did as she was asked. Harriet got to empty the liquor glass in peace. Nola returned and sat beside her. She slipped the cigarette between the woman's lips and lit it. Harriet took in the smoke like a bellows.

"Well?" said Nola.

"One of us must be insane. I don't know what the other is."

"Do you have—"

"Don't you know that every bitter woman my age has a wedding dress tucked away in a trunk somewhere. What are you asking for?"

"I'd like to be married before I die."

• • •

It was Johnny Dog who came to the house later that night. He had to slink his way along because of the curfew and the number of no account militia tramping the streets. He didn't see the women on that unlit porch until he was greeted with "You'd better hold it up, Mister. I got a lovely shotgun here for unwelcome guests and trashy so and so's."

"This sounds like Harriet Bloom talking…You know me, ma'am. I'm Johnny Dog."

"So you say…What you here for?"

"I'm carrying a packet of correspondence from the Americanus. A friend wanted me to give it over to Miss Nola Dye. I'll leave it at the screen door."

"Where'd you get it?" said Harriet.

"It was in the possession of a Mister Tobin. Before he was recently deceased. You must have read about it in—"

He saw the faintest outline of a person standing.

"Where is he?" said Nola.

"You Miss Nola Dye?"

"Yes."

"He's tucked away good and proper close by. He'd a brought it himself but he can't dodge about as good as me."

"I need to see him."

You'd have thought Johnny Dog carried extra shadows on his back he moved with such assurance and grace. Keeping up with him was the damnedest task, and don't think he showed Nola any consideration. He wasn't about to get his head chopped off even for some sweet pea.

He paced her through the trees, past the smelter fires, across the industry tracks, down a remote gully and into a torturous maze of wild berries where they slogged across a creek of icy waters up to their knees, and to the remains of a burned out church.

It had been church to the Christianized Utes, and close by some of their clan still lived in piss poor shacks and worked in the mines—when they could beg up a job. Beyond the roofless walls of Christiandom was a patched together shack—the castle of one Johnny Dog.

CHAPTER 92

Matthew kept watch from out the corner of a crude paper shade and who does he see coming through the smoke of a campfire and trailing Johnny Dog? For a moment every sign of sorrow on his face was erased. He heard Johnny tell her to march right in while he retreated to the campfire and joined his brethren for whiskey and poor man's poker.

She entered the hovel and there he stood, well back from the door, this lonely creature in the half glow of a lantern on the table, his shadow rising to the roof beams from the light.

The room smelled of old saddle leather and horse blankets, wood smoke and long packed earth. An odor of timelessness, if little else. Neither moved, neither spoke. They were living out a pure silence that kept the world at arm's length. But as with all things—

"Someone has to speak first," she said.

"I din't mean for ya' ta'—"

He stopped.

"You didn't mean for me to come here?"

"I din't mean it—"

"You didn't mean for it to sound that way?"

He nodded.

"I could not have said it better myself."

She came around the table and he moved toward her and in that one embrace there was a deep sense of completeness. What they felt there between them they would match moment for moment, feeling for feeling, with anyone who had lived from Genesis all the way down through time to this rinky mining town at the foot of the Rockies. They kissed there in the shadows, and they knew for the rest of their lives they would have the other beside them, even if that other were long since gone.

She rested her head against his chest and it felt to him like the perfect act of God. If only the world would let it be like that, but it was impossible, with so many poisons going around.

"Vandel," she whispered, "is out there preaching to anyone who will listen that you are the 'Coffin Maker.' A few pro mine newspapers will print it. The militia has announced they will hunt you. So will the Pinkertons."

He was thinking how everyone, short of Jesus Christ, would be hunting him, and told her so.

"Not everyone," she said.

He sensed she had not come just to steal a few more wishful, or even wistful, minutes together. She was walking a tightrope of something as yet unsaid.

"Dere' sumtin' else?"

She looked up and nodded. "I came to ask you something...I'd like to be married before I die."

He knew what she truly meant. She wanted to be married before one of them died. And when he told her this, she said only, "I knew you'd understand."

• • •

It was a feat to pull off. A Justice of the Peace was required. Fortunately, Harriet owned and rented a house on Chestnut Street to just such a Justice. He was a meek and gutless sort, so he had to be well paid and thoroughly threatened for his services.

The dress Nola Dye wore had been commissioned for Harriet and Neihart's wedding. It was a healthy size too large. And the best they could do was pin the hell out of it. Even so, it hung ungainly about the slim young lady's shoulders.

The couple was married on the steps of the roofless church in the slum camp where the Utes lived. Johnny Dog served as best man. He smoked through the service. As she looked on, Harriet thought the history of that dress now took on a touching bit of irony.

The service was simple and quick, with an emphasis on quick. There was good sun that day, and sharp white clouds. The light off the scorched building made the church timbers glisten.

Where the couple went for a few hours after the service, no one ever knew.

• • •

246

The camp was raided later that day. No one knew for sure who did the ratting out. Most suspect it was the Justice. A posse of thugs, Pinkertons, and good old fashioned American bounty trash half burned down the camp. They questioned, threatened, then beat its inhabitants for answers, but got none.

They broke into Harriet Bloom's house. She sat in the kitchen and smoked while they ransacked the hell out of the place. And when they came away with nothing, she laughed, and then the words that came out of her mouth as her ratgut oppressors left were so vile and descriptive that even the most foul of the men were not only shocked, but awed.

CHAPTER 93

Harriet was restoring order to the house when Nola returned. She was still in her wedding dress, though slightly more disheveled. Harriet greeted her from the kitchen doorway, leaning against the jamb, with the look of one decidedly curious.

Nola did not need the cyclone that had been through the house explained to her.

"They're all over the city hunting for him," said Harriet. "It's bad."

"There's a few questions I need answered from what I learned in that packet. Then I'll be back to help you."

Nola started for her room as if it all had its place.

"They're looking for you, too," said Harriet.

"I'll be easy enough to find." Nola turned for a moment. "I'm the one in the wedding dress."

She left at dusk. The city was in an escalating state of turmoil. The search for Crippled Jack—The Coffin Maker—brought out the seething undercarriage that supported every social and political action that expressed itself in blood and retribution. Outlaw, monster—hero, saint.

Animosity was rampant. Placards in windows for either side were met with bricks and bottles. Fights in bars, on the street, now no more uncommon than spitting on the sidewalk.

The Americanus was in total lockdown. Workers across the hill at the other mines grew restless and punitive because they saw a fight could be made. What Mary Jones preached from tent meeting to tent meeting— Poison the stock prices with protest, pull down the mine.

• • •

Nola knocked on the door of a small and inconsequential house with a patchwork garden and ill kept flowers. The door opened, and Nola was greeted by the deeply lined stare of a woman with pale and parchment like skin.

"Missus Smalls?"

"Who else?"

"My name is—"

"I know who you are."

"Good. Do you think I could talk to—"

"I think not. Go troublemake somewhere else." She closed the door.

Not to be deterred, Nola knocked again.

This time, the woman stood there with crossed arms. "Does the English language not apply to you?"

"Just a few minutes will—"

"A few minutes for you...a lifetime for us." She slammed the door.

Leaving now was out of the question. Nola knocked again. When the door opened this time, it was Jonah Smalls who answered.

"Mister Smalls—"

"Come in."

"Let her in, let the devil in," said the wife from somewhere in the house.

"Go to your room," the husband demanded.

As Nola entered the parlor the woman walked past her, saying, "The third time is the charm...not in this house."

"I can let the lady have a few minutes."

"The signs of sorrow have been over this house since the beginning. And tonight is living proof."

To Nola's eyes the woman was not wholly well. The bones in her hands and around her neck nearly pressed through a paper flesh.

"My husband could have died yesterday."

"Yes, I was there."

"Go to your room," said Smalls. "Now."

"I'm not about to be ordered about like an eight year old. Just because you're afraid of—"

"Would you like some coffee?" said Smalls.

"She'll get it in the face, if you make it."

"No coffee," said Nola, to try and kill the argument.

"Sit," said the husband.

"Yes, please," said the wife. "Our home is your home. Our life, your life. Look around...see what he sold our souls for."

Smalls could not contain the woman. "Get out!" he said, "before—"

"You're too late," said Missus Smalls. "And now you are adrift on your own indecision." She turned now her pale and labored face to Nola. "If something happens to my husband I will see you dead. And oh...if you believe half of what he tells you, you are a fool. Now it's just a matter of figuring out which half. It's something I've been working at for the last twenty years."

She glanced at the man she'd married with raw disgust. "Have I said enough?"

When he was sure she had gone, Smalls said, "I want to apologize for this."

"There's nothing to apologize for."

A voice from the hallway added one last touch. "That's where you're mistaken."

"Well," said Smalls, "why are you here?"

"I have been made aware of private conversations...between Misters Neihart and Gould...on...important...or secretive...matters."

"That could be so."

"Which might well have to do with the upcoming engineer's report on the estate of the Americanus."

"That too could be so."

"Do you have any idea what those conversations do entail?"

"No."

"That," she said, "I find hard to believe. You see, I have reliable information that all future correspondence between the two men is to come through you."

"Get her out," came that harridan voice from down the hall.

"Please go to your room," Smalls called out, "or I *will* be forced to lock you in."

The door slammed in response.

Smalls had to address the question. "If that were accurate, I would not be able to discuss it."

"Could this... correspondence...be related to the engineer's report?"

"Possibly."

"And is it possible Neihart had a reasonable idea what the report would say when *we* went down into the mine?"

"He's not an engineer."

"A new find of ore would dramatically increase the value of the stock."

"It better."

"And it would intensify the Federation's drive to unionize."

"Dramatically."

"Which means the conflict would grow more intense, more violent."

"More is at stake."

"It would also be a smart financial move to buy up all loose stock… before…the report came in."

"It would be a calculated risk."

"Unless Neihart knew already and passed the information on to someone…like Gould. You see…I am told the letter about the correspondence *predates* our going into the mine."

"I cannot validate that."

"Isn't it possible Mister Neihart wanted the strike?"

"That's gambling with destruction."

"I don't feel that's beyond him. What about you?"

"In regards to what?"

"Gambling with destruction."

Nola gathered up her notes. She stood to leave. "I have one last question," she said. "If I may?"

"Please," he said, standing.

"The newspaper man who was shot in the street. Was he paid to ask the question that he did?"

"I have no idea what you are talking about," said Smalls. But his expression was hopelessly at variance with what he said.

CHAPTER 94

Call it a miracle or sheer luck, but Nola managed to cross Leadville, pass streams of militia, and trek down Chestnut to the house without incident.

"You've had a visitor. A messenger," said Harriet, holding up an envelope. Both women knew it was from Neihart—the stationery said as much. Nola sat at the kitchen table and read, with Harriet there waiting, watching.

"It's a synopsis of the engineer's report," said Nola, "for release to the newspaper."

"It broke the bastard's way, didn't it?" said Harriet.

Nola slid the summary across the table and stood. She was extremely preoccupied now.

Before Harriet even finished reading she came out with a disgusted hiss.

Nola started for her room. "I have an article about all this I need to write up."

"And not much time," Harriet shouted after her.

• • •

She understood now that she had been baited into playing the fool, the unwitting pawn, the honest innocent, gulled to the political guillotine. Being brought down into the mine was part of the scenario. Being offered the press release first—every reporter's dream—just so much more manufactured gamesmanship.

She did not have enough facts to bring Neihart and the Americanus to its knees, but she had enough to put a crack in the wall of their corruptions.

She came from the bedroom with three envelopes, but was already charging headlong into the reality of being too late.

Members of the militia were double-timing it up the sidewalk, turning into the house, surrounding it.

Nola handed the envelopes to Harriet. "I have to entrust you with this...I'm sorry."

Harriet saw troops passing the windows, heading for the porch, screaming they could see the woman in there. She reached out.

"This one," said Nola, "is to go by courier…this one to Western Union. They may not send it, but get confirmation they received it. And this…it has papers taken from the packet. Make sure it gets to Mary Jones."

Fists were pounding the front door. You could hear the men scrambling up the porch.

They were in the house now. Harriet slipped the envelopes inside her blouse as a rat scramble of troops shoved past her and grabbed Nola.

"You act like she's goddamn John Wilkes Booth," said Harriet.

She was shoved out of the way without so much as a consideration. As Nola was being handcuffed, she recognized the youthful officer telling her she was being taken in for questioning about the Coffin Maker, as the one from the train in the desert.

"We've met before," said Nola.

"No," he said, "we have not."

He lied well, she thought.

"That's what the darkness does for you," said Nola.

As they led her out, she had a moment with Harriet as she passed. "I'm sorry," she said.

"I am now," said Harriet, "and always will be…your humble servant."

There were always newspapermen gravitating around Mary Jones' command tent, and that night it was even more so. Word had spread that the former Nola Dye, recently married to the man known as Crippled Jack—the alleged Coffin Maker—had been taken in for questioning by the militia, but no one knew where. Harriet arrived with Nola's envelope and within minutes Federation officers were being summoned, which told the reporters something of more than relative importance was in the wind.

All hunched together there in the tent, Mary and her people reviewed the article, the interview with Jonah Smalls, and the correspondence in Neihart's own hand to the railroad Czar.

Mary Jones stepped out into the night to face more than a dozen hungry, waiting newspapermen. On one side of her stood Harriet Bloom, and on the other a Federation officer holding a lantern above the small woman to give her the light to read by.

"What I am about to read to you," she said, "was written by one of your own…the former Nola Dye. And it was secreted here just minutes before her arrest. If that is in fact what happened, and not something much more predatory."

She took a moment to clean her glasses and to let the newsmen wait a bit, let them get hungrier for the story, give their anticipation a chance to simmer.

"The article is titled… CORRUPTIONS AT WORK."

Mary Jones read on. "The article, the Smalls interview, and Neihart's correspondence to the Czar suggest to this reporter Neihart well knew what the engineer's report would say. And that was before he went down into the mine."

The woman looked up from what she was reading. "A descent the former Nola Dye was witness to," she said. "And if true, Neihart did not share that knowledge with his investors and partners, as they would never had sold out at the prices they did."

Mary Jones paused, addressed the reporters with a look, then she read on. "At this moment, there are corruptions at work here. And if so, what corruptions lie ahead? Tomorrow the engineer's report will bring about a dramatic rise in stock prices. Even so, the Americanus might well be on a collision course with tragedy. Not only for the everyday stock buying public, but for the union as well. And then what about the city of Leadville, and the state itself?"

CHAPTER 95

Neihart was at the Americanus field office when Smalls showed up nearly incoherent. He had escaped his own house just heartbeats ahead of the press who were hunting him out. He'd left his wife in an upstairs bedroom. The last he'd seen of her she was being shouted questions at from the reporters in the street, with her rabid shadow against the curtains holding the sides of her head and ordering them away.

There were newsmen on the Hill, but they could not get past security. There was nothing Smalls could tell his boss as Neihart had read the article. A manager from Western Union who was on his payroll had immediately brought him a copy.

"You should not have given the interview," said Neihart. "You're not good at it."

"She twisted my words. It's important you know that."

"Sure," said Neihart. "She was just too good at her job."

Neihart got out pen and ink, and stationery.

"Are you going to fire me?"

"On the contrary, Jonah, I'm going to give you a raise and a better title."

He wrote out a note. Folded it, tucked it into an envelope, which he sealed. Then he offered it to Smalls, held between two fingers. "Find Vandel or McSorley and give them this."

"I don't know where they are."

"That's why I said 'find them.'"

Smalls took the envelope.

"I heard," said Smalls, "it was Harriet Bloom who brought the article and correspondence to that Jones woman and the Federation."

"You have to give respect where respect is due. But make sure not to turn your back."

"Are we in trouble?"

Neihart looked at his executive as if the question were not only irrelevant, but out of touch. "Do you know why you were not successful as an independent? Do you, Jonah?"

What could Smalls really say, but "No."

"You're that type not equipped to even know when you've won the fight."

• • •

Nola had been secreted across Leadville to a warehouse on 13th Street. Just across the road were the railyards of the Denver and Rio Grande. You could call out for help here all you wanted, but rest assured, no help would be coming.

Nola was made to stand in a dim and dusty light facing a long table where nearly a dozen men sat and presided over her questioning. Some were in uniform, others were civilians. Nola was tired, but quietly defiant.

"You bring me here and question me without representing who you are, and by what authority you do this."

"We are trying to capture the murderer known as the 'Coffin Maker,'" said the officer. "And who goes by the name of Crippled Jack."

"I request a lawyer," said Nola.

"You were married today to the murderer known as Crippled Jack," said one of the civilians.

"I was married to the marksman known as Matthew Drum."

"Who is wanted for murder."

"I demand a lawyer."

"If you can convince him to surrender," said the officer, "we have the power to grant him life imprisonment, rather than death by hanging."

"By what authority," said Nola, "that of the Middle Ages?"

"Do you want to see him hung?" said one of the other civilians there.

"You'll never see him hung," said Nola.

A lone civilian at the far end of the table in the guttering light afforded by a dying candle said, "You'll never see him at all."

She looked down that row of deeply shadowed and resentful faces. "You may have the power in this warehouse. Or in this city. But it doesn't extend as far as God."

A passage of looks went from one to the other of her jury, all in silence. The turn of a head, the slight movement of a hand, a nod...ending, finally, with a whisper.

Then the officer in charge motioned for a trooper to lead Nola to the warehouse door, where she was cast out into the night.

She knew the night was far from over. She was walking down streets through various degrees of darkness—be not afraid. She did not try to keep herself from missing him. There was beauty in that, and she hoped it never eluded her. That jury back there, to attain that much animosity tells you how much you've accomplished in so little time.

"Missus Nola Dye Drum."

She stopped and looked back. Two riders came down that street of shadows. She knew who they were before she knew who they were, because they had been there since the beginning, and even before then.

She told herself her husband was somewhere thinking of her. She set her mind on him, hoping he would feel her at that moment.

The two men did not bother to announce or introduce themselves. The one with the beard, who was daubing his mouth with a bandana, said, "He didn't even have a last name. He had to take Ledru Drum's name."

"In America," she said, "you can choose any name you want."

"I wonder," said the other man, resting his forearms on the cantle of his saddle, "if you are determined as they say."

You could almost hear ghosts the street was that quiet.

"I faced one jury tonight," she said. "I have it in me to face another."

• • •

Harriet waited in the house she kept dark for her own safety. She paced room by room, sneaking a look out windows. The wind had picked up and the windows rattled. She hated it when the windows fuckin' rattled, as they set her on edge.

There was a sudden knock at the front door that startled her so that she spun around and almost fell. She grabbed the pistol off the table where she kept it and opened the door. A merchant she recognized stood before her.

"Miss Bloom," he said.

"What is it?"

He pointed to the street, and oh, how his voice was shaky. "There's a woman lying in the road outside of your house."

Harriet set the gun down and rushed into the night. A handful of people amidst the wagon tracks where the body lay. She pressed past the people and pleaded they step back. She dropped to her knees where lay Nola Dye Drum—shot through the heart.

Harriet Bloom felt herself begin to break apart. She clenched her jaw and she clenched her fists and she used her anger to dam the flood of agony coming out of her.

She looked around her and shouted, "Do you know what is happening here? Do you? You should. Because something is."

CHAPTER 96

Matthew was waiting in the cold camp east of the Ute shanties that he'd set up with Johnny Dog. He stood, leaning against a tree on a ridge. With the sun coming upon the landscape like an unknown force, he could see Johnny's approach a long ways off.

When he arrived and dismounted, Johnny took off his hat. It was a battered thing with feathers in the banding and he slapped it hard against his leg repeatedly, he was that despondent.

"They took her to a warehouse out by the tracks. They questioned her hard, then let her go. She was shot down on the road, Matthew. They killed her."

Matthew nodded silently. He looked off to where the trees bent violently with the wind.

"Harriet Bloom owns a funeral parlor on Harrison," said Johnny. "She's taken the girl there and sent word to her parents in San Francisco. But if you're thinking to go and see her, put it out of your mind. They got the place under guard, bounty men everywhere."

"It doesn't mata'," said Matthew. "I see her sun 'nough."

He turned and started to limp off.

"I nee' a faver."

"Yeah?"

"Amm'nition…for my Vet'alis."

"How much?…A saddle bag?"

"Five tousen rounds."

This got Johnny's attention. He started after Matthew. "I don't think there's that many goddamn men in all of Leadville, friend."

"Gonna be lot lez."

• • •

He meant to force them to a place of his choosing to match blood. Leading two mules loaded down with ammunition he and Johnny Dog ascended the foothills north of Turquoise Lake. Up toward the Stripe, burying crates

259

of .38 rimfire, food, and pouches of water along the way. Leaving markers to find them, he would be able to stand ground then retreat, stand ground then retreat, all the way up to where patches of snow marked the crest and his last chance at escape. He intended to make their killing of him—priceful.

Across the city, hostilities escalated. The shooting down on the street of a white woman was not part of the violent lexicon, unless the woman was a whore, or of an inferior race. People began to show up at the funeral home to pay their respects. A thin stream at first. Most were miner women. Among their number were the ones who had thrown feces on the reporter, and now felt repentant.

The reality—the Nola Dye Drum murder brought a much more fevered interest to the press releases, and the Americanus had the finest rise in its stock price since the initial public offering, even with the stranglehold of the strike.

This is where Neihart proved his financial genius. He did not bring in strike breakers to reopen the mine. He did not solicit blacks or foreigners, or any of the other social tribes that were desperate enough to cross the picket line. He let the mine sit empty. He relied on people's greed to boost the price. "It may take a week to break the strike, it may take a month, or a year. But one thing is sure...the silver will be there and the miners won't."

As for Mary Jones and the Federation, of two things they were certain. The Businessman's Association of Leadville would turn virulent against the Federation when they began to dramatically suffer from all those lost paychecks. And then there was the price of silver on the American market. Something neither they nor Neihart could control. A recession would prove devastating for one, and deadly for the other.

As Smalls had discussed with Nola Dye during the interview, a strike is "gambling with destruction."

• • •

Everyone knew the murder was the start of a war and now Vandel and McSorley kept their newly hired trash with them everywhere they went. It made for sly mockery when word got out... "the bodyguards needed to hire fuckin' bodyguards to keep alive."

McSorley was so disgusted by the wisecracks that when they were drinking down at Vulture Alley one night he brazened to go to the jakes alone and take a piss—that was the last seen of him. And don't think it did not unnerve certain bastards.

The next night a poorly threaded kid of the streets walked into a crowded Vulture Alley bar and up to the table where Vandel and his people downed drinks and dinner.

"You Mister Vandel?" said the boy.

Vandel looked the kid over. Saw he was carrying a leather pouch. Wondered, what the hell?

"If I am?"

The boy held out the pouch. "A man paid me two bits to see you got it."

It made a funny clacking sound when the kid offered it.

"Two bits, hey?" said Vandel.

Well, in that smoke filled nothing of a bar, the drunks and other shades of miscreants began to circle the table. Curiosity may have killed the cat, but it was a hell of a chaser.

Vandel took the pouch and shook it and there was that clacking sound again. And he saw those faces all pressed together in the din, seeing…did he have the sand to open it.

"Fuck you," he said, and unloosed the pouch strappings and emptied the contents, and did that kick off a shudder or two.

On the table were twenty, maybe twenty-five human teeth. Some rotted, some oddly cracked, but all bloodied up having been torn from the mouth of their owner. There was a badge that Vandel saw had belonged to McSorley. And a note—that was also bloody. Where was written:

— The Coffin Maker—

Vandel glared at the kid. "The man who gave this to you. Was he young? Crooked up hand? The one they call Crippled Jack?"

The boy's face squinched up and he shrugged and looked around. "He was just a fella on a horse. And…he wanted me to tell you…that you should come to Turquoise Lake and have at it."

CHAPTER 97

Soon enough Vandel would discover Turquoise Lake was a graveyard. Before the leather pouch was even delivered, Matthew had been in the high grass a few hundred yards from the cabin by the water, setting up his shooting sticks for the rifle to rest on, while Johnny went Indian and crawled his way to the shanty. He slipped the corral latch and the gate drifted open and the horses, smelling something in the air, slipped off into the night while he set a stick of dynamite by the front door and lit it.

When the dynamite blew out the front part of the cabin it turned into a rain of burning slats and timber that fell as far as the lake, where the bits hissed then smoldered as they sunk into the blackness.

Men came stumbling out of that hell, wounded, some with their clothes on fire, others naked and dazed, holding their heads as the explosion had rocked their skulls. One of them staggered through the fire's shadows holding the remains of his torn apart arm.

They were gunned down to a man like carvings against a curtain of flame, and by the time Matthew and Johnny Dog had circled the lake, the cabin walls collapsed in on themselves and set off a storm of cinders and ash that looked like fireworks reflected on the still cold waters.

He was looking back, Matthew was, when Johnny Dog wondered what was he thinking.

"Ta' church...wher' we were marriet. Ta' church..."

• • •

Matthew set up his shooting sticks on a low slope where the trees clustered and he had a clear view of the lake.

Vandel and half a dozen hireds came shortly after dawn and right behind them—newspapermen on horseback, in buckboards. Even that picturetaker with his gypsy wagon.

The cabin was just charred wreckage by then, giving off dying gasps of smoke. Men fanned out over the death site. And that photographer, it looked to Matthew, he was setting up to get a picture of the dead bodies laid out in front of the torched cabin.

Even at this distance Matthew could pick Vandel out from among the increasing number of men arriving. About a dozen started a trek around the lake. Led by what had to be a tracker, as he kept leaning down over his mount's withers, watching the ground, pointing. Vandel was not among them. He'd stay back and let the rabbits run first. The men coming on were not much to regard from the looks of them, but they were heavily armed. They would all be heavily armed from then on.

Those men came around the short side of the lake. They were maybe four miles out. Small parties of men were arriving by the hour, reports of militia on the way circulated.

A command post had been set up near the sorry remains of that cabin to be run by the Pinkertons. This hunt was meant to be an overwhelming statement of force and a political warning.

The twelve followed the trail Matthew had left in a long and slender line moving slowly up from the shore. The first shot echoed across the lake and caught everyone by surprise. The last rider in the line slumped from his rickety saddle and when the others realized, they scattered.

What followed was an intense run of shots that cut into the ranks of the hunters. They could not scatter fast enough. Some were driven from their saddles, some had the mounts cut out from under them. The wounded on the hill were trying to crab their way to safety, but there was none.

Through field glasses, Vandel could see a continuous rope of smoke rising from the trees where Matthew was hidden away. He could hear the Pinkertons ordering men up the west side of the lake—about twenty in number. It was near to eleven miles and would take hours. Others were ordered to support those that were being slain, and a wagon was to go with them to pick up the wounded, if they could.

Vandel watched the fight and knew this was nothing. He looked with his field glasses farther up. When they climbed up through the lamp black country of the Stripe, that's where the real killing would take place.

CHAPTER 98

Johnny Dog was farther up the hill where he had two horses picketed. He was scanning the countryside on both sides of the lake. More men were arriving from Leadville along with a wagon load of militia. He shouted down to Matthew that twenty riders had begun the long sweep up the western shore, and about a half dozen were following the trail east up to where there was still sporadic gunfire.

Matthew was covered with sweat and drank from a water bag. He raised an arm to let Johnny know he'd heard him, then he went back to the business at hand.

The first of them he'd let come well within range, hoping to give the next riders a false sense of security, which is what he counted on. When he blew out the skull of one of their mounts and the rider's face was spattered with blood and brain matter, and another took a shot to the thigh, they knew better. They veered their horses away from each other, they looked for any swale or ravine to escape the rifle fire. The Pinkertons had ordered another group up the eastern trail with mapped orders, and another group after that. They came on over the soft round shadowless hills like vermin escaped from a cage.

Johnny Dog saw the youth could not hold that position much longer. He could not humanly shoot any faster. And the return fire was leaving great puffs of dust in the earth around him as it closed in.

One of the riders breached the treeline firing away with his pistol like some mindless journeyman. Johnny Dog leapt onto his mount and charging downslope passed into that slim glade of aspen to dispatch the bastard before he had a chance to trample down over the youth.

Matthew saw now his position there to be hopeless and he shouldered his rifles and loosed his shooting sticks from the ground. Johnny hoisted him up onto the horse like a grain sack with gunfire hounding after their asses.

The air was thin and the horse nearly collapsed from the weight and the climb, but gasping, made the Stripe where they had the second horse and buried ammunition.

As Matthew pulled away the tarp that covered the hole where the ammunition was hid, Johnny Dog went about surveying the valley with field glasses. And was it a sight. More men arriving, for Christ's sake, and wagons with militia and supplies. Groups of riders ascended the hills from both ends of the lake. And there were campfires now along the shore by the cabin. Fires for coffee and food.

"It's a tent camp down there. A fuckin' revival. All they need is the tambourines."

Matthew drank from a water bag in huge gulps and then he put his head back and doused himself to clear away the sweat and powdersmoke.

"We can beat it outta here, now," said Johnny, "before them charlatans reach the crest and close the door."

Matthew spotted two riders well in advance of the others and coming on quick. He hauled up one of his Vetterlis, shouldered it, took in the wind, and fired. The shot echoed down the mountain and one of those poor fellas had suffered his last worry, the other turned and fled.

"What's it to be?" Johnny shouted.

Matthew looked down into the rugged emptiness of that valley now swarming with men. He'd been bound up and left in a place like this— once upon a time.

He turned to Johnny. He asked him to take the extra horse and picket it at the crest. And could he beg one other favor.

"Such as?" said Johnny.

"Vandel don' die up here—"

"And won't he be surprised when I show up some dark night," said Johnny.

And with that, he swung his horse about and was gone up the mountain on that slim pass along the edge like a creature born to it.

Alone now, an exhausted Matthew set up his shooting sticks. He then sat and waited for time to catch up with him.

CHAPTER 99

The Pinkertons who arrived at the base of the Stripe believed that one vigorous, well-planned assault would take the killer down. There were about a hundred payrolled and heavily gunned hunters on the ridge. This did not include stretcher bearers, newspapermen, and an artist with charcoal and oils.

They mapped out a plan. After all, they arrogantly thought, how much ammunition could a cripple carry with him up into that god forsaken emptiness? When Matthew saw how they arranged for the assault, he took up his shooting sticks and rifles and trudged farther up into the Stripe to a nest of rocks where he had left more ammunition and could snipe hell out of them on the trail itself.

When they charged, it came from a dozen angles. They'd kept marksmen back, enough to lay down a wall of gunfire.

They rode with their heads down low against the withers and came on like thunder, blighting a landscape whited with puffs of smoke where Matthew aimed his rifle. His spent cartridges tinging against the rocks at a fevered pace.

He could hear the clatter of hooves over the stone trail up into the Stripe and where he fired off rounds riders tottered from their saddles or had their mounts collide with the earth. The shadows of men and horses enormous against the rockface pressing on up a passway barely wide enough for two horses abreast and when shot, lost their footings and skimmed over the edge, turning in space, legs flailing, the riders' screams through the fall to disappear in voids of blackened stone.

The assault had been a waste of life, blocking the trail with corpses of men and animals. In the blue dusk his adversaries slithered along and dragged away the dead, then in small groups they went about the business of pushing carcasses from the ledge or chopping them into parts where that was necessary. Matthew did not shoot at them as they went about this tragically futile exercise.

He was filthy and bloodstained from a wound to his forearm and another to his leg just below the knee. His eyes were dark and hard and the flesh beneath them burned by the heat of the barrel from hours of shoot-ing. He swiped two fingers of grease taken from inside an ammunition box and made a black oily stripe across each cheekbone to quell the pain.

He took up his shooting sticks and rifles and water bag, and hobbled his way up to where he cleared the Stripe and reached open ground just beneath the crest. There he collapsed from exhaustion.

CHAPTER 100

He lay there looking at the stars until he finally had the strength and sat up. They were still carting away the dead down below, and tending to the wounded.

Newspapermen were writing up their stories, and everywhere along the mountain men were closing in across a cold blue evening. Judgment would come with dawn.

He tiredly stood. There were patches of snow and he bent awkwardly and scooped up a handful. He put it to his lips and bit off a chunk and then he pressed the ice against the bone where he'd shouldered the rifle for how long—how many hours?

He walked to where Johnny Dog had picketed the extra horse and the last crate of ammunition was buried. Matthew loosed the animal's leather strappings and then he went about removing the saddle. He took the horse blanket and waved it and slapped it across the animal's rump and the horse took off free into the night.

He stood there entirely alone now, except for those he carried around inside him. And that made him feel suddenly as if he were privileged with some great secret.

A flare cut across the night sky and he knew this must be a signal. Flares were being fired off up through the Stripe, lighting the way for men to make the fight. And if that were not enough, fireworks were being set off higher yet above the passage. There was gunfire soon after. Hunters were shooting into shadows they thought to be Crippled Jack.

From Turquoise Lake, it made for an unreal scene. Great shocks of light like cannon fire and smoke billowing across the blackness, as if the Stripe itself were some ancient fortress under siege. The painter there would live to see his renderings of that scene copied, embellished, altered by others endless times. But no truth would emerge from any of them.

• • •

Matthew sat among the bastion of rocks on the crest where he would make the fight. He closed his eyes. Another flare lit up the night sky down below where he had been. Volley after volley of gunfire. Wild and random. He aimed at the pricks of light from their weapon barrels. One hour bled into the next. The ground around him was littered with empty shell casings. Another flare and the shooting stopped. All was quiet except for voices calling out…"Crippled Jack"…"Coffin Maker"…"Crippled Jack"… Just to let him know they were everywhere and the end was near.

Matthew thought of Sweeny and what Johnny Dog had said, and quietly spoke out… "Ya wa' right…We shutta kep' Sweeny's ha'monka."

With dawn unveiling around him he could now see the dead along the edges of the crest. Horse and man alike. He scooped up handfuls of empty shell casings. Dusty as they were, they still glistened some. He let them just pour from his hand.

He rested his head against his staked up rifle barrel. He was played out. He closed his eyes again and he found himself just drifting. Somewhere in that dark, he heard a voice, "Son."

His eyes opened and he looked up. There was Ledru Drum.

"What is it, Matthew?"

"I failt'."

"How'd you come to that idea?"

"I camit'd ta' ultimate sin."

"And what sin was that?"

"I outliv'd my amm'nition."

Drum reached out. "Remember back, son…to the desert where I found you…*It's up to God now.*"

The youth nodded and as Ledru Drum grasped the boy's arm, there came a flare.

Matthew's head jerked up. He saw the flare arcing like a comet across the heavens. Had it been a dream, a hallucination, just flat out human exhaustion?

The Pinkertons had ordered marksmen to begin with first light. An assault would follow. There were reports of gunfire all along the crest for a relentless hour. No matter how many shots were poured into the position where Crippled Jack was thought to be holding out, no shot was returned. They soon thought him dead, or mortally wounded.

What happened next would be a point of conjecture and debate. He was seen from a dozen quarters rising up behind the rocks where he had hid. A rifle in each hand, the smoking barrels resting on each shoulder, walking toward his hunters across open ground with that odd hitch.

He was seen raising his rifles. Was he surrendering as some thought? Others believed he was getting ready to fire, to make one last fight of it. Some, who had a closer view, held that he was raising the rifles as best he could over his head to form a cross. But why a cross, was the question.

CHAPTER 101

Harriet was about to enter the funeral parlor when she saw a commotion far up the street. A man on horseback was waving his hat, shouting. He was coming on at a fast clip.

"They killed him up on the Stripe," he yelled. "Crippled Jack...the Coffin Maker... They're bringing him in now."

Harriet knew what came next. She turned to the two men who had been protecting the parlor, and the girl's body against any kind of degradation. Both were Utes.

She told one to get Johnny Dog and have him bring back a dozen armed men. The other was ordered to get up on the Hill. Inform Mary Jones what had happened and that men were needed. Armed men...and now.

There was soft daylight coming through the open parlor doorways when Harriet entered. The funeral director she employed stood there with hands folded. A quiet man, old before his time, said, "We'll need another casket."

"Yes," said Harriet, looking into the room where Nola Dye Drum lay. "Place it beside his wife."

• • •

The sidewalk outside the Western Union office was crowded with businessmen and news reporters trying to pick up any scrap of information on the Americanus that came across the wire.

A runner was handed a telegram with news. He had to fight his way past an unrelenting mob that pawed at him. He hustled into the Clarendon Hotel next door and sprinted up the stairs.

Minutes later a second story window fronting the street opened and Neihart leaned out flashing a telegram. He was assaulted with questions and threats which he utterly disregarded.

"You want to hear the news or just make fools of yourselves." He started to read from the telegram... "Stock prices soaring... Stop. May set one day trading record... Stop.

"As for the rest. Meet me in the dining room. And you're welcome."

Neihart had taken over the dining room. There was enough booze on the tables to grease the rails for what Neihart had to relate. He held up a number of dispatches and went about the business of hardcore finance. Everything else—the death of Nola Dye Drum, the slaying of the Coffin Maker—was nothing.

"I want you all to hear our most recent correspondence from San Francisco." He read, "Consortium interested in buyout... Stop. Will arrive in Leadville tomorrow... Stop. Believe deal within striking distance... Stop." He held up a last dispatch. "And this... is the most telling." He read again. "Believe deal can be struck with union that will *guarantee further rise in stock prices...* Stop."

• • •

From far up Harrison Street you could hear the raised voices. Shouts, cheers. A huge drum beating out a slow metronome.

You could see the Pinkertons on horseback turning the corner, followed by the militia, followed by a freight wagon.

From the rooftops and upper floor windows one could look down into the back of the wagon where lay the body of Matthew Drum ringed in by hired trash.

Then came a train of buckboards and wagons bearing the wounded and dead. And they made a long, long train indeed.

The procession continued down to the funeral parlor. There was quite a crowd of townspeople following them, but all was not well. It began with children darting out into the street, throwing bottles and rocks at the Pinkertons and militia, then disappearing back into a wall of watching bodies.

Harriet was on the sidewalk when the wagon pulled up with the body. She walked around the back of it and there lay Matthew. She refrained from reacting to what she saw.

An officer called to her, "We're commandeering your building... temporarily. So we can get pictures of the murderer with everyone who—"

Harriet cut him off. "You're commandeering nothing. I'm taking the body. Here and now."

"I don't think you understand," said the officer.

She stepped back. Armed Utes came out of the parlor doors and formed a battleline on the sidewalk. On the rooftops miners appeared, from alleys they appeared, muscling through the crowd more appeared. All with weapons. A new reality settled in.

"You wanted your pound of flesh," said Harriet. "And you paid a fortune for it. How much more are you willing to pay?"

The officer saw he was sitting on a potentially violent riot.

"Let her take the body," he said.

Johnny Dog and a number of his men leapt into the wagon. Vandel was there, screaming in rage at this acquiescence. Johnny Dog took special note.

CHAPTER 102

Fate casts a wide net.

The death of Nola Dye had aroused suspicions in fellow newspaper-men. And after Nathan Neihart sold his rights in the Americanus to an eastern syndicate for a quiet fortune, a rumor began to circulate that the engineer's report might have been, at the very least, doctored. How the engineer had been in the employ of the syndicate that bought the mine. And when they sent a second crew down, it was discovered the Americanus was an empty hole. That the ore taken from it had been seeded there. That the Americanus was, for all practical purposes, a scam.

This caused a catastrophic downturn in stock prices, the Leadville mines bearing the worst of it.

Before the engineer could be questioned regarding all this, he left for Europe on a long sabbatical. Reporters found out he had been hired by Smalls, who was in contact with the syndicate. Neihart never hired engineers. He allowed investors to supply their own.

When Smalls was to be questioned about all this by lawyers he was found in his study...the victim of a suicide. He left no note, only a wife who bordered on madness, claiming her husband had been murdered and it was the fault of Nola Dye and her interview, where she dramatically altered her husband's words.

As for Neihart, he had bought out Colonel Gheen and his investors at great risk, or so he claimed. He had allowed the syndicate their own engineer. With the fortune he made during the surge in stock prices he invested in each of Leadville's major mines, not only to support their stock prices, but to see they had cash to stave off disaster. It was another brilliant tactical business move on his part as it diversified and increased his power and quelled many of the resentments against him. He had also defeated Mary Jones and the Federation. This too bought him favor with the forces that be.

As for his correspondence with Gould that Nola Dye wrote about, the railroad Czar defended Neihart to a fault. He even had Western Union release copies of telegrams between Smalls and the engineer, which led to the credence of a possible conspiracy between them. Some newspapers questioned the convenience of such reports, but Western Union was too powerful.

As for Mary Jones and the Federation—you cannot strike a closed down, useless mine. They believed Neihart had forced the strike to temporarily drive up prices on word from the engineer's report, while he consummated the deal.

When asked, Mary Jones said, "We accept this temporary defeat with greater resolve."

CHAPTER 103

Harriet laid Nola out in her wedding dress. She bought Matthew a suit, nicer probably than anything he had ever worn in life. She found in his possession a page torn from the Bible about Abraham and Isaac and written in script across it:

—It's up to God now—

She was going to slip it into Matthew's pocket but decided to keep it. She did not know why, it was just some unassailable feeling.

• • •

Nola's parents were old, polite, and gentle souls, who could never have fathomed their daughter would be at the center of such a political maelstrom.

While Nola's mother stood in the quiet of the funeral home beside her daughter's coffin, holding the child's hand and softly weeping, the father took Harriet aside.

They stood in the open doorway to the sidewalk near where Johnny Dog sat at the entry. He had been maintaining a steady vigil on the chance of some foul action. He'd kept himself busy by sharpening one end of a wooden stake with his knife blade.

"I want the two of them to be buried together," said the weary gentleman. "With one headstone. And I'd like it to read something special. And I'd appreciate any thoughts you both might have about that."

Harriet was caught off guard, Johnny Dog no less so. She looked at the coffin, at the brokenhearted woman, then at Johnny Dog, who'd kept right on sharpening that stake.

"What I'd put on the stone," said Harriet after due consideration… *"They made the fight."*

CHAPTER 104

A wily Vandel never got to lure Matthew into the trap he'd set for him back at the shooting contest by intentionally missing his target from a certain distance. But Johnny Dog made good on his promise.

A drunken sleeping Vandel lay in bed on his back. The door to his room opened slowly and a pair of bare feet passed through a bit of moonlight cast upon the floor. A hand carrying a wooden stake with a sharpened edge rose out of the dark.

Vandel's eyes shot open when the stake was driven into his throat. He tried to pull free as he choked on his own blood.

Johnny Dog used his full weight to press down on the wood dagger. As Vandel fought for his life, a voice whispered, "Crippled Jack sends his regards."

Johnny Dog then rode to the top of the Stripe to get drunk beneath the stars.

CHAPTER 105

You'd have thought the future had fallen by the wayside, and life went back to its own grand state of inequality, without so much as a whisper. But not so. The future was near at hand and bearing its own brand of miracle.

It was during the Christmas season that things began to be set right. It had all started when Nathan Neihart brought in a renowned architect to build an Ice Palace that he would finance. It was to be constructed on Constitution Hill. A property that Neihart owned. The idea was to turn Leadville into a winter resort, a tourist attraction that would employ local citizens. It would be a castle made of ice. The turrets that flanked the drawbridge would literally be five stories tall, taller than any building in Leadville. It would have a skating rink, a merry-go-round, popcorn machines, a restaurant, dance floor, gaming rooms, even a theatre.

Harriet Bloom left her house well before the dawn slipped over the rim of the world. She walked up Fryer Hill. She stood before the remains of the Americanus. Its deep still shadows a terrible omen of all that was to come.

"What do you think of all that went on here?"

Harriet turned. There stood a young woman, neatly dressed, collar up, carrying a notepad.

"I work for the *Chicago Times*," she said. "I was sent here to cover the labor wars."

Harriet looked the girl over. She flashed on a moment like this from her own past. Harriet went back to wandering the remains.

"I heard you knew Nola Dye. That she actually lived in your house."

Harriet did not answer.

"And Crippled Jack... You knew him also."

"You mean Matthew Drum."

The reporter followed Harriet, but at a courteous distance.

"Do you think Neihart orchestrated the whole scam? Or was it Smalls and the engineer who conceived it?"

Harriet still did not answer.

"The fortune Neihart made in that two day selloff. Everyone hating him. Then he turns around and invests in those mines on the Hill. Saving them, and Leadville during the recession."

Again, she did not answer.

"What do you think of his Ice Palace?" said the reporter.

With the light coming off that castle on the hill, it was a magical sight. Like some wonderment from a fairy tale. What Harriet wanted to say would have scorched the girl's soul.

"He goes skating up there in the morning. Alone. Before it's open to the public. That's what money does for you, I guess," said the girl. "That's how I ambushed him for an interview."

"Like you're trying to ambush me now."

"Yes, ma'am."

"I don't ambush," said Harriet. And with that she walked away.

• • •

The next morning Harriet put on men's clothes. She tucked her hair up in a railroad cap. She put on one of her father's overcoats. She got out a scarf that would cover her whole face, leaving her nothing but a set of eyes. Then she checked her revolver to make sure it was loaded and ready to serve.

The shop windows she passed along the way were all decorated for the holiday season. She caught glimpses of her reflection in the glass. She could be anybody, but she knew who she was.

She entered the Ice Palace through the drawbridge with its imposing towers. Strangely enough, it made her think of *Ivanhoe,* which she had read as a girl many lives ago.

Neihart was there skating, and he was alone. He was a fine and stylish skater. But, of course, he'd had much practice, as he had skated through every criminal act, every corruption, every one of life's pitfalls, with the grace of a great skater.

He did not know he was being watched until he made this elegant turn. His blades just skimming the surface as he came to a stop. He had no idea who this person was, until he saw the House revolver.

"You can't run away on skates," she said.

She could see from the froth coming out of his mouth that his breathing had quickened.

"When I kill you," she said, "it will be for all of them."

He tried to escape. It was a ridiculous sight. His skate blades chopping wildly at the ice to make good getting away.

She shot him twice. The first bullet deflected off his hand. The second proved fatal.

As he lay dying, she knelt over him. His blood steamed as it touched the cold white ice, then pooled into an expanding burgundy map. If you did not know what it was, you'd have thought the image quite beautiful. Almost painterly.

She pinned a note to his chest. All it said:

—The Coffin Maker—